# Warriors of Gaia: Rough Justice

## D. S. Northrop

RIO FLOJO PRESS

www.rioflojopress.com

This book is a work of fiction. Names, places, and incidents are products of the author's imagination. Any resemblance to actual events, locales, or persons is entirely coincidental.

Cover art by Bradford Northrop

ISBN: 978-0-9883424-4-6

This book is dedicated to the many students I've had the privilege of teaching over the years. The characters in this book have been inspired by them.

Thanks to Barbara and Kristin. Your help and unceasing effort have made this book possible.

# Prologue

# Farmington, New Mexico, February 13, 2013

Eddie's week had been a rough one, a real egg-sucking ripsnorter of a week. First, the power company had shut off his electricity. Then, his fat-patootied wife had called. She was going to turn him in for nonsupport, which meant Eddie was going to jail. Again. And Eddie didn't like jail. He didn't play well with others, so he spent his entire sentence recovering from one beating or another.

He swallowed the last of his Wild Turkey and slammed the glass down on the bar. Another couple shots and he wouldn't care about his week, one way or the other.

"I'll have another one, Henry," he called.

"No, you won't," replied Henry, the barkeep. "You just drank up the last of your credit, Eddie. You owe me fifty dollars and twenty-five cents. No money, no booze."

"Aw, come on, Henry, you know I'm good for it. My disability check's comin' in any day now."

Actually, Eddie had lost his disability pay two nights ago playing acey-deucey at Frank's Tavern. He'd drunk up all his credit at Frank's, too.

In point of fact, Eddie wasn't even disabled, but old Doc Spencer had vouched for his bad back. Doc Spencer was a good ol' boy. He drank a lot, and he didn't have much of a memory anymore, but that worked out pretty well for Eddie. Doc kept confusing Eddie with another guy who *did* have a bad back, and that gave Eddie instant access to free government money.

Eddie looked around the bar as he got unsteadily to his feet. The TV was turned to the NFL channel, but the sound was off. A couple young kids were shooting pool. They were too young to be in the bar, but nobody cared as long as they didn't order anything to drink. Albert Snarm sat in a booth in the corner belching and nursing a Coors. Albert was too cheap to buy a friend a drink, so there'd be no help for Eddie in that direction.

Options exhausted, Eddie staggered out into a cold New Mexico night. He turned his collar up against the bone-chilling wind. Eddie lived a mile and a half from Henry's Place, and his car had died months ago. If that cheapskate Henry hadn't cut him off, Eddie would be feeling no cold. As it was, he was freezing his tush off.

As he staggered down Chinley Street, Eddie noticed a black shape in the shadow beside Gold's Pawnshop. Eddie hadn't thought it could get any colder, but the closer he got to that shadow, the colder he got. His teeth began to chatter, and he pulled his collar shut even tighter.

It was only when the shadow began to move toward him that Eddie realized he was going to die. He screamed, and then he screamed again.

\* \* \* \* \*

Art Shanker hated 1:00 a.m. phone calls. But he was the medical examiner, so every time a dead body showed up unexpectedly, the police rousted him out of bed. Art never understood the hurry. The body was going to be just as dead at 9:00 a.m. as it was at 1:00.

Having been on the scene for half an hour, he knew this case was a strange one. Eddie was a young fella, so death from natural causes seemed unlikely. But Art couldn't find a single thing wrong with the body. No wounds, no bruises, no cuts, no blunt-force trauma, no blood anywhere.

Everything about Eddie looked just fine except for the expression on his face. Art had never seen a person look as terrified as Eddie looked. The load that Eddie had dropped in his shorts reinforced Art's preliminary finding, that he had been scared to death.

And that black rose gripped tightly in Eddie's left hand was just plain weird.

# 1

My friends and I watch the villagers celebrate. They've just won a remarkable battle against their erstwhile masters, the Court. They've effectively ended countless centuries of servitude. I feel lighter than air, because I played a role helping them achieve this victory.

The musical instruments of the villagers are primitive: flutes made from hollowed reeds and drums crafted from animal skin stretched over a round wooden base. The music is pleasing nonetheless. The flute players are masters of harmony, and their spirited melodies resonate through the night air. The drumming is insistent, urging us to dance.

I resist the call to dance because my last forty-eight hours have been exhausting. But I love watching the villagers. They are dervishes, spinning wildly to the pulsing rhythm of the drums. They are wearing their finest clothing, threadbare and faded, but special to them.

"We only wear our finery on the feast days," explains Falstaff. Falstaff commands the militia that dealt the damaging blow to the black-uniformed soldiers of the Court. "We celebrate two feast days a year, one on longday to honor the Mother, and one on shortday to honor the Father. And now we're celebrating on the day we defeated the blacksuits in battle. None of our ancestors have ever danced for this reason. We are the first!" He throws both fists up.

* * * * *

My friend Tyler and I stumbled into this world by passing through a thin membrane in space-time that separated our twenty-first century world from this hellish future earth. Global warming, melting polar ice, ocean acidification, and the exhaustion of Earth's limited fossil fuels created pandemonium and led to a series of wars in which nations fought one another over increasingly scarce resources. Weapons became ever more deadly as billions of people starved. Biological weapons, chemical weapons, nuclear weapons, and plague destroyed what was left of the world's crumbling civilizations and turned cities into abandoned wastelands.

In the aftermath of the collapse, the only law was the law of the mighty. The strong enslaved the weak. My friends and I are trying to bring an end to the rule of the powerful in this one small corner of our brutal future world.

My friends and I sit on the edge of the village square, comfortable in chairs that fit our larger bodies. The villagers are short, most of them under three feet in height.

In the centuries following the collapse of civilization, men grew smaller as they adapted to an all but nonexistent food supply. The only tall people in this future world are the members of the Court and their lackeys, because they've lived off the labors of the others. Since it controlled the military, the Court could do whatever it wanted, and it wanted to preserve its pleasures.

My friend Tyler was captured by the blacksuits on the day we came through the brane. I passed back through the brane into my twenty-first century world to recruit our friends to help rescue Tyler. We were successful in that endeavor, but when we attempted to return to our world, we found the brane closed. So we're trapped in the future. The villagers have been keeping an eye on the clearing where the brane used to be, and they promise to let us know if it reopens.

\* \* \* \* \*

Tyler and his girlfriend, Eva, are dancing along with the villagers. Ty was crippled and blinded in one eye by the blacksuits, so his dance steps are no match for the lithe young villagers, but I give him points for effort. My friends Kenny (short for Kennedy) and Chase are also dancing, although their moves are more twenty-first century than futuristic. Bree is sitting next to me. She's never liked to dance, although she smiles as she shares this evening's joy.

My friends return to sit with us, exhausted, but laughing. I notice Kenny has a pink barrette in her hair.

"Are you making a fashion statement?" I ask, pointing at the barrette.

"A girl has to mind her appearance," Kenny responds. "You never know when you might run into a handsome stranger."

Her statement is odd, because in this world of scarce water, we're filthy most of the time, and it's a struggle just to keep our hair from becoming dangling spikes of sticky grease. Still, Kenny has always liked the boys. And the boys have all liked Kenny.

From time to time, groups of villagers come to our table and thank me. I think of myself as Erin Taylor, junior-to-be at Sierra Vista High School in Tucson. For reasons I've never understood, the people of this world think I'm the "Daughter of Gaia," the mythical one who will free them from bondage. At first, I rejected the role. How could I possibly free these people when the Court commands huge armies? But the villagers are insistent, so I've reluctantly accepted the responsibility.

"Now that we're all together, I have a treat for you." Falstaff produces a jug sealed with a cork. "This," he says dramatically, "is honey mead." He pulls the stopper from the bottle. He fills each of our snifters. The beverage is sweet, thick, and delicious.

"I've been saving this since my wife made it twenty years ago," says Falstaff. "Mead is precious, because we seldom harvest enough honey to make it. I thought I'd open it to celebrate the birth of my first child, but the blacksuits murdered my wife when our village failed to pay proper tribute to the Court. But our victory today is as precious to me as children would have been. So drink up!"

Falstaff refills my snifter, and I sip again. I notice the mead has quite a bite, so I wonder if it might be alcoholic. I'm fifteen (or maybe sixteen; it's hard to count days here), and my parents would throw a fit if they knew I was drinking alcohol. As I ponder this thought, a man rushes across the town square to us. He is breathing hard, but unmistakably excited.

"Begging the Daughter of Gaia's pardon," he says, gasping for breath, "but the brane is open."

For a moment, we sit in silence, absorbing the news. And then we all try to talk at once.

"Play the time game," says Kenny. "Pick your future."

"We can go home!" shouts Bree.

"I'm staying here," says Grizz. That's not a surprise. Grizz knows I've committed to living in this world, and he won't leave without me. I wait anxiously for the others to decide.

"I'm going back," says Bree. "I love you all, but my home is in Tucson." Tears run down her cheeks. Bree is our mechanical genius. Her expertise will be sorely missed.

I jump up, embrace Bree, and kiss her on the forehead. "Good luck, Bree. I'll miss you." The others follow suit. Tears form in my eyes as well. I wipe them from my cheeks with the back of my hand.

"I have to run," says Bree. "I don't want the brane to close before I get there."

"Do you know the way?" I ask. "Can you find it in the dark?"

The messenger who brought the news volunteers to guide her.

"Don't forget to smear on some wolf bane!" I cry as Bree and the messenger disappear through the door. Wolf bane is a scent Kenny cooked up to repel dreadwolves. Without wolf bane, nobody survives a night in the forest.

We all look on sadly as Bree leaves. We've known her since we were children; the thought of never seeing her again fills me with grief. The Tucson Ramblers have now been reduced from seven to five. *If* the other three choose to remain. We lost the first member of our septet when the blacksuits killed Jules at the Battle for the Sanctuary. Losing Bree is hard, but at least she's leaving us alive and in one piece.

"I have forts to build. The Sons of 1776 are going to come across the saddle one of these days, and when it happens, these people are gonna need our help. Besides, I can't leave my homies," Chase says with a grin.

15

Tyler is in quiet conversation with Eva. "I can't leave Eva," he says at last, "and I don't think she'd be happy in our world. Life in Tucson would be too fast and too strange for her. How could she adapt to cars, and talking heads, and school?" Eva kisses Ty on the cheek. I've never seen Ty happier than he's been since he met Eva. And nobody in the world deserves to be happy more than Tyler.

Kenny sits quietly, contemplating her decision. "If there were any boys my size in this place, this would be an easy decision. I need someone to squeeze."

Chase raises his hand, palm out, and wiggles his fingers at her.

Kenny eyes him and says, "I like you too much to have you for a boyfriend, Chase."

"Oskar Salieri is looking for a wife," I say, referring to the chief justice. Salieri is our number one enemy.

"He wouldn't make it past 'I do,'" says Kenny, grinning.

She sits quietly for a moment. "I'm going to stay," she says. "I could have a really great future in Tucson, but nothing I could do there would be nearly as important as the things I'm doing here. *Noblesse oblige* and all that stuff."

"So we're still a team," I say. I'm deeply relieved that my friends are staying. Grizz and I would have been lonely without them.

"Darn right," says Kenny with a grin. "I'm gonna turn Oskar Salieri into my butler. 'Oskar dear, go get me a bowl of strawberries and cream. And after that, polish the silver.'"

I smile at the mental picture Kenny's words bring to mind, of Salieri in a suit with a bow tie, fetching strawberries. But Oskar Salieri will never be anybody's butler. He's a strong and formidable man.

16

Despite my hate for him, I respect him. He's a formidable enemy. When Salieri goes down, he'll go down fighting.

Helen and Falstaff, who have been sitting with us, diplomatically silent, break into smiles.

"Mother bless you all," says Helen. "We will miss Brianne, of course, but with the five of you staying, we're still a formidable force. We will continue to fight the Court until we are rid of them."

\* \* \* \* \*

Centuries ago, as civilization was collapsing, a huge consortium of survivalists from all over the country built a chemistry lab and a workshop to help them achieve a position of dominance in the future world. They stocked these facilities with weapons and ammunition, explosives, tools, and the raw materials they knew they'd need to become rulers of the new world order. Unfortunately for them, they were swept away by another, more powerful group before they were able to establish themselves. Plague decimated the group that drove the survivalists away. Now, centuries later, they've returned to their lands only to find they no longer have the knowledge to solve the riddle needed to open the locks on the doors of their workshop and chem lab. My friends and I were able to solve the riddle. Inside the workshop and chem lab, we've found resources that may help us defeat the Court and free the villagers.

The Sons of 1776, as the survivalists call themselves, have become our implacable enemy. They want their resources back. So in addition to trying to overthrow the tyranny of the Court, we must defend ourselves against the Sons. Toward that end, my friend Chase is overseeing the construction of forts to defend the tools we must have to defeat the Court.

\* \* \* \* \*

The hour is late, and the villagers' victory celebration is winding down. Grizz and I haven't slept in nearly forty-eight hours, so we excuse ourselves and head to our dormitory in the Phoenix village hall.

The night is warm and, with only a sliver of a moon, dark as well. We pass villagers who are exhausted from their revels, many too tired to find their way home, sleeping in the town square.

The villagers have thoughtfully provided mattresses that are sized for us, and mine is soft. One seamless mattress is far superior to pushing together four mattresses that were designed for small people. I hear the others come in quietly as I float off to sleep.

We sleep in late the following morning. I wake near noon with my head still foggy. I lie on my mattress, staring at the ceiling, which, like the ceilings of all the villagers' buildings, is less than five feet from the floor. I clear the cobwebs from my head.

I amble out into the town square and find my friends eating lunch around a trestle table. Villagers hustle about, busily attending to their affairs. They greet me with friendly waves as I pass. Sort of like the paparazzi, I think, and immediately reject the analogy. The villagers are much better behaved. I've long since grown to accept that, in my role as Daughter of Gaia, I'm going to attract attention wherever I go. I've almost gotten to the point where I'm not embarrassed anymore. Almost.

I join my friends and tear into a lunch of peas, squash, potatoes, and wild greens. The villagers have obviously been trading food. With the destruction of the blacksuits' village forts, villagers can now grow anything they like. They won't harvest newly planted crops for a while, but they can trade with their neighbors. The Court wanted to keep the villagers docile, so they allowed each village to grow only one crop. Vitamin deficiencies kept the bodies of the villagers weak. But nothing could weaken their spirits. I'm hoping a balanced diet will cure them of the vitamin deficiencies and malnutrition they've suffered.

I've just finished eating when I'm greeted by a sight that arouses a dozen conflicting emotions. Walking toward our table are Bree and my adorable, towheaded twin brothers, Han and Luke.

D.S. Northrop

# 2

"What are you two doing here?" I blurt.

"Nice to see you, too, ET," says Han.

"I didn't mean it that way," I apologize and embrace them both.

In the months I've been here, they've grown another two inches. They must be at least six feet tall. They still have the blond hair, big ears, green eyes, and the button noses that make them so adorable.

"I've missed you two!" I say honestly. "But why are you here? Why aren't you back in Tucson?"

"He dared me," says Luke.

"Dared you to what?" I ask.

"He dared me to climb Midnight Mesa," explains Luke. Midnight Mesa is the place where the brane connecting our twenty-first century world with this future world occasionally flickers open.

"'Cause nobody ever goes up there any more since all you guys disappeared," says Han.

"Everybody's parents are like, 'If you ever go up there, you're grounded for the next five years,'" says Luke.

My brothers have a confusing habit of completing each other's thoughts. The tag-teaming is often bewildering.

"Well I'm glad you two geniuses had a good reason for coming here," I say, my voice tight. "This world is *dangerous*. You have to go back. Think what losing you two will do to Mom and Dad."

"Oh," says Luke, "that's not a problem."

"We left Mom and Dad a note before we walked into the weird light," says Han.

"We told them we were looking for you, and we were OK. We told them not to worry," explains Luke.

"Don't you think having all three of us missing might be just a tiny bit hard on them?" I ask.

"Heck no," Luke responds. "When they read the note, they'll know we're all *alive*."

"Yeah," says Han, "I told them in the note that we'd be coming back as soon as we rescued you."

"So you two are rescuing *me*?" I bristle.

"Of course! That's what brothers are for! Only I didn't have any paper, so I carved the note on a piece of wood with my pocketknife," says Luke.

"'Cause *somebody* stole my knife," says Han, giving me a meaningful look.

It's true. I took his pocketknife the day I passed through the brane.

"I never meant to keep it," I say defensively. Then I realize they're doing what they always do when they're in trouble: they're shifting the topic of the conversation.

I give them my sternest big sister look. "OK, smart guys, how's anybody gonna get that note if nobody ever goes up on the mesa anymore?"

"The police go up there all the time," says Luke, "looking for clues to explain what happened to you guys."

"And we left the wood sticking up in that big pile of rocks in the middle of the medicine wheel."

"You two are going to go straight back to Tucson," I say sternly.

"No way!" says Luke. "Bree was telling us all the cool stuff you've been doing. We wanna help, too."

"Did Bree tell you Jules and Charity are dead?" I ask pointedly.

"Yeah," replies Luke.

"And she told us you wasted Jared the Jerk," says Han.

I squint and stare daggers at the two of them. "None of that matters. This is no place for a couple of fourteen-year-olds."

"We're fifteen in a month," says Luke.

"And three days," adds Han.

"Talk some sense into these two, Grizz." The boys worship Grizz.

"Hey, Uncle Grizz!" they say in unison. Although Grizz is only a year and a half older than they are, they call him "uncle." The reason for this has never been clear to me.

Grizz looks at them thoughtfully. "Your sister is right, guys. This is a very dangerous place to be. You really should go back."

"You're a traitor, Uncle Grizz," says Luke.

"Not gonna go," says Han.

"Grizz and Chase," I say, "can you carry these two knuckleheads back through the brane?"

"They're a little too big for that," says Grizz.

Grizz is right. The twins have long since passed me in height and in weight. They're six-footers now, and still growing.

"And even if we could wrestle them back," says Chase, "how could we keep them from coming right back the minute our backs are turned?"

"So what if this is a dangerous place?" says Luke. "We're not scared."

I've watched my brothers skateboarding, rock climbing, and dirt biking, and they have absolutely no fear. I've spent my entire life trying to drill this fundamental mathematic truth into their heads:


No Fear = No Brain


Obviously, I've failed. There must be a special angel keeping watch over demented twins, or they wouldn't be here now.

I decide to play my trump card. The boys are at an age where they've begun to notice girls.

"There aren't any girls on this side of the brane. The girls here are all three feet tall," I say.

"What do you mean?" says Han. "There's Kenny."

Kenny snorts.

"You and Kenny!" I stammer. "You and Kenny go together like pickles and Frosted Flakes. That's just ridiculous!"

"Did you just call me a pickle?" asks Kenny. "Cause if you did, I'm gonna sprinkle itching powder on your bed."

"No!" I object. "*They're* the pickles."

"Itching powder," says Han, laughing. "Now that's a good one. ET, do you remember when we put frogs in your bed? That was sooo funny!"

"Hilarious," I grumble. I have to give myself credit. When I saw the frogs, I didn't scream. But I jumped about three feet straight up in the air.

"But she got us back," says Luke.

"Yeah, she waited till we were asleep, and then she put our hands in bowls of warm water," says Han.

"We peed," says Luke.

Helen looks at me with a strange expression.

"This was a long time ago," I explain.

And, I realize, they've just done it again: they changed the subject. I have an urge to stomp away and kick something.

"Fine," I say, fuming. "You can stay. But here's what's gonna happen. You're gonna go to the mines, and you're gonna train with the militia. If you stay here, you'd better learn to defend yourselves."

"And," says Falstaff, looking gruff, "if you fail to follow orders, you'll be washing dishes all day, every day. A soldier always follows orders." Falstaff gestures at a soldier standing guard by the door. "Show these new recruits where they'll sleep."

"So we can stay?" asks Luke.

"You're the bomb, ET," says Han, hugging me and nearly knocking me over.

I'm not sure the militia is ready for Han and Luke. I guess we'll find out.

In the entire ruckus over the twins, Bree has been standing quietly, observing the drama.

"Bree!" I say, at last. "Why are you here? Did the brane close?"

"No," she says calmly. "I sat in front of the brane for hours, thinking. When the sun came up, I decided that as much as I miss my family, I would miss you guys more. I had just gotten to my feet when Heckle and Jeckle came through the brane."

We smother Bree with hugs. "I'm really glad you came back," I whisper in her ear. "We would have missed you terribly."

Helen welcomes Bree as well. "I'm so relieved," she says. "We would have missed you, child. You have skills we could not have replaced."

No sooner have we welcomed Bree back than I receive another surprise, although this one is much less pleasant. Standing in the doorway is a man I dislike intensely: Officer William H. Kremke, one of Tucson's finest. The policeman who worked the Sierra Vista High School beat.

* * * * *

"What the devil is going on here?" hollers Kremke. "Who are these little people, and what are you delinquents doing here?" His face is fire-engine red, and the veins of his forehead are standing out.

"Hello, Officer Kremke," I say evenly.

"Taylor!" he shouts, turning to me. "I should've known you'd be a part of this!"

"Welcome to the future," I say, voice cool.

"The future! What the devil do you mean by that?"

"Just what I said. When you walked through the funny light, you walked into the future. You're still in Tucson, Officer Kremke. But it's a little different from the Tucson you left."

"This can't be Tucson," says Kremke. His anger is rapidly turning into shock, perhaps even fear. Beads of perspiration dot his forehead. "Where are all the buildings? The temperature is too hot! Where did the desert go? The mountains are too tall! Why are the people so short? How can *this* be Tucson?"

Despite my dislike of the man, I can't help but feel a twinge of sympathy. I remember how frightened I was when I first passed through the brane and found myself trapped in this brutal world.

"As I said, things are a bit different now. Please, Officer Kremke, come to our room, and I'll explain what's happening."

Kremke, cowed for the moment, follows us quietly. I lead him to the Village meeting hall, where my friends and I are staying temporarily.

"Watch your head," I say as we enter. The ceiling of the room is only a little over four feet high. I've bumped my head on it more than once. My friends and I sit in a circle along with Helen and Margaret, the captain of the Daughter's Guard.

"Please have a seat," I say.

Kremke sits. "This room is filthy," he says.

"Actually, the room is spotless," I disagree. "The floor is packed dirt. They don't use flooring here."

"You're going to be in big trouble when I get you back to *my* Tucson." His eyes range wildly from one of us to the next.

"Getting back to *your* Tucson may be a problem," I explain. "After you passed through the strange light, what happened?"

"I ran into one of these tiny people."

"And what happened to the light?"

"It kind of flickered, and then it went out."

"Then you're stuck here with us," I say evenly.

"Stuck here! No. That's not possible. I don't *want* to be here!"

Tears form in Kremke's eyes. He loses his bluster, and all that's left on his face is fear and confusion.

"That funny light was a doorway into the future," I explain gently. "It turns itself on for a little while, and then it winks out. Unfortunately, it's hardly ever on. When it's off, you can't get back to the twenty-first century."

"I'll go back and wait for the light to come on again," says Kremke, regaining his composure.

"You could wait for weeks or, more likely, months," I say. "And then there's the problem of dreadwolves. Let me explain where you are or, more precisely, *when* you are."

I proceed to give Kremke a very short sketch of the world's history for the last thousand years or so. I describe what I've learned about global warming, fossil fuel depletion, wars, and the collapse of civilization. And finally, I tell him about our war with the Court.

The expression on Kremke's face goes from confusion to fear and back again.

"So I'm stuck here," he says softly.

"I'm afraid so," I say. "You're welcome to stay here with us. Or, if you'd prefer, we can arrange for you to join the blacksuits. They may be more to your liking than we are."

"The devil you know is better than the devil you don't," he whispers.

"Glad you're so enthusiastic about staying with us," says Kenny, sarcasm dripping from every word.

"You say the Court treats people as slaves?" Kremke asks.

"Yes, but they'd probably make you an equal. They seem to respect tall people. They'd probably make you one of the elite." I'd prefer Kremke go over to the other side. With us, he'd be a source of constant discord at best. At worst, this man who seems to hate us could be downright dangerous.

"Hard as it may be for you to believe," says Kremke, "I don't approve of slavery. I don't approve of governments that repress their people. I fought in the marines, for Pete's sake! I fought against that crap."

"So you'd rather stay with us?" I ask.

"Yes, I would," says Kremke. "I don't like you, Taylor. And I don't like your snob friends. But you sound like the good guys in this world. So I don't have much choice, do I?"

"No, you don't. Helen," I say, "can you find some mattresses for our new…friend…?"

"Yes, I can."

"You're welcome to bunk with us," I offer.

Kenny and Grizz roll their eyes. Chase shakes his head in disbelief.

"Where else would you put him?" I ask.

"At least we can keep an eye on him if he's here with us," says Grizz grudgingly.

"Keep an eye on *me*!" rages Kremke. "Why you little jackanapes, I ought to give you a thumping!"

Kremke stands, and a second later, so does Grizz.

"Take your best shot," says Grizz.

"Margaret, will you arrest Officer Kremke if he attacks Grizz?" I ask.

"Yes, Daughter of Gaia, I'd be glad to. Guards!" she hollers over her shoulder, and two dozen warriors from the Daughter's Guard enter the room.

"Arrest *me*? You must be joking. And what's this 'Daughter of Gaia' crap?"

Margret addresses Kremke. "You will find, Officer Kremke, that the person in this world you should respect most is the Daughter of Gaia. If she wants you arrested, you will be arrested."

Kremke blusters, but he sits down. Grizz follows suit.

"I bunk here," I say, pointing at my mattress. "Grizz bunks there. Why don't you sleep right between us?"

"Do Kenny, Chase, and Bree sleep here too?" asks Kremke, incredulous.

"Yep," I reply simply.

Kremke turns to Helen. "You allow these children to sleep this way? All of them in the same room? Why, there'll be hanky-panky all night long!"

"There is no 'hanky-panky,'" says Helen. "I'm not familiar with the word, but I know what you are implying."

"I'll just bet," mutters Kremke.

Moments later, the villagers drag in a mattress for Kremke.

"If you'll excuse me, Officer Kremke, we have business to attend to. Helen, can you find Officer Kremke something to eat?"

"I'm not hungry," says Kremke. "Perhaps I should stay while you 'attend to business'?"

I wrestle with this decision.

"You've been a marine," I say finally. "We may find you useful. Margaret, post a guard on Officer Kremke. If he's truly one of us, I want him to know our plans. But I don't want him escaping and taking our plans to the other side."

Kremke is clearly unhappy about having guards watching him.

"If we find we can trust you, I'll recall the guards," I say. "Until then, we'll be watching every move you make. This will be your last chance to go over to the other side. Once you know our plans, we'll jail you if you try to leave."

Kremke turns his options over in his mind. "No, I'll never fight for slavers," he says at last. "I don't like you, but I'll never throw in my lot with despots."

"Fair enough," I reply.

The reason I hesitate to let Kremke in on our plans is that I've been burned before. I don't want Kremke to pull a Zoe Kerber on us, listening to our plans and then going over to the other side. Zoe and her boyfriend, Jared, came through the brane and pretended to join our cause. But they decided that a life of luxury with the blacksuits was a more attractive proposition than a life of hardship with us, so they deserted. I got partial revenge for their treachery, however. I slew Jared in the recently fought Battle at the Forest's Edge.

* * * * *

"Grizz, have you told them about our time as captives of the Court?" I ask.

"I thought I'd leave that for you," Grizz replies.

"Please tell us," asks Helen. My friends and I are joined by Helen, Falstaff, and Gretchen, who has become Falstaff's right hand. Falstaff has a few other officers present, and I recognize them from the days I spent recovering my health at the fort near the mines, Fort Taylor.

I launch into a description of our kidnapping, the days we spent as captives, and our escape. My friends listen with rapt attention. I can see everyone become squeamish as I describe our escape through the sewers and into the sewage lake.

When I'm done, Helen says, "I think we should stop now and celebrate our many victories. Human nature constantly directs our focus to the future, but I want to be sure we don't lose sight of all that we've accomplished since the Daughter of Gaia and her friends joined us."

Helen ticks off the accomplishments on her fingers as she talks. "We have unlocked the secrets of the workshop and the chem lab. We have taken the Court's mines away from them. We have destroyed the blacksuits' village forts. We have begun to eat a healthy diet. We have ended the gleaning of our young people. And, we have defeated the blacksuits on the field of battle." Helen pauses for a moment. "We have much to be proud of."

Kremke looks confused.

"Let me explain what Mother Helen has said," I say to Kremke. "People cannot travel at night because fierce dreadwolves rule the forest after dark. A night in the forest is certain death. But Kenny discovered a scent that keeps the dreadwolves away. Using the scent, we can travel by night whereas the blacksuits cannot. Traveling by night enabled us to capture blacksuit forts used as the way stations to their mines. We burned the forts, so the blacksuits can no longer travel to the mines. The mines are now ours.

"When Mother Helen talks about gleaning, she refers to the blacksuits' practice of raiding villages and kidnapping thousands of our young men and women for use as slaves in the blacksuits' cities. Now that we own the night, we can lay ambushes for blacksuit columns as they approach our villages. So the blacksuits can no longer glean our children. Using Kenny's wolf bane, we can now travel from village to village so we can trade with our brothers and sisters."

I turn my attention to the others.

"We've accomplished many things. And we should celebrate our victories. But we need to plan for the future as well. When the blacksuits kidnapped me, I saw the inner-ring forts and New Washington myself. There's no way we can take those forts without at least fifty thousand soldiers and some new, more powerful weapons. The walls are made of reinforced concrete, and on top of the walls, they have embrasures and murder holes, where their archers can loose arrows from behind cover, firing down on us as we approach. They have clear fields of fire, and the way they've built their corner turrets, as we approach the walls, we'll be taking fire from the front and both sides as well."

I pause for a moment to let my words sink in.

"How many soldiers do we have right now?" I ask Falstaff.

"We had fifteen thousand, but we lost four thousand in battle yesterday."

"How many soldiers can we feed if we use all the food we grow at the mine site?"

Falstaff pulls on his beard and says, "We could probably feed twenty thousand. The farms near the mines were mostly intended to feed miners, but they also exported some food to New Washington."

Falstaff pauses and leans in. "Also, we must remember that our militia has only been in training for a few weeks. We were able to fight the blacksuits yesterday because we surprised them with flanking attacks. But we'd never stand up to them if we fought on even terms. With their discipline and training, the blacksuits are more than we can handle right now."

"So what I'm hearing," I say, summarizing, "is that we need to increase our food production, we need more soldiers, and we need time to train our militia."

"That's true," confirms Falstaff.

I look directly at Helen. "And it's also true that we need to continue paying a food tax to the Court so it remains dependent on us. If we don't pay the food tax, they'll simply burn our villages to the ground, and everybody will starve."

"Sadly, that is true," answers Helen.

"How do we increase the size of our militia?" I ask.

"Remember that our people must work in order to eat," says Helen. "We can't take villagers away from their fields for long periods of time without endangering our food supply."

"If we want to increase the size of our army, there are tens of thousands of slaves working inside the outer ring of forts. They'll join us in an instant if we call on them," says Gretchen.

"But how would we feed them?" I ask.

"We lost four thousand fighters in the Battle at the Forest's Edge," Falstaff reminds us. "And we can feed another five thousand with the surplus we produce in our fields near the mines. That would bring our militia to twenty thousand."

"Can we get word to the slaves that we'd like them to join our army?"

"I can make the arrangements," says Helen. "We can't have a massive defection of slaves without attracting the attention of the blacksuits. We'll have to recruit them a few at a time. The people we send to do the recruiting will be in constant danger, but we'll have no shortage of volunteers. I can send dozens of agents inside the outer ring. The blacksuits think we all look alike, so they won't know our agents from their slaves. I estimate we could send out enough agents to recruit a hundred fighters a day."

"Then that's settled. Now, what can we do to increase food production?" I ask.

"Can we clear more land and plant more crops?" asks Chase.

"Once again," says Helen, "if our people are clearing trees, they are not working in the fields. And if they don't work in the fields, they don't eat."

"Could we slightly reduce the taxes we pay the Court?" asks Chase. "Just enough to free a few people to clear more land in each village?"

"Clearing trees is hard work," says Falstaff. "It'll take a long time to bring more land under cultivation. But it's a good idea."

"I will send word out over the radio net. Within a week, every village will know," says Helen. There are fifty villages ringing blacksuit territory, one for each state in the old United States.

"I have lots of metal at the workshop," says Bree. "I could melt it down and use it to forge plows."

"And I can probably figure out a way to produce fertilizer," says Kenny.

"Those are both great ideas!" I say. "I don't know a lot about farming, but metal plows and fertilizer should help boost food production."

"Just one little thing," says Kenny. "I need pee."

"Pee?" I ask.

"Yeah, pee. It's rich in urea, which makes great fertilizer. I'd have to refine it and crystallize it to make it water soluble, but it's very doable. And the nice thing about pee is it's *really* easy to make. I also need poo."

"Oh my," says Helen. "Delivering a constant supply of urea to the chem lab will be hard work. There will be no shortage of volunteers, but the job will be...unpleasant."

"I can help with that as well," says Bree. "We've been building carts with wheels at the workshop. Two people pulling a two-wheeled cart will be able to carry much heavier loads than they're able to carry on their backs."

"We have our work cut out for us," I say. "I suggest we break for dinner and then come back together to discuss our next set of attacks on the blacksuits."

\* \* \* \* \*

We reconvene after dinner and dive right back into our discussion. We're filled with ideas tonight.

"When will each of the villages have their trebuchets delivered?" Our trebuchets are similar to catapults, but more powerful. Bree is building them with help from the villagers stationed at the workshop. The trebuchets are needed for our assaults on the outer ring of forts.

"In another week or two, every village should have a trebuchet and the training to use it," says Falstaff. "We should be ready to attack the outer ring of forts well before the next full moon."

"How are you coming on the hot air balloon?" I ask Kenny.

"I've figured out how to rubberize softbark," she replies. "The slow part is sewing the balloon together. We have a dozen people working on it. Bree is working on a loom, and that should speed things up. Even without the loom, we should have enough material for a small balloon ready in a few weeks."

We decide Kenny will go back to the chem lab to work on fertilizer and her balloon, Bree will return to the workshop to make plows and carts, and Chase will continue working on the construction of forts. Ty and Eva will go to the chem lab with Kenny. Tyler is a physics genius, but he's also done a lot of reading on chemistry. He'll be a great asset for Kenny. They'll all leave in the morning.

"Before everybody goes, I'd like to fill you in on my thoughts for our next attacks on the blacksuits. Falstaff, how many troops do you have here at Phoenix right now?"

"We have three brigades here, three thousand fighters. I've already sent the rest back to the mines."

"Do we know when the blacksuits will do their next gleaning in a village in this area?" The blacksuits glean each village at least once a year. They take thousands of our best young men and women and turn them into slaves

"I believe the next gleaning for Baltimore is scheduled for the quarter moon," says one of Falstaff's junior officers.

"Baltimore is four dayswalk from here?" I ask.

"Less than that if we march both day and night," says Falstaff.

"OK," I say, "here's the plan."

\* \* \* \* \*

We arrive at Baltimore two days before the gleaning. This gives us plenty of time to prepare our ambush. We'll have almost fifteen hundred fighters on either side of the road. They'll remain in hiding until the blacksuit brigade reaches us. Then they'll catch the blacksuits in a cross fire, what Falstaff calls "enfilading fire." Grizz and I will lead a smaller party to block the trail behind the blacksuit column. We want to keep them from retreating back to the safety of their fort.

Officer Kremke is with us, and he is making Falstaff nervous.

"I'm an old marine," he says, "and I know a thing or two about combat. If these blacksuits are the professional army you tell me they are, then your ragtag militia doesn't stand a chance."

"You didn't see our 'ragtag militia' standing toe-to-toe with the blacksuits at the Battle at the Forest's Edge," I point out. "And it was the blacksuits who came off second-best."

"Yes," says Kremke, "but you surprised them with flank attacks. That's not a real test of what an army has inside."

"We're going to surprise them again today," I explain. "So today won't be much different from the last time."

Still, Kremke's doubts have made Falstaff worry. He worries his fighters many not be ready for the fight. Enfilading fire is tricky, because if you're not careful, your arrows will travel straight across the road and hit your own people on the other side. We find an ambush site where hills on opposite sides of the road look down on the road itself. Shooting arrows downhill should reduce casualties from "friendly fire," but Falstaff worries nonetheless. I make a mental note to give Falstaff more time to train our fledgling militia.

We take up our positions at dawn. Falstaff treads up and down the road between our positions, ensuring our people will be invisible to the blacksuits. When he finds fighters with inadequate cover, he barks harshly at them.

"I'm telling you," warns Kremke, "this fight is a mistake."

Kremke fuels Falstaff's own doubts. Falstaff mumbles about how green our brigades are. I point out, once again, the fact that our men and women committed themselves with honor during the Battle at the Forest's Edge. We took everything the blacksuits could dish out, and we won. This seems to calm Falstaff a bit.

Grizz, Kremke, and I are surrounded by one hundred members of the reconstituted Daughter of Gaia Guard. They are sworn to give their lives to protect me, a fact that still causes me terrible discomfort. Daughter of Gaia or not, I still identify myself as Erin Taylor, teenager. And Erin Taylor, teenager, struggles with the notion of people dying for her. My previous Guard came to a very unhappy ending on the day I was kidnapped. I can still hear their cries as the blacksuits slaughtered them. This heightens my sense of unease.

We settle in and wait for the blacksuits. Grizz, Kremke, and I are posted at the extreme northern end of our line. I watch Kremke very carefully. I don't trust him. The minute he looks as though he may make the slightest noise to give away our ambush, I've ordered Margaret, the commander of the Guard, to use her knife to silence him quickly and quietly.

I'm lying flat on my belly with my AK-47 in front of me. I peer out from beneath a scraggly bush and can just barely make out the trail below. Like everyone else, my face is blackened with mud so it won't stand out against the forest background. I swat insects and wipe sweat from my forehead. Periodically, I scoop up a handful of forest loam, spit on it, and use it to darken my forehead where runnels of sweat have dissolved the camouflage. Even in the shade, the heat is overwhelming. There is no sound except birdsong and the chirring of insects. Our fighters are absolutely silent. If anybody is coughing or sneezing, they're doing an excellent job of muffling the sound.

We hear the blacksuits coming long before we see them.

# 3

The blacksuits march with fifers and drummers. We hear the marching cadence softly at first, but the songs become louder with each passing minute. I become more and more nervous as the blacksuits approach. Soon we hear the sound of marching feet and the uniquely military sound of metal rhythmically touching metal. The blacksuit column emerges from the trees along the trail. Can our "ragtag" militia defeat these seasoned veterans again?

If the blacksuits are concerned about the loss of their village forts, you'd never guess it by looking at this column. In the lead are two officers, chests colorful with ribbons and medals. Behind them, the blacksuits, wearing their high-crested military hats, march with the easy gait of a veteran brigade, brass buttons shining in the sun. They talk and laugh among themselves, showing no concern about their mission.

We know there are usually a thousand blacksuits stationed at each of their outer ring of forts, and we know they typically leave only a token force behind when they march off for a gleaning. We don't know if they've changed their practice since we've burned down their village forts. My guess is, because everything has happened so fast, they probably haven't had time to make many adjustments to their routine.

I watch as the blacksuit column passes by below me. By my rough count, there are about nine hundred of them. Next to me is an anxious young officer who has the job of blowing the horn when the last of the blacksuits has passed us by. This is our signal to attack. Unfortunately, nerves get the best of our bugler, and he sounds too early. There are a dozen blacksuits who have not yet passed. With two thousand of our fighters loosing arrows against nine hundred blacksuits, even our less-than-perfect marksmanship drops all but a handful of blacksuits within seconds. The survivors are confused and disorganized. They go down beneath our second volley.

The blacksuits at the end of the line are stunned, and this gives Grizz, Kremke, and me the chance to pick off all but five of them with AK fire. The five survivors turn and run northwest, toward the safety of Fort Gentry. Grizz and I are up in an instant and running after them.

"You stay here," I shout to Officer Kremke over my shoulder. Kremke's guards were up and ready to run, but stop cold. I can tell from Kremke's eyes that he's angry, but I don't trust the man behind me with a loaded weapon. His animus for us runs too deep.

The rest of the Daughter's Guard follow, willy-nilly. Since most of the blacksuits are less than three feet tall, Grizz and I can easily outdistance them with our longer legs. My plan is to pass them and squeeze the five survivors between Grizz and me in front and the Daughter's Guard behind them. I don't want any blacksuits getting home to tell the story of what happened to them. I want them to disappear, which will help our cause psychologically, but I also want the blacksuits in the ring forts clueless and unable to change their tactics to avoid future ambushes.

Grizz and I sprint a hundred yards down the trail without seeing a single blacksuit. They've taken to the forest, which will make it much harder to hunt them down.

"You go right, I'll go left," I yell.

Grizz turns east and disappears in the trees. I sprint another fifty yards and then turn west. I move twenty yards into the trees as quietly as I can, concealing myself behind a tree. A blacksuit is running well in front of me, with another right on his heels. Taking careful aim, I drop the first blacksuit, slide the selector for rapid fire with my thumb, and take out the second blacksuit with a short burst. I hear a shot from the east. Grizz has one. Two more to go.

I walk quietly back to the south. None of the blacksuits has passed me by; they simply aren't fast enough. Hearing noise to my left, I spray a burst of fire in that direction, and watch as another blacksuit crumples. Standing still, I listen carefully. I can hear the Daughter's Guard approaching from the south. I walk toward them. The last blacksuit is either trapped between us or somewhere on Grizz's side of the trail.

In the blink of an eye, I'm caught flat-footed by a blacksuit who has concealed himself behind the trunk of a tree. It's all I can do to block his sword cut with the barrel of my AK. I bring the stock of my rifle around with my right arm and catch the blacksuit on the side of his head. He goes down in a heap, unconscious, but still breathing. His strategy was a good one. If he could have gotten past me, he would have been in a foot race with the Guard, and he'd started with a lead. I wait until the Guard reaches me and ask them to take care of the wounded blacksuit.

Half an hour later, I'm standing with Falstaff, Grizz, and a sheepish-looking Kremke. Our warriors are celebrating. For them, repressed by the blacksuits since memory began, this is heady stuff. The elimination of an entire blacksuit brigade is an experience they never dreamed they'd live to see. I struggle, as I do after every battle, with the guilt and depression that accompanies the taking of life. I hope I never reach the point where I take killing for granted.

Kremke shakes his head. "I was wrong about your militia," he admits. "They committed themselves well. You should be proud of them."

I'm a little startled by Kremke's easy apology, but he seems sincere. Could I have been wrong about him? Is he really a decent human? Other than being a pain in the butt, he's done nothing to make me think he's anything more than an earnest ally.

We've had lively discussions about the treatment of enemy wounded and prisoners. Many villagers want to either kill them or put them to work as slaves, but I forbid this. Compassion is one of the many things that morally separates us from the blacksuits. I order our people to take the wounded to Baltimore for the best medical care we can give them. When they're able to travel, they're to be taken, under guard, to the mines and set free. This presents the prisoners with tough choices: They can't go home; the dreadwolves would get them long before they reached a friendly fort. They can head over the saddle to the waterless desert on the other side. They can sit in a jail cell. Or they can go to work farming for us. The few prisoners we've taken so far choose to farm. By all accounts, they adapt and settle down.

Falstaff and the army will quick-march to Trenton, where, in ten days' time, they'll ambush another blacksuit brigade. After that battle, our people will begin to carry their food taxes and deposit them at the edge of the forest, near the closest outer-ring fort. The message to the blacksuits will be clear: Come to our villages to collect your taxes, and you may die in an ambush. Better to let us bring the taxes to you.

Once the second ambush has been completed, Falstaff will take his warriors back to the mines, where he can give them further training. We need an army that can stand up to the blacksuits in an even fight. To get to that point, we need more training.

The Daughter's Guard, Grizz, Kremke, and I head back to Phoenix. I debate sending Kremke with Falstaff to help him train our troops, but think better of it. I want to keep an eye on Kremke, and Falstaff and Kremke mix like oil and water. I'm afraid I'll find Kremke in the brig on my next visit to Fort Taylor. Falstaff is well-known for his temper.

During the hike back to Phoenix, I take time to meet the members of my Guard. Their commander is a young girl named Margaret. She explains that Falstaff has assigned his finest warriors to protect me.

"We will keep you safe, Daughter of Gaia," Margaret promises.

I recall the wretched fate of my last Guard, but I don't say anything to Margaret. I'm sure she knows the story already. Nonetheless, the members of my new Guard are a confident, swaggering bunch.

We march hard and reach the friendly walls of Phoenix in four days.

Kenny left several weapons she's been working on for us to test. We found tens of thousands of gallons of gasoline at both the chem lab and the workshop, but it had degraded during the hundreds of years it sat unused. Nonetheless, Kenny was able to convert most of it into a highly flammable jelly that she seals in pottery jars. We refer to the content of these jars as "Kenny Gas." In addition, Kenny was able to chemically revive the tear gas we found at the workshop. We also have a large stash of the plastic explosive C4, along with detonators, Kenny's electric voltaic piles, and the wire needed to carry the electric current from the voltaic pile to the detonators. And finally, Kenny found some night-vision goggles on a back shelf of the chem lab.

We spend two days learning to use these weapons. With practice, Grizz learns to use the tear gas launcher with accuracy. I train

Margaret and three of her officers how to work with the C4. We experiment with the night-vision goggles, and they work well. They capture ambient light, and although the goggles make everything look green, they enable us to see objects that would otherwise be lost in darkness.

"Might I ask the Daughter of Gaia what plans she has for using these weapons?" asks Margaret.

"We're going to pay a visit to the blacksuits," I reply.

"With due respect, ma'am, Falstaff told us our job was to keep you safe. Paying the blacksuits a visit doesn't sound very safe."

"Margaret, the Daughter of Gaia leads by example," I explain, simply. "I've decided I can't ask others to do things I'm unwilling to do myself."

Margaret is worried, but I'm not about to sit around and watch others do the fighting.

\* \* \* \* \*

*George and Maureen, the owners of the Shake 'n' Burger, are patrons of the arts. There's a wall in the restaurant reserved for the drawings and paintings of young artists, mostly high school kids from Sierra Vista High. Anyone looking at the wall is bound to conclude that there are a lot of very talented teens in Tucson. They also encourage writing and poetry. The first Monday of the month is reserved for a poetry slam, and the Tucson Ramblers usually gathered to listen to Grizz's poetry on nights when he performed. On this particular night, the Ramblers consisted of just Jules and me, as it was finals week.*

*Grizz likes to work under blue and red lights, which gives him an almost eerie appearance. He's a versatile poet, but likes to write about life's mysteries. Lots of kids participate in the poetry slam, but the biggest rounds of applause always seem to go to Grizz (or perhaps it just seems that way because I'm biased).*

*One night in particular during our freshman year, Grizz was onstage and on a roll. Face intense, eyes closed, beads of perspiration on his forehead, Grizz was reciting his latest. His poetry was passionate, almost magical, and every eye in the room was riveted on him. That is, they were riveted on him until Donnie Horvat and his buddies crashed the party.*

*There were six kids in Donnie's crowd, and they worshipped Donnie. Donnie's a huge guy. He's easily six feet six, with a barrel chest, thick neck, and the muscular arms of a man who spends a lot of time lifting weights in the gym. Donnie and his friends never got along well with books and schooling, so when Donnie dropped out of high school, it was only a matter of time until his friends joined him. Life after high school was a steady roll downhill for those guys. Without a high school education or any useful skills, they had a hard time finding work. They worked the odd construction job and took whatever other work they could latch onto, but basically, failure in life made them mean and bitter. Everybody knew that when you saw Donnie or his friends walking down the street, you crossed over to the other side.*

*Donnie is in his midtwenties now, and recently, he seems to have money to burn. He spends his money mostly in Art's Bar, which is a few doors down from the Shake 'n' Burger. Most folks think that Donnie's seemingly endless supply of money comes from selling drugs. I've seen him myself, lurking in the shadows on the edge of Sierra Vista High, doing business with high school kids. It's common knowledge that Donnie works the middle school crowd as well.*

*On this particular night, Donnie's gang decided to visit the Shake 'n' Burger. They'd obviously been drinking, and they were clearly out to make trouble. They were so noisy when they came into the restaurant that nobody could hear a thing Grizz was saying. They took a table right up front and began razzing Grizz.*

49

"Come on, fag boy, give us some poetry," yelled Donnie.

Grizz tried to continue, but whenever he began to recite, Donnie's crew drowned him out with catcalls.

"Real men don't write poetry, fairy boy," Donnie sneered. Turning to address the whole room, Donnie, who had obviously been drinking, slurred, "All of you in here are faggots. And you girls"—he looked at our table—"you're nothin' but a bunch of butch Lesbos."

From behind the counter, George asked Donnie's crew to leave.

"Why don't you come out here and make us, old man?" hollered Donnie.

"Maureen, call the police," said George.

Maureen picked up the phone, and George took a bat from under the counter and walked out from behind the counter, softly smacking the barrel of the bat into the palm of his left hand. I don't know whether it was Maureen calling the police or George looking like the angel of death with a Louisville Slugger, but Donnie and his friends decided to leave.

"You queers have a good time," Donnie hollered over his shoulder as he walked out the door.

Grizz finished his poem, but the magic was gone.

After he was done, Grizz sat down with us and seemed genuinely unconcerned about Donnie's interruptions.

"Those guys have a hard life," he said simply. "You gotta consider what they're dealing with." We stayed a few minutes longer, finishing our macadamia-coconut shakes before leaving.

When we left the Shake 'n' Burger, we were unpleasantly surprised to find Donnie and his pals waiting for us on the street corner. Standing with them was Officer William H. Kremke of the Tucson Police, probably responding to

*Maureen's call to the police dispatcher. They were all laughing at some joke when they caught sight of Grizz.*

*"My, my," said Donnie. "Fag boy and his Lesbo friends."*

*"I'm not a fag," said Grizz simply.*

*"Sure you are," said Donnie. "You write poetry, don't you?"*

*"Writing poetry doesn't make you a homosexual," said Grizz evenly.*

*Donnie walked straight up to Grizz and planted his face mere inches from Grizz's. "You wanna prove it?" asked Donnie. "Let's see if you're man enough to fight."*

*As a sophomore, Grizz was a big kid, but even so, he was no match for Donnie. "I don't want any trouble," he said calmly, looking Donnie straight in the eye.*

*"Well, you've got trouble whether you want it or not," said Donnie, and he punched Grizz in the stomach. Grizz doubled over, and Donnie took advantage of it by hitting him with a wicked uppercut. The force of the blow sent Grizz reeling backward, blood spurting from his broken nose. Donnie was on him, cat-quick, and doubled him over with another blow to the stomach.*

*I went screaming after Donnie, but one of his friends caught me before I could get to him and pushed me down hard, sending me skidding across the concrete sidewalk.* This sidewalk rash is gonna hurt tomorrow, *I thought.*

*"Do something, Officer Kremke," hollered Jules.*

*By this time, Donnie had landed several more blows.*

*Officer Kremke looked at Jules as though she were some ignorant form of alien life. "The boys are just letting off some steam," he said, and turned back to watch Donnie as he continued to demolish Grizz.*

*I was up off the sidewalk in an instant and went after Donnie again. I was rewarded with another trip to the sidewalk, face-first this time.*

*By this time, Grizz was bleeding from nose, mouth, and ear. His eyes were already beginning to swell shut.*

*Fortunately, Donnie was winded. He gave Grizz one more shot to the stomach, turned around, and walked off down the street with his buddies trailing behind.*

*I was up again, screaming at Officer Kremke. "How can you let them do this? Why didn't you stop them?"*

*Kremke eyed me coolly. "It's a hard world, darlin'," he said. He turned on his heel and walked away.*

*Over the next several days, we nursed Grizz back to health. The amazing thing is, to this day, he doesn't hold a grudge against either Donnie or Officer Kremke.*

*"Donnie and Kremke are being the only people they know who to be," he explained.*

*I wish I could be as philosophical. I hated them then, and I hate them now.*

\* \* \* \* \*

I arrive back in Phoenix to find the villagers have walled off a portion of the village council chambers so my friends and I will have a bit more privacy. They've already installed our mattresses and have moved in chairs and tables. They've created a small office for me with a desk and several chairs, some sized for "giants" and some suitable for villagers. I sit in my chair and smile for a moment, but I have business to attend to.

During the Battle at the Forest's Edge, several hundred slaves working in the fields were within hearing distance of the fight. They brought their shovels and rakes with them and joined our ranks. Most of them perished, but a few survived. We brought the survivors back to Phoenix with us. I spoke with one young man, Bardolph, on the march. He's a fierce young man with fiery eyes, dying to fight against the blacksuits. He has no training; none of the slaves within the circle of outer-ring forts has any military training. They are too closely watched by the blacksuits to do the surreptitious training done by the villagers outside the ring. He has knowledge, however, and I intend to use it. I ask one of my guards to find Bardolph so I can talk with him.

A few minutes later, while I am stuffing AK ammunition clips in my backpack, Bardolph appears at my door. He stands hesitantly in the doorway.

"Come in." I gesture to him. "Please have a seat."

Bardolph takes a seat on one of the smaller chairs.

"Bardolph," I begin, "we're gonna launch a raid on the blacksuits. I want to destroy buildings of value to them. What targets can we reach in a half dayswalk from the edge of the forest?"

Bardolph's eyes flash with excitement. "Will you take me with you?"

"Of course. We'll need you to guide us to our targets."

Bardolph lists several targets of opportunity.

\* \* \* \* \*

We march at sunset and camp for the night at the edge of the forest. We'll be entering blacksuit country near Fort Gentry, but since we eliminated most of its garrison during our ambush, I doubt they have the resources to guard the fort and chase after us at the same time. From their perspective, we could have three brigades waiting out of sight, in the forest, ready to attack as soon as they open the gates. I'm confident the blacksuits will sit on their hands, but as a safety precaution, our little force of just over one hundred warriors will invade blacksuit territory out of sight, a couple miles west of the Fort Gentry.

Officer Kremke has cautioned us against the raid. "Only veteran soldiers should try to fight behind enemy lines. It's too easy to run into a larger force, or to end up cut off from behind."

I take a deep breath and hold my temper. "The Daughter's Guard is a crack fighting force," I counter.

"Sure," says Kremke, "they're great on the parade ground or in an ambush, but face-to-face with veterans, they won't have a prayer."

"You may stay behind if you wish, Officer Kremke, but the raid is going to happen."

Kremke grumbles, but he comes with us as we begin our march.

Within twenty minutes of entering blacksuit land, slaves see us. They drop their tools and swarm around us. The slaves have been burned dark brown from their hours spent working in the fields. They are poorly dressed, and few have a complete set of teeth. Their poverty is readily apparent. This is why we're fighting, I remind myself.

"Has the Daughter of Gaia come to liberate us?" an elderly man asks. He is wearing threadbare woolen pants and is shirtless. His old brown skin sags.

"Not today," I answer. "We have much work to do, but the Court's days are numbered."

As we march deeper into blacksuit country, we see an occasional blacksuit overseer, but the minute they see us, they turn and run. Their flight brings rousing cheers from the slaves.

Our progress is impeded by slaves, who constantly gather around us as we travel. Margaret asks them politely to let us pass. "We have work to do today," she says. "Please let us through so we can fight the blacksuits."

Within an hour, we reach our first target. A small blacksuit fort serves as home for overseers who patrol the surrounding fields. From the fort's diminutive size, I know there can be no more than twenty blacksuits stationed inside. Like all blacksuit forts in the outer ring, it's made from wooden poles buried vertically into the ground. Holes between the logs are chinked with mud. A desultory plume of smoke rises in the still air. We hear the blacksuit in the guard tower sound his horn as soon as he sees us, and within seconds, a dozen blacksuit heads peer at us from the top of the wall.

We move quickly to within fifty yards of the fort. Blacksuit guards loose arrows in our direction, but we are outside their effective range. Grizz loads a canister of tear gas, raises the launcher to angle thirty degrees above horizontal, and pulls the trigger. We watch as the canister rises in an arc, reaches its peak, and falls just inside the walls of the fort. Even at a range of fifty yards, we hear the hissing sound of discharging tear gas. For a brief moment, nothing happens. Grizz launches a second canister for good measure. This one clears the wall and falls inside as well.

The gate to the fort flies open, and nine blacksuits tumble out, coughing and wheezing. They look in our direction, and I raise my AK in case they decide to attack. I could easily kill some of them, but I'm not interested in killing people today. I just want to burn things down. Realizing we outnumber them by more than twelve to one, the blacksuits make the prudent decision and retreat.

"Your turn," I say to Margaret.

We have gone over our tactics a hundred times, and our fighters are ready. Four teams of two head for the fort. Each team takes its own wall. One team member throws a jar of Kenny Gas, the jellylike substance Kenny has refined from aged gasoline, at the wall. The jar shatters, and Kenny Gas slowly trickles down the wooden posts. While this is being done, the second team member lights a fire arrow and shoots it into the gas-soaked wall. We are rewarded by four nearly instantaneous *whoosh* sounds. Kenny Gas has a very distinctive sweet smell when it is first ignited. Within minutes, the fort is blazing. The Guard cheers, and their roars are matched by slaves in the fields, who have stopped work to watch the show.

I can't resist a sideways glance at Kremke. He seems impressed with the businesslike way the Daughter's Guard carried out its assignment. I inwardly gloat.

There's not much surface water in the forest, and what little there is to be found is undrinkable, poisoned in the wars that ended civilization. But this is the monsoon season, and we approach a vast swamp and find it wet and impassable. The brown, fetid pools of quicksand bring back unpleasant memories of my first day on this side of the brane, when I nearly sank into a bog. The only way across the swamp is over a wooden bridge. The blacksuits have posted sentries on both sides of it, but they flee when they see us coming. The swamp is evil smelling, and I'm relieved when we reach the far side of the bridge.

Fifteen minutes later, Bardolph points at a huge gray barn. Its walls are well worn, and the roof looks on the verge of collapse.

"That's your next target," Bardolph says.

"You're absolutely sure that barn has nothing in it useful to the slaves?" I ask. "No food?"

"That barn is used for storing cotton," says Bardolph. "Only the city people and the blacksuits wear cotton clothing."

Except for Helen's acolytes, I've never seen any of our people wearing anything but homespun woolen clothing. Still, I open the door to the barn and check inside. The barn is filled to the rafters with cotton bales. I see a few wheeled carts and some farm tools, nothing of value to the slaves.

"Do your job," I order Margaret.

In less than ten minutes, the fire is raging. We pause for a few moments to examine our handiwork. The barn burns hot. The tremendous heat forces us to back away. Raw cotton burns slowly and generates lots of smoke. Flames and dark clouds of smoke billow high into the sky, and wisps of flaming cotton rise in the air above the doomed barn.

Our next target is a second blacksuit fort. Grizz empties it with tear gas, and Margaret's fighters set it on fire. As we watch it burn, I see movement on the road to our right. Through my binoculars, I see a blacksuit column. They're moving at the double. I hear the telltale military sounds of marching feet, fifes and drums, and metal clanking on metal.

＊ ＊ ＊ ＊ ＊

"What are they doing way out here?" I ask.

"They must be heading for Fort Gentry," Bardolph offers.

Some of the survivors of our attack must have gotten through. This column seems to be headed out to inspect the carnage. Bugles sound, and I watch as the blacksuit column leaves the road and heads in our direction.

"They may have been heading for Fort Gentry, but they're after *us* now. They've seen smoke from the fires." I quickly determine that there are several hundred of them. Even with Grizz and me wielding AKs, we're no match. There are just too many of them.

"I told you so," says Officer Kremke, looking smug.

"Stuff it," I reply irritably.

"That ends our raid for today," I say. "Margaret, quick-march our people back home."

We have a lead of about half a mile. I check every few minutes, but the blacksuits are not gaining on us. Even with the Guard marching at double time, Grizz and I need only walk at a brisk pace to keep up. When we approach the bridge over the swamp, I order Margaret to have her people lay C4 charges on the center span of the bridge.

"Sound off when the bridge is ready to blow!" she orders.

The rest of us take up defensive positions. Grizz, Kremke, and I unsling our AKs and lie prone. The Guard, which will be using bows and arrows, drops to one knee. I watch anxiously as the blacksuits approach. Our people are working frantically to set their charges, but I can tell they won't be done before the blacksuits are in range. The long black line quickly closes the distance between us.

When the blacksuits are less than one hundred yards away, Grizz, Kremke, and I open up with AK fire. On automatic fire, we tear three holes in the blacksuit lines, but they keep coming without hesitation. The blacksuits are cruel, but there's no questioning their courage. I can see an officer, sword drawn, leading the charge. I toggle single-fire, draw a bead on him, and squeeze the trigger. The officer goes down, but the black line continues to advance.

At forty yards, Margaret yells, "Fire!" and fifty blacksuits drop. The blacksuits' archers pause for a brief moment as they string their bows. A rain of arrows falls around us, and several of our people are hit.

"Charges ready!" hollers the officer commanding the explosives party.

"Go!" I order Margaret.

I look around. Many of our people are down, but only two of them are moving. Grizz picks up one and throws her over his shoulder, and I carry the other. Dozens of our fighters pick up their dead comrades. The Daughter's Guard never leaves a fallen comrade behind.

We are running as fast as we can, and since the enemy archers need to pause before they fire, we suffer only one more volley before we are out of range. Unfortunately, bunched up on the bridge, we are an easy target, and more of our warriors go down.

We reach the far side of the bridge and sprint until we pass the explosives party. I turn and survey the situation. A few of the blacksuits have made it across the bridge. But at least two hundred of them are on the bridge when I hear the *crump* sound of plastic explosive detonating. The center span of the bridge falls into the swamp below. Dozens of blacksuits fall with it. The few blacksuits who made it across the bridge realize they are trapped between us and the swamp. Outnumbered, and with no place to go, they drop their weapons and raise their hands.

We've taken losses, but the blacksuits have lost many more.

"Not too bad for a ragtag militia," I say, looking Kremke in the eye.

"You got lucky," he replies.

I suppress the urge to throttle him.

\* \* \* \* \*

One of the prisoners is a junior officer. He's a burly, good-looking man with a salt-and-pepper mustache. I fall in beside him as we march back to Phoenix. I strike up a conversation, hoping to gather military information from him, but he is too well trained to provide me with anything useful.

"Where are you from?" I ask.

"I am village born," he says. "I was gleaned when I was thirteen."

I think of my brothers, who are nearly the same age, how wrenching it would be if I were to see them ripped from our home by strangers.

"Why do you fight for the Court?" I ask, genuinely curious.

"I could either fight for the Court, or I could be a slave working in the fields. The choice wasn't difficult."

"Does everyone who is gleaned have the same choice?"

"No," the young officer replies. "First of all, the girls are not allowed to fight. And the blacksuits are only interested in the biggest and strongest boys. I was big, so I was lucky."

"And you never thought of defecting?"

"At first, I thought about it all the time," he replies. "But a soldier's life is a good one. We eat well, we live comfortably, and when we grow too old, we marry and live in a nice veteran's apartment in the outer suburbs. If I defected, I'd have lived in a village and spent my days farming. I'd be malnourished and hungry half of the time. And if the blacksuits recognized me as a defector, they'd kill me, slowly and painfully."

"How would they know you were a defector?"

"Easy," he replies. He rolls up his sleeve and shows me a tattoo covering his forearm: VB. Village born.

"Will you fight for *us* now?"

"Would you switch sides and fight these people?" he asks, gesturing at the Daughter's Guard. "You hate blacksuits, but to me, they are friends and comrades. No, I won't kill them."

# 4

Back in Phoenix, we check by radio the status of our preparations for our attacks on the outer ring of forts. Everything has gone well. The villagers have had time to practice with their trebuchets, and they're confident they can do what they have to do. We set the night of the full moon as the date for our attack. With plans in place, I decide to rest and relax. I've been on the move nonstop for weeks now, and I'm ready for a respite.

Chase radios in a report that the Sons of 1776 have been sending scouting parties up the saddle. I realize it's only a matter of time before we'll have to deal with the Sons. Right now, we're doing everything we can. Chase is building strong fortresses at the saddle and also at the chem lab and the workshop. Hopefully, we'll be ready to put up a fight when the time comes.

I've suffered several wounds in the last couple months, but most of them have healed. My cracked ribs have mended, and the wound in my side has gone from angry red to a benign light pink. My broken pinkie finger still protrudes at a peculiar angle, but I can use it, and there's no pain when I bend it. Grizz was bitten by a snake during our escape from New Washington, and he has nothing but two tiny circular scars on his leg to show for it.

Being with Grizz every day has been bittersweet. We enjoy each other's company, but there is always an emotional tension present. The longing I have to hold him near is never far from the surface. I can tell he is suffering as well. But, since nothing can be done, we soldier on. I'd rather spend a day with Grizz, painful as my yearnings may be, than spend a day without him.

The two of us travel from Phoenix to the Sanctuary so that we can meet with Helen.

The Sanctuary is located in a vast system of underground caverns buried beneath a small, rocky hill. The Disciples of the Mother hid from the blacksuits here, as the location lies far from the area the blacksuits used to patrol. Now that the blacksuits are unable to launch patrols, the Sisters will continue to use it because it lends itself to the quiet, contemplative lives many of them lead.

Helen asked me to join the order. I gave her offer long and serious consideration. I finally decided to join the order for a number of reasons, but the most important was my growing devotion to the villagers' cause. Although I don't understand why, the effect I've had on their morale and fighting spirit is undeniable. I don't know what makes me special, but I am, at least to them. So, I've been inducted into the Order and am officially a Sister. I took a vow of celibacy when I was inducted, and that really complicates my relationship with Grizz. I didn't fully understand the depth of my feelings for him when I took my vows. I'm torn inside, my conflicting emotions constantly at war.

I have a burning question for Helen. Finding her alone in her chambers, I knock politely. Helen is elderly, but beautiful. Her beauty is not so much a matter of form and figure as it is of soul. She looks at me with her bright blue eyes, full of compassion, as always. Her silver hair gleams in the torchlight.

"Come in, Daughter of Gaia. You look troubled."

"Helen," I begin, "on three occasions now, I've seen Jules." Jules, one of my friends from Tucson, died months ago during the Battle for the Sanctuary. Seeing her, therefore, is troubling. "I saw her once when we were trapped in the blizzard atop the saddle and twice while I was being pursued by the Apaches."

Helen absorbs this information. "What were your circumstances when you saw her?"

"In all three cases, I was at the end of my endurance. I was ready to quit. I was ready to die."

Helen smiles. "But obviously, you did not give up, or we wouldn't be having this conversation."

"That's true."

"Do you remember when I told you that you would be capable of seeing visions, just as I do?"

"Yes, of course."

"When you saw Jules, you were having a vision."

I work on this revelation for a few moments. "Then that would explain why my friends didn't see Jules. During the blizzard, she appeared in front of all of us, but the others didn't see her."

"Your friend Jules loves you very deeply," says Helen. "She has clearly decided to postpone her journey in order to stay with you."

"What do you mean she's postponing her journey?" I ask, confused.

"Death is not the end of a spirit's journey," explains Helen. "The spirit simply moves from one plane to another. Usually spirits are

65

anxious to begin their next adventure. That's why I say Jules must love you very much to postpone hers."

This concept is so foreign to me that it takes me a while to process Helen's words. "So death is not the end of things?" I ask.

"No, child. Death in this world is the end of *this* phase of your journey, but your spirit moves on to a new phase."

"Is heaven the next step?" I ask, remembering my Methodist upbringing.

"Yes and no," says Helen mysteriously. Seeing my confused look, she continues. "The spirit takes many journeys. Spirits may linger in a particular state for as long as they wish. Since some of the phases are gloriously pleasant, some may elect to remain in them for a long time. But most spirits elect to continue their journeys."

"So Jules is staying in this world to help us?"

"Yes, child. Jules was channeling energy to you so you could go on when you were unable to continue on your own. This can be done, but it was very, very exhausting for Jules. She would have to rest for weeks after such an energy transfer."

Helen's revelations are exhilarating. I know I'll need time to fully integrate this new knowledge, but thank Helen for her guidance.

"There is no need to thank me, Erin. Just imagine what your capabilities will be once I have *trained* you to use the gift of visions."

\* \* \* \* \*

Grizz and I have a daily running routine we've kept up ever since our first few days on this side of the brane. We run at least five miles, ten if time permits, and at sunset, we like to climb to the top of the hill above the Sanctuary and watch the sun set. The sunsets here are gorgeous. I don't know whether they're caused by climate change or by something done during the war, but they're beautiful.

Tonight, as Grizz and I watch the sun sink in the west, we finally have time to speak about our experience as hostages in New Washington.

"How did they treat you in New Washington?" I ask.

"Actually, they treated me very well. Since they were using me to make you cooperate with them, I thought they'd throw me in a dungeon somewhere and feed me bread and water, but they didn't. I ate better in New Washington than I did in Tucson."

"I wonder why they treated us so well."

"I think it's because they view us as equals. We're tall like they are. And it doesn't hurt that you're the Daughter of Gaia. The Court is very class-conscious. I talked with the maids who came to my room every day, and they told me there's a very rigid hierarchy in their society. The justices are on top, of course, and then there are the other folks who live in New Washington, the senior military officers, the heads of government, and the managers of their businesses. They're all tall, so they must have eaten well, even during their days wandering the wilderness."

"My maids called them 'the elite.' They said it takes ninety-nine workers to keep each member of the elite living in comfort."

Grizz is pensive. "The people who live in the suburbs are shorter, but they live fairly well. The Court uses them for its own purposes, and they're definitely on a lower rung of the social ladder, but they seem happy enough."

"And then," I say, "there are the slaves and the villagers. They're on the bottom."

"I don't think the Court even views them as being totally human," Grizz says. "They work them hard, and they don't place any value on their lives. If they die young, it doesn't matter because there are always more slaves to be had."

"You know, since we've stopped the gleanings, the Court may have to treat the slaves better because now they can't replace them so easily."

"Or they'll make the women have babies faster."

We sit in silence for a while. I slide over and sit next to Grizz. He puts his arm around me, and I rest my head on his shoulder. This feels as right as anything can feel, and painful at the same time. Tonight I let my demons go and concentrate on enjoying the warmth of our contact. The warmth has nothing to do with temperature.

"How did you keep from going crazy when you were stuck in that room all day?" I ask.

"That was the worst part," says Grizz. "I nearly went stir-crazy. I know what people mean now when they talk about cabin fever."

"Yeah," I agree. "I moved all the furniture in my room to the sides and made myself a little runway. I ran crunches for hours, sprinting ten yards, stopping dead, and then sprinting ten yards the other way. I did this over and over again, until I was ready to drop."

Grizz laughs. "I did the same thing. Hours and hours of crunches. Plus I wrote some poetry. The maids were really kind. They brought me some paper and a pen and ink. The pen was a bird's feather, and the ink was in a jar. I had to keep dipping the point of the feather into the ink."

"You wrote poetry?"

"Yep. Some of the best poems were about you."

"You wrote poems about me? Can I read them?"

"You could, but I left them in my room the night we escaped. I was in such a hurry, I didn't think to pack anything. After all, I had no idea you had an escape plan. I was sleeping peacefully when you started banging on the balcony, and after that, everything moved really fast."

"So Salieri has your poems?"

"Let him eat his heart out," says Grizz. He leans in and kisses me on the forehead. "I love you, ET."

"I love you too, Grizz." Inside I feel that unsettling, but deeply pleasant warmth again.

\* \* \* \* \*

We leave Phoenix on the day of the full moon. The attacks on the forts of the outer ring are going to be carried out by villagers, except for our attack on Fort Gentry. We have the Daughter's Guard to carry out the mission. But everywhere else, villagers are rendezvousing in the forest near a blacksuit ring fort. I can only imagine the excitement they must be feeling. A good dollop of fear must be included, because even though they're wearing wolf bane, hundreds of howling wolves will still surround them, albeit at a respectful distance. The luminescent gleam of their yellow eyes will be visible although their bodies won't be. Being surrounded by crying wolves still gives me the willies, even though I've been through the experience many times. I can only imagine what the villagers must be feeling.

Because there's a full moon tonight, we can see what we're doing without torches. Kremke and I accompany one group of ours as it enters the clearing a hundred yards west of Fort Gentry. Grizz and a second group enter the clearing on the east side. The watchmen in the towers see us immediately and sound their bugles. We hear the sound of hundreds of blacksuits rolling out of their beds and rushing to man the walls. I don't think anyone inside the fort was sleeping very soundly, considering the wolves have been howling ever since darkness fell.

By the light of the full moon, the blacksuits in the fort can see us clearly. But they're powerless to stop us. We're out of range of their arrows, and they dare not open the gates of their fort because the wolves would be after them in a matter of seconds.

Each of our groups has two trebuchets. Bree has made them modular so they can be easily disassembled and carried through the forest. The Daughters quickly and efficiently assemble their trebuchets. We've practiced setting up our weapons every day for a week now. Two guards pull back on the lever, which causes the hydraulic piston that powers the trebuchet arm to contract with a hissing sound. Another fighter adjusts the range finder to a distance of a hundred yards. This causes the trebuchet arm to rise. The bucket at the end of the firing arm is loaded with a jar of Kenny Gas. Margaret, the commander of the Daughter's Guard, releases the launching arm. With a *whoosh*, the hydraulic piston releases, and Kenny Gas is on its way. We watch as it shatters against the wooden wall of Fort Gentry. One of our trebuchets was aimed a little low, so the fighters adjust the range and fire another jar at the fort. This one shatters near the top of the wall, splashing the blacksuits near it.

I watch the faces of the blacksuits on the wall through my binoculars. There is curiosity on their faces, but also fear. They have no idea what we're doing. They have never seen a trebuchet before, and have no concept of what Kenny Gas is. I can hear their officers shouting commands.

The Daughters reset the trebuchets. They load the buckets with fireballs: woolen balls, soaked in Kenny Gas, wrapped around a rock in the middle, which provides heft. The fighters light the fireballs, and the trebuchets once again hurl their missiles at the walls. The fireballs hit the wall and ignite the Kenny Gas, which catches fire with a loud *whoosh*.

Grizz's group has been busy as well. Both sides of Fort Gentry are in flames.

The blacksuits frantically try to put out the fires. They dump water, a scarce commodity here, on the flames. This is ineffective because Kenny Gas burns like grease; water runs right off. The only way to tame Kenny Gas is to smother it. As long as it has oxygen and fuel, Kenny Gas burns.

Within moments, the blacksuits realize their quandary. They can't put out the fire. If they stay in the fort, they'll burn. If they open the gates, the dreadwolves will attack. Most vault over the walls and run north, toward safety. We see the gray shapes of dreadwolves in the moonlight running them down.

The front gates are thrown open, and a group of about two hundred blacksuits charges directly at my party. I didn't anticipate this tactic. I guess they figure they're going to die one way or another, so they may as well take some of us down with them. The dreadwolves mow down more than half of the blacksuits, but the remainder closes in on us. Once the blacksuits are among us, the dreadwolves halt their pursuit, frightened by the scent of the wolf bane our people carry.

The blacksuits outnumber us. All we can do is close ranks and fight back. I curse myself for not bringing my AK. I draw my bowie knife and cut down the first blacksuit I find. Luckily, the blacksuits had no time to form up, so they reach us in small clusters. Still, I see the guardsman on my left go down, and I hit the next in the face with my shield as I parry a sword cut from yet another. A blacksuit approaches me from the right, but he has no sword. He dives at my ankles and knocks me down. I roll and come up fighting, but there are now three blacksuits in front of me. The Daughter of Gaia draws a crowd. Margaret, seeing my predicament, cuts down the blacksuit to my right. I block a sword thrust with my shield and sidestep away from the lunge of the other attacker, hacking at him as I move.

Kremke had the forethought to bring a handgun with him, and he downs a dozen blacksuits before he runs out of ammunition. He drops his gun, now worthless, and scrambles to find a sword and shield left by a fallen guardsman. He picks up weapons in time to parry the blow of a blacksuit officer.

Fortunately, our comrades who had been attacking the fort from the east have seen the blacksuits' charge and react quickly. Trapped between my group and Grizz's, the blacksuits fight on bravely, but the issue is no longer in doubt. Within minutes, the blacksuits are all on the ground.

"I think some of the blacksuits who climbed over the wall got away," says Grizz. The dreadwolves won't venture any farther than a mile from the forest edge, and there may have been more blacksuits than dreadwolves, so some of them almost certainly escaped.

"That's OK," I say. "When they tell their story, it'll put fear into the rest of them. They'll know they have a fight on their hands, and we're not afraid to come right after them."

I look around the battle site and find that fifteen of our own warriors have fallen. Still, we can't help but cheer as we watch Fort Gentry burning, a fiery beacon on a bright moonlit plain.

"I didn't think they'd come after us the way they did," says Kremke. "That was very un-marine-like of me. I'll have to carry a sword and shield next time

Officer Kremke is learning.

\* \* \* \* \*

Back at the Sanctuary, a group of Sisters are jammed into the radio room, waiting for news of the attacks on the other outer-ring forts. Excitement saturates the air. We've already announced the burning of Fort Gentry. We hear static on the radio, meaning somebody is ready to transmit. We wait tensely for the call sign.

"This is Council Chair William calling from Charlotte. Repeat, Council Chair William from Charlotte."

Helen lifts the microphone and toggles the button to speak. "This is Sister Helen at the Sanctuary. We hear you, Charlotte." The tension in the radio room is visceral.

"Fort Thomas is burning!" says William. "Repeat, Fort Thomas is burning!"

A rowdy cheer goes up in the radio room.

Over the next few minutes, congratulations flow in from all of our radio stations. I recognize Chase's voice from Fort Kennedy and Falstaff from Fort Taylor, near the mines. Bree and Kenny chime in, as do the other council chairs on the network. Two ring forts are gone. We hope to hear from Fargo and Boston tonight. They're a few hours' walk from their ring forts, just as we are. The other four ring forts are a six dayswalk from the villages with radios, so we won't know their fate tonight.

Within an hour, Boston calls, announcing victory at Fort Salieri. Shortly after that, Fargo radios to announce the fall of Fort Roberts. Our losses have been minimal. The mood in the room is ecstatic. Sisters waiting for news outside the door hear the cheering from inside the radio room and add their voices to the chorus.

We adjourn to catch a few hours' sleep. I'm keyed up and must wait hours for sleep to come.

After breakfast next morning, we all meet in the Great Cavern of the Sanctuary.

"We've won a great victory," Helen says, "the greatest victory in the history of our people. But we can't rest on our laurels."

"I agree," I reply. "The Court will try to rebuild their forts. They won't build them near the forest again, because they must now realize that the dreadwolves give us an advantage in any night fight near the forest."

"There is irony here," says Helen. "The dreadwolf curse was created by the Court to keep the villages from communicating with one another, but now the wolves keep the blacksuits from traveling and fighting at night, while we move and fight with impunity. The blacksuits are victims of their own creation."

Happy smiles greet this remark.

"That's true," I agree. "But the dreadwolves won't help us as we move the fight away from the forest. As I said, the blacksuits will rebuild. Our job is to make that task as difficult as possible."

"The blacksuits won't build with wood this time," says Grizz. "Now that they know we can easily destroy wooden forts, they'll try to rebuild with stone."

"But the Court does not have enough stone to rebuild eight forts quickly," says Helen. "I don't know how quickly they can quarry stone, but I'll wager it will take them many months, or even years."

"And while they're rebuilding, we need to harass them every step of the way," I say.

"What do you recommend, Daughter of Gaia?" asks Helen.

"We'll soon have an army of twenty thousand warriors," I begin. "And I estimate the Court has no more than twenty-five or thirty thousand blacksuits left. Salieri said he had ten thousand troops guarding New Washington. They'll have smaller garrisons in the three inner-ring forts."

I look around the table and see nods of agreement.

"If they try to rebuild all eight of the outer-ring forts at once, they won't be able to station more than two thousand troops at each without seriously reducing the garrisons of the inner ring and New Washington."

"And they won't do that," says Grizz. "Right now, they must be very worried about an uprising of the slaves in their inner-ring cities."

"I'll send more agents to New Washington and the inner-ring forts," says Helen. "If the blacksuits draw down those garrisons enough, we can be certain the slaves will rise."

"Since the blacksuits won't be able to send more than two or three thousand men to each of the outer-ring forts as they rebuild," I say, "I recommend Falstaff divide our militia into four divisions with five thousand fighters in each. Then we should distribute them around the outer ring. We'll outnumber the blacksuits anywhere we choose to fight."

"We can also use our militia to launch raids like the one we made with the Daughter's Guard," suggests Grizz. "Burn down their bridges and warehouses. Take out their supply trains."

"We'll harass them at every turn!" exclaims Helen. "We must keep our militia equipped with Kenny Gas and firebombs. If we do, over the next few moons, we will bleed the blacksuits dry. With a hundred slaves joining us every day, we'll soon have them outnumbered."

"Will Falstaff have enough fighters trained to carry out our attacks?" asks Margaret.

"He should have them ready soon," I answer. "We'll pay him a visit and see how the training is coming along. I'd like to visit my brothers as well."

"Do we all agree on the Daughter's plan?" asks Helen.

All answer in the affirmative.

That afternoon, two radio messages come from Kenny. The first is good news. The second is chilling.

The first message is: "The balloon will be ready to test in a week or two. Tell ET to get her butt over here if she wants a ride."

I radio back, "I'm on my way!"

The second message is: "Something has been bumping off our sentries at night. Eva seems to thinks it's a thing called a 'skinwalker.' Whatever it is, we're taking countermeasures. I'll fill you in when you get here."

"Somebody has been killing our sentries?"

"Somebody or some *thing*."

"I'll be right there."

# 5

The road between the Sanctuary and the mines is becoming a familiar one. When we reach the place where Jared and Zoe kidnapped me, I pause, and tears come to my eyes. I can still hear the cries as the blacksuits butchered my vastly outnumbered Daughter's Guard. I pause in the clearing and lower my head.

Later that afternoon, Kremke falls in beside me. This is surprising, because he usually works hard to give the impression I'm not really there.

"You may have the pygmies of this world fooled," he says, "with your Daughter of Gaia save-the-world crap, but I know what you really are."

"Really," I counter. "And just what am I?"

"You and your friends are stuck-up snots. You've been handed everything in your lives on a silver platter. You think you're better than everybody else."

"You don't know a thing about me, Officer Kremke. My parents were poor as church mice. And nobody has handed me a single thing on this side of the brane. Everything I've had on either side of the brane, I've had to work for."

"That's not what I mean," says Kremke. "You were born with brains and looks, and your parents taught you all the hoity-toity upper-class manners. Now my boy and I didn't have any of that going for us. We came up rough and dumb, and let me tell you, life's been hard for both of us."

I can tell this conversation is going nowhere, so I resist the temptation to argue. Anyone who thinks my life has been a bowl of cherries is sadly mistaken. But I guess everything is relative. If Kremke thinks he was born holding the short end of the stick, I'll never convince him otherwise.

* * * * *

On the second day of our journey, I am talking with Margaret when I hear a loud explosion. One of the warriors in front of me has disappeared amid a flaming shower of dirt and rock. Another explosion follows, and a second fighter is gone.

"Drones!" shouts Margaret. "Take cover!"

I dash toward the trees ahead. I hear another explosion and am pelted by a shower of dirt and pebbles. I reach the tree line and dive under a tree. Margaret, who was just behind me, dives and lands on top of me.

"What's going on?" I ask, bewildered.

"Look up there," says Margaret, pointing toward the sky.

I look up and through the tree branches I see a silver metallic vehicle shaped like a swept-wing aircraft hovering above the clearing. Listening carefully, I can barely hear a humming noise coming from the drone. There is a single blinking red light on the bottom, near the nose of the craft. The drone circles slowly above the clearing. Suddenly, it streaks off to the south.

"Drones are left over from the old wars," explains Margaret. "They only harm people in the open. Under trees, we are safe."

"If that thing has been shooting people for hundreds and hundreds of years, it must go somewhere to reload its munitions. I wonder where it goes."

Margaret shrugs. "We don't see them often. Maybe one or two times a year."

I want to find the place where the drone rearms.

When we reach the mines, we find them a hive of activity. Falstaff is building a series of defensive strong points around the perimeter of our fields. Anyone attacking us here will have to pay a high price. He's fortified the flanks of the northern twin so attackers can't climb up and fire down into our positions below, and he's expanding Fort Taylor itself, heightening the walls and adding turrets and murder holes.

The southern fields are covered with men and women in training. In the largest field, fighters are practicing with their bows and arrows. Next to them are warriors hacking and stabbing burlap bags filled with seeds. The obstacle course is jammed. Grizz and I can't resist the temptation to run it as well. I've run it before, but the physical challenge is always enjoyable.

Falstaff finds us as we are catching our breath after the run.

"Falstaff, my friend," I say, "you're keeping our fighters busy." I embrace him.

"We make rapid progress, Daughter of Gaia. Let me show you around."

In one field, our trainees are practicing an assault on mock city walls. Some provide covering fire while others throw grappling hooks over top of the wall, climb the ropes, and pull themselves over the top. In another field, our men and women are learning to use trebuchets, although these are much bigger than the ones I've seen.

"Bree thought we'd need bigger machines to attack the concrete walls of the inner forts," Falstaff explains.

"We're going to need something stronger than trebuchets to breach the walls of New Washington," I comment. "But these may be useful against the forts of the inner ring. We'll have to test them."

We pass fields where our fighters are doing calisthenics. Their clothes are soaked with sweat as they do chin-ups, push-ups, crunches, and other forms of muscle-building physical exercise. In another corner, trainees are lifting weights, ingeniously made with rocks mounted on sturdy tree branches.

"By the time I'm done with them, they'll be ready to march for twenty-four hours and launch an attack without rest," Falstaff says.

I can't help but peer at Kremke from time to time. He appears impressed by the preparations we've made.

We pass the military grounds and tour the farms. I can tell our people have cleared new land for farming.

"Our farmers work with remarkable energy," says Falstaff. "We've told them we need more food to grow our militia. We practically drag the farmers out of the field at night so they sleep. We'll

82

double the acreage under cultivation within two moons. I've already radioed Helen and told her to increase the flow of freed slaves, so our militia will be growing even bigger and stronger every day."

As we head back to Fort Taylor for dinner, two towheaded missiles strike and nearly knock me off my feet.

"ET!" cries Han.

"Hi, sis!" says Luke.

We embrace, and I don't want to let go.

"Hey there, Uncle Grizz," they say when they notice Grizz beside me.

"What happened to your hair?" I ask.

"This is what you call a mullet," says Han.

"No," I answer evenly, "it's what I call a mess. Let me guess. Your brother cut your hair?"

"Yeah," Luke admits. "Looks like a mullet to me."

I sigh.

"We're getting really good with the weapons," says Han.

"Yeah, Han shot an onion off the top of my head," says Luke.

"What?" My jaw drops. "What if he missed?" I ask incredulously.

"He's not gonna miss," says Luke. "He's way too good."

Falstaff shakes his head. "They are as stubborn as their sister," he says with a rueful smile.

"Are they ready to fight yet?" I ask, hoping the answer is no.

"Yeah! We're ready," they say in unison.

"Not yet," counters Falstaff, "but they're getting there. They have great natural ability. Han is excellent with the bow, and Luke will be one of our finest swordsmen."

"Not one of the finest," Luke objects. "*The* finest!"

Falstaff rolls his eyes.

"Let's see how good you are," I say to Luke.

We find wooden swords and shields.

"I don't wanna hurt you, ET," says Luke.

"Just worry about yourself."

I launch a flurry of thrusts at Luke. He parries them all and gives no ground.

"Not bad," I admit.

He goes on the offensive. He's fast, and he's good, but he can't penetrate my defenses. We fight on, and he gives as good as he gets. Finally, I'm able to break through and nick his shoulder.

"Gotcha!" I crow.

"Just a cut," Luke responds.

Undeterred, he continues to attack. It takes me more than ten minutes to wear him down and score a killing blow. He's going to be a great one, but he needs to work on his stamina.

"You're good," I concede, breathing hard. "When you can beat your sister, you'll be ready to fight blacksuits. In the meantime, you need to improve your staying power. And concentrate on your shield work against a backhanded cut"

"Fair enough! I'll be ready to beat you real soon. You wanna try, Officer Kremke?" offers Luke.

"Sure," says Kremke. "Why not?"

Luke needs less than twenty seconds to score a killing blow with his wooden sword.

"I guess I better practice," Kremke, admits sheepishly.

"I'd be honored to train you," says Falstaff.

"I'd be honored to have you as my instructor," returns Kremke. So it's settled. Kremke will stay at Fort Taylor with Falstaff and learn to fight with the weapons he'll need in this cruel new world. I can't help but admire the way Kremke has managed to morph from a know-it-all blowhard to a man who admits he has a few things to learn. But I still don't trust him.

"I'll leave your guards here," I say to Kremke . I turn to the guards. "Keep an eye on him."

Kremke bristles with anger, but holds his tongue.

"Let's go run the obstacle course," says Han.

"Loser has to kiss the frog," says Luke.

In a flash, they're gone.

"They have a frog?" I ask.

Falstaff shrugs. "We don't have many animals that make good pets."

"When they're ready to fight, send them to me," I tell Falstaff. "I want to keep an eye on them."

"Begging your pardon," replies Falstaff, "but being near the Daughter of Gaia has not been the safest place to be. Trouble follows you wherever you go."

I can only smile. He's right. "Even so, I want 'em where I can see 'em."

Falstaff leads us to his office in the fort.

"How many trainees are ready to fight?" I ask when we're seated.

"I've taken three thousand of our oldest fighters and sent them to garrison Fort Kennedy and the forts at the workshop and the chem lab. They're good fighters, but they're too old to march with the youngsters."

I nod.

"We have about ten thousand more ready to fight. The rest will need to train a few weeks more."

I tell him about the plan to harass the blacksuits as they try to rebuild their outer- ring forts.

"Great plan," says Falstaff. "We'll bleed them white. They'll have to rebuild their forts or lose control over their fields. And we can make sure rebuilding costs them dearly. We'll have them outnumbered wherever we choose to fight. Are you planning to travel with our fighters?"

I demur. "I'm going to visit Kenny and see her hot air balloon."

"I thought, since you have actually attacked forts and led a raid, you could help our people as they learn to do these things," says Falstaff.

"I can join them," says Grizz. "I can help our fighters while ET gets her balloon ride."

I'm surprised by the strength of my physical reaction at the thought of leaving Grizz. I literally throb inside. But his plan makes sense.

With that settled, we join Falstaff and his officers for dinner. Just as we are finishing, our fighters drag a prisoner into the mess hall.

"We caught one," the leader says. "He was with a party that killed a bunch of our people near the mines. Most of them got away, but this one was wounded."

They push forward a limping man whose hands are bound. His pant leg is wet with blood. His hair is long, black, and shiny. An Apache. The Sons are sending their scouts to reconnoiter.

\* \* \* \* \*

I ask the Apache to sit.

"My name is Erin," I say pleasantly.

The Apache glowers in response.

"Would you like food or water?" I ask.

"I need nothing from you. I know you. You are the One Who Got Away," he says.

"Yours are not the only people who can run hard," I say evenly.

"One day we will catch you," he says. "And then we will see what you are made of."

"Perhaps," I reply. "In the meantime, I have a few questions for you."

"I will tell you nothing," he says, and his eyes flash insolently.

"Why are you here?"

He sits in silence.

"Are the Sons of 1776 planning to attack us?"

His silence continues.

"Your people are called Apaches, but many of the ones I saw had blond or red hair. Why do they call you Apaches?"

I'm startled when he begins to speak. "There are very few N'de left," he says. "So we train others who show promise. They are not as strong as the N'de, but they are good."

"They weren't good enough to catch a girl," I say. If I make him angry, he may say something he otherwise wouldn't.

"Your day is coming," he hisses viciously. "And it will be coming soon. Very soon."

*Very soon?* I think. *That's bad news. I'm glad we're improving our defensive positions.*

I know I won't get any more from him. "Watch this one carefully," I say to Falstaff. "He's dangerous."

"We will tend his wounds and guard him well," replies Falstaff.

The next morning I leave with the Daughter's Guard. Falstaff has brought our strength to one hundred again by replacing the fighters we lost during our raid and our attack on Fort Gentry. The monsoon season is winding down, so I'm not as worried about being caught in a blizzard again as we approach the crest of the saddle.

By midday, we reach Fort Kennedy, where Chase greets me fondly.

"ET," he says warmly, "I can't wait to show you what we've accomplished!"

"Mother Helen has suggested we call this place Fort Kennedy in your honor, I say. (Chase's last name is the same as Kenny's first name.)

Chase blushes and grins. "What an honor! Imagine that, a fort named after me."

The fort is impressive. It's built on the western side of the saddle, so it won't attract attention from anybody traveling along the eastern side of the mountains. The walls stand twenty feet tall and are topped with murder holes. Two-story bartizans are built at all four corners, and at the midpoint of the walls as well. The bartizans will ensure anybody trying to scale the walls will be caught in plunging enfilading fire. The gates look solid and sturdy. All the trees, shrubs, and rocks have been cleared from the area, creating good fields of fire in all directions.

"What are those people doing?" I ask, pointing at a group of men and women who seem to be painting the fort black.

"The black stuff is a gift from Kenny," Chase explains. "After we saw how easy it was to set a wooden fort on fire in the dry season, Kenny decided we should coat our wood with fire retardant. The only problem is, she can't make it fast enough to coat Fort Kennedy and the ones at the chem lab and the workshop all at once. So she's given Fort Kennedy top priority."

"Why is that?" I ask.

"Do you see those blockhouses there and there?" Chase asks, pointing at two buildings to the south of the fort. I see others to the north as well. "Those are there to keep our sentries safe at night. The Apaches have been coming through here for a couple of weeks now, and they were playing havoc with our sentries. So now, we keep the sentries safe in the blockhouses and set out torches all the way across the saddle, but the Apaches still get through."

"I know. We caught one near Fort Taylor yesterday," I say.

"I assume with all the traffic around here, the Sons of 1776 are planning to attack us. I think the Apaches are scouts measuring our strength so the Sons will know what they're up against." Chase looks worried. "The fort is a strong one, and Falstaff sent me a thousand warriors to hold it, so we'll put up a good fight when they show up."

"The fort looks like it can accommodate a lot more than a thousand fighters," I note.

"We've built it for a garrison of up to five thousand," Chase responds.

"It'll be a while before Falstaff can send that many soldiers up here."

"I know. But look at what else we've done." Chase leads me into the fort, and we climb the steps into a bartizan. We peer out the narrow window of a murder hole. "Do you see that pile of rocks over there?" he says, pointing at a pile about fifty yards from where we're standing.

"Yes," I reply.

"Watch this." Chase dips a copper wire into a jar containing a liquid solution. The pile of rocks disappears amidst a huge explosion. When the smoke clears, the rocks are gone, and there's a large hole in the ground in their place.

"Holy cow!" I exclaim. "What was that?"

"That's a mine. Bree made fifty of them for us. We'll set them off when a crowd of enemy fighters gets close. We have them hidden all over the place. Bree will make more, but she's up to her ears making wolf bane and plows."

I can see many more piles of stones now that I know what to look for.

"How are the forts at the workshop and the chem lab coming?"

"They're all about done," says Chase.

I enjoy the tour Chase gives me. The barracks for housing the troops are in various stages of completion, but there's a large mess hall and an armory that are finished. Chase points out an exercise yard, which doubles as a parade ground for training fighters.

"I can't believe you've accomplished so much in the short time you've had," I say.

"All the credit goes to the workers," Chase responds. "Our people are hard workers. They seldom take breaks, and they work from sunup to sundown. They know the Sons are coming, and they know we need this fort to keep them away from our farms below."

I decide to spend a few days at the fort to rest and watch as our people put the finishing touches on our defenses. I also spend two nights in the guard tower looking for Apache infiltrators. Torches are burning clear across the saddle, but I don't see any activity. Have they finished scouting, or have I just picked a couple of slow nights?

I hope for the latter because if the Sons are done scouting, the attack is coming, and it's probably coming soon.

\* \* \* \* \*

We descend the east side of the saddle, and on the trail to the workshop, we pass a party of our people headed west toward the saddle. They are heavily burdened, each person carrying several jars of wolf bane strapped to their backs. They are headed back toward the villages. Our people still need the wolf bane to travel safely at night in the forest. I wonder if it's possible to manufacture the wolf bane at the Sanctuary so we won't have to haul it over the saddle.

We spend several days with Bree in the workshop. She has been busy. There is a huge workroom in the there, and it's filled to capacity with people mass-producing wolf bane. In the main room, Bree has a large furnace fired up. As we watch, she and her helpers place a large square of metal into a cauldron and push it into the fire using a long insulated rod. A half hour later, they remove the cauldron from the fire and pour the molten metal into a mold.

"When it hardens, we'll have another plow," Bree explains. "The people who built this place left us tons of metal to work with, but we'll need more if we want to produce enough plows to really improve our farming efficiency."

"The Court was mining iron ore," I say.

"We'll have to find a source of carbon to turn the iron into steel," replies Bree. "Iron is brittle. An iron plow will work, but it'll break down after heavy use."

"So we need a coal mine?"

"That'd be ideal," says Bree.

I ask Bree if it would be possible to transfer our wolf bane production to the Sanctuary to speed up delivery to the villages.

"I've been intending to suggest that," she says. "But I wanted to be sure we had a surplus before we interrupted production to move the whole operation. Hauling our heavy equipment over the saddle will be difficult."

I think about the places where the path up the saddle is almost vertical. Manhandling heavy equipment and delicate lab supplies will not be easy.

"Let me know when you're ready to move," I say. "I'll see if we can get you some extra hands to help."

I enjoy our stay at the workshop. The place is alive with the energy of our hardworking people. The mood is a happy one. Our villagers know they're doing important work, and I admire their work ethic. They're fast and efficient, pausing only to eat and sleep. Bree tells us she has to force them to go outside for exercise once a day.

* * * * *

We leave Bree and start the two-day trek to the chem lab. When we arrive, Kenny greets me with a hug. Tyler is there as well, and we embrace warmly.

"I'm glad to see you guys," I say. "If there's one thing I hate more than anything on this side of the brane, it's that I don't see my friends nearly enough."

"This world keeps us busy," says Kenny, in an understatement.

Once we've cleaned off the dirt from the road, Kenny leads Tyler, Eva, Margaret, and I into a small room that she uses for an office. Kenny has somehow fashioned a small desk, a couple tables, and five chairs. All are loaded with stacks of papers, chemical paraphernalia, and jars full of smelly things. As a chemist in the lab, Kenny is scrupulously clean and tidy. To make a lab work, she has to be. But you'd never know it by looking at her office.

"Please, take a seat," she offers, gesturing at the chairs.

Realizing there are piles on the chairs, she scowls at them. She has an owlish look of confusion on her face, as though the piles had magically appeared or been placed there by some mysterious intruder.

Seeing us smiling, she says, "Oh, just put that stuff on the floor. A neat office is a sure sign of a small mind."

I'm not sure I agree with her, but decide to change the subject. "Tell us about the skinwalker."

Eva explains, "Ancient Navajo legend tells us skinwalkers are witches who can change their shape at will. When they need to hide, they turn into snakes and hide beneath rocks. When they want to travel fast, they become eagles. And when they want to kill, they take human form."

"Do you believe this myth?" I ask.

"I didn't at first," says Kenny. "But now I'm not so sure. Our problems started one morning when we found our sentries dead. Back then, we posted a single sentry on top of the hill, another by the hatch, and a third one out by the old highway. One morning we found all three of them dead. They had the most terrible expressions on their faces, as though they'd been frightened to death. We examined each

94

sentry from head to toe and couldn't find as much as a bruise on their bodies. And their killer left a black rose in each sentry's right hand."

"That black rose is her trademark," says Eva. "She gives all her victims a single rose."

"Is this skinwalker an Apache?" I ask.

"No," says Eva emphatically. "The skinwalker *frightens* Apaches. They won't even say its name. And Apaches are fearless."

The thought of something that makes an Apache afraid gives me a little shiver.

"The second night," continues Kenny, "we stationed three sentries at each post. In the morning, all nine were dead. Expressions of horror on their faces, black roses in their right hands. We searched around the sentries' posts, but couldn't find a single footprint. Nothing coming in, nothing going out. We looked for hours. Whatever it was, it didn't leave a trace."

"The skinwalker killed *three* people before they could react and defend themselves?" I ask incredulously. "And she did it to all three groups?"

"Like I said," Kenny continues, "I was skeptical at first, but after the second night, I became a believer. I don't know what's out there, but whatever it is, it kills, and it kills fast."

"Has anything happened since then?"

"After the second night, we put six guards at each post, and we set out enough torches to light up half the desert. We haven't had any problems since. We don't know if the skinwalker left or whether she can't kill so many people at once, but we're not going to let our guard down."

I turn over what I've heard in my mind. I'm not willing to believe this skinwalker has supernatural powers, but she's obviously going to be a formidable opponent.

"We're going to need to figure out who's doing this," I say at last. "I don't know how, but we'll have to find a way. Eva, how do you kill a skinwalker?"

"The legends say it's almost impossible," she answers. "You can kill a skinwalker when it's in human form, but it's so fast and so silent that you'll never see it coming."

I change the subject. "So tell me about the balloon. Does it fly?"

"Yes!" says Kenny. "I've taken it up to a height of fifty feet and kept it there for an hour. No sign of leaks, and the burner works like a charm. I've extracted a gas very similar to propane from the decomposed gasoline in the workshop. It burns well, and it's very efficient at giving the balloon lift."

"Let's take a look at it."

Kenny leads us outside. The balloon isn't inflated, but even lying on the ground, it looks enormous.

I touch the balloon with my hand. I'm surprised when it makes a loud crinkling sound. "It's noisy."

"Yes," says Kenny. "When I started the balloon project, I began by making the balloon from softbark alone. But when I filled the balloon and increased the pressure, molecules of gas escaped, and over time, the balloon deflated. So I tried to rubberize the softbark using very light material. I solved the problem of escaping gas, but the material is crinkly. It's quiet once the balloon is inflated."

"You stained it black," I note. Not only is it black, it's flat black. No sheen at all.

"Yeah," says Kenny. "A blacksuit arrow or two can bring this baby down, so I figure we'll probably want to fly at night so they can't see us. I've managed to mask the burner, so the only thing to tip off the blacksuits when we're around will be the sound of the burner, and the burner's not very loud."

"Good thinking. I'm impressed, Kenny. When will you give me a ride?"

"Tomorrow morning suit you?"

"Tomorrow morning suits me just fine."

"That thing really flies?" asks Margaret doubtfully.

"That thing really flies," says Kenny. "Now let's get some dinner."

Kenny lays out a feast for dinner. We have stewed eggplant with goat cheese, snow peas, and a salad with fresh greens, tomatoes, carrots, and onions. I crave meat, but the villagers need their sheep for wool and their few goats for cheese and milk. And there's not much game in the desert around the lab.

Kenny has built a table tall enough for "giants" with booster seats for the villagers. Bree has used the woodworking machinery at the workshop to craft comfortable chairs. Kenny has added soft pillows for the seats.

As we're eating dinner, one of the sentries from our lookout post on top of the chem lab hill bursts in.

"There's something you need to see," he says breathlessly.

"What is it?" I ask.

"I don't know, but it's very big, and it's headed this way."

# 6

We leave our half-eaten dinners behind and run for the hatch.

"You can see it best from the top of the hill," advises the sentry.

We scramble up to his post.

"There," he says, pointing to the southwest.

The sentry is correct. Our visitor is enormous. It appears to be a robot built from metal. It gleams in the evening sun. The robot moves quickly, and the distance between us rapidly shrinks. As it comes closer, we can literally feel the earth shake with each step it takes.

The robot is an android: two arms, two legs, and a large torso. Its head is square and seems to be attached directly to its trunk. It has no neck. Its walk is peculiar. After a moment, I realize why. When he walks, his arms don't move. They're probably there for the sake of appearance. They make it look more human.

"What do we do about *this* thing?" I ask.

"Hope it's friendly?" Kenny suggests.

"As fast as it moves, I'd hate to try to outrun it," adds Tyler.

I rack my brain, but none of our weapons will be of any use against this colossus. AK fire, I'm reasonably sure, will simply bounce off.

"Keep the hatch open," I holler down to the warrior guarding the door. Fortunately, the hatch is on the opposite side of the hill from the approaching automaton. We'll have at least a few seconds to scramble back to safety before the robot can walk around the hill. "If that thing starts shooting missiles or bullets, we'll need to get off the hill and into the chem lab, pronto. In the meantime, we wait and watch."

The meantime turns out to be very short. Within minutes, the giant robot stands at the foot of chem lab hill. It's gigantic. Standing on the crest of the hill, we look straight into the glowing red eyes of its massive head.

"My name is Garganto, killer of killers. Look on my power, ye mighty, and despair!" His deep, gravelly voice is thunderous. His mouth moves as he speaks, but when it opens, we see no teeth.

"Well, that's just great," whispers Kenny. "The killer of killers is standing right here on my doorstep."

"We mean you no harm," I say, doubting it'll do much good.

The giant laughs. The roar of his laughter literally shakes the ground beneath our feet.

"No one harms Garganto," he roars. "Garganto is the killer of killers!"

"So you're the killer of killers. Does that mean you kill only killers?" Kenny asks.

"No!" bellows Garganto angrily. "I kill everyone! I am the greatest of all killers. That is what Garganto means when he says 'killer of killers.'"

"Well, you should be more specific," says Kenny, sounding downright cheeky. "You can take that 'killer of killers' thing two ways."

"You are impudent!" thunders Garganto. "I will enjoy squashing you, little female insect."

"Kenny, what are you doing?" I whisper urgently. She ignores me.

"OK, Garganto," says Kenny, "go ahead. Kill me."

"Garganto kills by squashing little bugs like you beneath his feet."

"And you can't climb up this hill to squash us," taunts Kenny.

"I will wait for you to climb down."

"And what if we decide to wait up here and not come down?"

"Garganto will wait. You little creatures need food and water. Sooner or later, you will come down."

"We have food and water right here on this hill," counters Kenny.

"Garganto's father instructs Garganto to be patient. Garganto's father says, wait three hundred sixty-five days, if necessary."

That's very bad news. We don't have enough food to last a year, and I don't want to be trapped here for a year even if we did.

"Before I squash little insects like you, Father instructs me to ask three questions. Garganto has mercy for some," he rumbles.

*Well, that's good to hear*, I think. Maybe we can wriggle out of this thing on a technicality.

"Are you robots?" asks Garganto.

"No," I respond.

"Are you British?" asks Garganto.

"No." What does that mean? Why does he care if we're British?

# D.S. Northrop

"Are you my father?" asks Garganto.

This one causes me to hesitate. What happens if I answer yes?

"No," I reply after careful thought.

"Good!" bellows Garganto. "I will squash you like bugs."

"Wrong answers, genius," hisses Kenny.

"How old are you, Garganto?" I ask. We have to find a way to wriggle out of this quandary. Perhaps we can talk our way out.

"Garganto is nine hundred eighty-six years, seven months, three days, five hours, seven minutes, forty-two seconds old."

"Wow. You're pretty old. How many people have you squashed?" I ask.

"Garganto has squashed 127,416 little creatures."

"You're nothing but a big fat bully!" hollers Kenny.

I'm not certain, but I don't think making him more angry is a good strategy.

"Cut it out!" I hiss.

"What is 'bully'?" asks Garganto. "I do not have the word 'bully.'"

"A bully is a big can of prunes like you who picks on people smaller than he is."

"Yes, that is right. I kill little things. Garganto is bully. Thank you, little creature. Garganto. Bully," he says with relish. "Bully. Bully." He happily turns the word over and over again.

"Do you have conversations like this with all your victims before you squash them?" I ask.

The hill shakes with Garganto's laughter. "No. People run from Garganto. People don't talk to Garganto."

"You asked us if any of us were your father," I observe. "Don't you know what your father looks like?"

"No," says Garganto. "My father was human. He died long ago. But he promised to pass my secrets down through generations."

"Oooh, Oooh," whispers Kenny. "I have an idea."

"Well, by all means, try it out," I whisper urgently.

"You have done well, my son," says Kenny. "I *am* your father."

My jaw drops. Oh my God. Kenny is really going to make him mad now. What's she up to? What's she *thinking*?

"Harrumph," says Garganto. "If you *are* my father, then what is your name?"

"Well, here goes nothing," Kenny whispers. "My name is Percy Bysshe Shelley." She manages to tell him this last part with a straight face.

*What the…?* I think. Tyler and I exchange glances. He's as mystified as I am.

"Father! Is it you? After all these years?" rumbles Garganto, excitement in his voice.

"Yes, Garganto," says Kenny, "I am your father."

"Then you will know the password," says Garganto suspiciously.

"Of course I know the password, my son," says Kenny. "The password is Ozymandias."

"Father! Father! It *is* you!"

Tyler and I trade looks of amazement.

"Oh…my…God," whispers Kenny. Then she speaks to Garganto. "Yes, son. It is me."

"Why did you not tell me when I asked if you were my father?"

"I didn't tell you because I was testing you. I wanted to see if you were following my instructions after all these years."

"Yes, Father. I follow your instructions to this very instant," says Garganto with feeling. "I love you, Father. If my arms were real, I would embrace you."

"Oh jeez," whispers Kenny, "am I glad his arms aren't real!" The she turns to Garganto. "I love you as well, son. Will you follow my orders right now?"

"Yes, of course," thunders Garganto with joy and devotion in his voice.

"My orders are to stay right here. We humans are tired. We need sleep. And, oh yes, don't squash anybody."

"I will not move," Garganto agrees happily. "I will not squash."

"And remember, Garganto, 'Naught may endure but mutability,'" says Kenny.

"Oh, what a splendid day!" says Garganto, who begins to recite:

What is Heaven? A globe of dew,

Filling in the morning new

Some eyed flower whose young leaves waken,

On an unimagined world.

"I have found my father," rumbles Garganto. "There can be no doubt!"

We work our way down the hill and into the chem lab as Garganto happily recites poetry.

"What was that all about?" I ask, overwhelmed by curiosity. "How did you *know* that stuff?"

"The way Garganto introduced himself," Kenny explains. "'My name is Garganto, killer of killers. Look on my power, ye mighty, and despair!' I knew I'd heard those words before. And then it occurred to me. The lines are almost identical to those in a poem by Percy Shelley."

"Don't tell me. Let me guess," I say. "The name of the poem is 'Ozymandias'"

"Bingo."

"Where on earth did you read the poem?"

"What, you think the chemistry genius can't read poetry? I think I'm insulted."

"No, no…It's just that, well…" I'm at a loss for words. "Kenny," I say finally, "you're the greatest!"

Kenny grins. "Garganto's kinda cute once you get to know him, don't you think?"

"If you say so," Tyler snorts. "Really cute for a mass murderer who calls himself 'killer of killers."

"Don't be so critical of my boy. Think what he can do to the blacksuits!" says Kenny. "And I'm his beloved daddy! He'll do anything I say!"

"OK, Pa. He'd be awesome fighting blacksuits. But how do we get him to the other side of the mountains? Remember, he said he couldn't climb," I say.

"We'll worry about that later," says Kenny. "Right now, I'm hungry. I didn't get to finish my dinner."

My friend Kenny. Father of the world's most vicious robot. Life on this side of the brane keeps getting stranger and stranger.

Over a late snack, we discuss our new friend, Garganto.

"Why won't he kill the British?" I ask.

"Percy Shelley was British," says Kenny. "But since he's been dead for over a thousand years, I doubt he built Garganto."

"Maybe the men who made him were British?" suggests Tyler.

"The British were our best friends, back in our day," I say. "Maybe Americans made him and wanted to protect our allies."

"If that were the case, why wouldn't they have programmed him not to kill Americans either?" asks Kenny.

"Beats me," I admit. "How do we get him to the other side of the mountains?"

Kenny scratches her head, thinking. "The mountains must end somewhere. Why don't we tell him to walk north for a couple weeks? As fast as he moves, he'll cover hundreds of miles. If he can't find a way around the mountains to the north, I'll have him come back here, and send him off to the south."

We climb back to the top of the hill, and Kenny gives Garganto his marching orders.

"Yes, Father," rumbles Garganto happily. "As you wish. And I will be warmed by my love for you every step of the way!"

"Good boy," says Kenny. "I'm proud of you."

Garganto stomps away, heading north.

* * * * *

I awake the next morning excited. I've never flown in a balloon before, and I'm looking forward to the experience. I have confidence in Kenny's abilities as a chemist, so I'm not frightened at the thought of flying, although my general fear of heights gives me pause.

We eat a hurried breakfast and head outside.

"Will you take me up, too?" asks Tyler.

"Sure," says Kenny.

"ET, I'd like to introduce you to Merry," says Kenny. "Merry is the gal who supervised the crew that sewed the softbark together. They worked thousands of hours on it. I promised Merry she could ride along."

"Pleased to meet you, Merry," I say.

Merry looks down. "I'm so excited to meet the Daughter of Gaia," she says as she shuffles her feet nervously.

"And I am pleased to meet you, Merry," I reply, smiling.

Merry lifts her eyes and looks at me, devotion on her face.

"Step inside," Kenny says. Tyler and I hop into the gondola. Merry carefully climbs up the side of the basket and drops in.

Kenny carefully attaches the bottom of the balloon to the gondola, which houses the burner. Cylinders of gas are attached to the sides of the basket. She ignites the burner and turns the valve on a propane cylinder. Slowly, the balloon begins to fill.

"I have a vent inside which prevents the balloon from taking off. When I open the vent, the hot compressed gas is released, and the balloon takes off like a missile. I figured we may need to take off in a hurry some day."

"Good idea," I say. I have a mission in mind for the balloon, and a quick takeoff will be a necessity.

Even with the vent closed, the compressed gas causes the balloon to climb very slowly. Kenny watches carefully to make sure the balloon material is spread out evenly and won't get snarled.

"Hold on tight," she warns.

Despite my faith in Kenny, my pulse begins to hammer. Tyler looks amazingly calm. Merry's face is a mask of terror. The villagers have never even imagined flying.

Kenny opens the vent, and the balloon shoots up like a rocket, just as she predicted. Its crinkly material lets out a thunderous roar as the balloon fills and expands instantly. Before I can even catch my breath, we're over a thousand feet high and climbing fast. I watch as the people below dwindle in size, and soon, the hill above the chem lab shrinks to a speck. The temperature drops rapidly. Within moments, I'm shivering with cold. Tyler is grinning like an idiot. Merry's eyes are closed, and she's hanging on to the rail of the gondola with a death grip.

"We're OK," I say, throwing my arm around Merry's shoulders.

As soon as I say this, things begin to go *very* wrong.

# 7

The balloon begins to move horizontally at breakneck speed. The wind that is carrying us is so strong that it tilts the gondola sideways, and when I look to my right, I'm looking almost straight down. I realize that I'm crushing Merry beneath me. With an effort, I roll off Merry, who is wailing in terror.

Even Tyler looks troubled.

"What's going on?" I holler so Kenny can hear me above the wind, which is blowing my hair straight up from the top of my head.

"Jet stream!" hollers Kenny.

With the gondola sideways, the burner is no longer beneath the balloon, but aimed at the horizon. Kenny has no control over the balloon whatsoever.

I watch as the mountains disappear behind us at incredible speed. If this is a jet stream, it's a jet stream on steroids. The ground below flashes by in a blur.

With no burner to keep the air inside the balloon warm, the balloon begins to deflate. Within a few moments, we begin to drop like a rock. Just when I've accepted the fact that I'm going to die, we fall below the jet stream. No longer buffeted by the wind, the basket rights itself. But the momentum of its motion carries the bucket past vertical, and we find ourselves falling toward the opposite side of the gondola.

Merry begins to fall out of the basket, and I grab her by the hem of her tunic. Tyler helps me keep her inside the gondola, which has righted itself again. It swings past vertical again, and for a few seconds, it rocks back and forth like a pendulum, bouncing us from side to side. Finally the gondola settles, and the balloon is once more directly over the burner. Kenny is back in control.

"Can you fly us back?" I ask.

"Not unless we can find a jet stream blowing back the other way," says Kenny.

"You can't steer this thing?"

"I wasn't planning on going anywhere," says Kenny gruffly. "I thought we'd go straight up and come straight back down. There are never any clouds above the chem lab, so I had no idea there was wind blowing up here. Global warming must have set off some low-altitude windstorms."

Below me, the desert spreads flat to the horizon to the south. To the east and north, I see green-colored land. Plants? People? Far off to the north and east, I see thin ribbons of blue. Rivers? To the west are our home mountains. I can barely make out the twins and the saddle. Below us, the ground is no longer moving. The balloon is just hanging, motionless, several thousand feet above ground.

"I guess we should go down," says Kenny, "since we're not going anywhere." She turns down the burner, turning it up only when we begin to descend too quickly. Within a matter of minutes, we're back on the ground.

Kenny hops out of the gondola and kicks the ground. "Nuts! Nuts! Nuts! Ouch!" The last expletive comes after she kicks a large, unyielding rock.

I want to holler at Kenny for scaring the stuffing out of me and for getting us into this predicament, but it's not her fault. She's right. She had no way of knowing there'd be such high winds aloft.

Tyler, as always, looks unflappable. "We have a little hike in front of us," he observes mildly.

I take stock of our situation. I can't know exactly, but judging from the size of our home mountains, I guess we flew about sixty miles. Tyler is a slow walker because of his injured knee, and Merry is a shade less than three feet tall. We'll be lucky to cover fifteen miles a day.

Ever since I was chased by Apaches, I've made it a habit to take two canteens of water and weapons wherever I go. Having been caught without my AK at the battle of Fort Gentry, I now carry an AK as well as my sword. Paranoid after the skinwalker attacks, my friends are also armed to the teeth. Tyler and Kenny have AKs slung over their shoulders, and Merry, whose size makes it impossible to carry an AK, has a bow and arrows. I always carry dried food in my backpack, too, just in case.

"Did anybody else bring food?" I ask. Tyler and Kenny have brought their backpacks, standard practice when leaving safety.

"I didn't think I'd need any," says Kenny. Merry shakes her head.

Tyler rummages through his backpack and finds a small container of dried potatoes. "There's enough here for a couple meals," he says. I'm not surprised. Tyler eats nonstop. He's never far from food.

"We can't leave the balloon here," says Kenny.

The gondola and the propane tanks are a write-off. There's no way we can carry them. I watch as Kenny draws her knife and begins to slice away at the balloon. In a few minutes, she has cut it into three roughly even pieces. Softbark is incredibly thin and light, but I'm still amazed: when we fold it carefully, it fits snugly in our hiker backpacks.

We inventory our water supplies. I have two full canteens, Tyler has a full canteen, and Kenny's canteen is half full. Merry didn't bring water.

"I think it'll take us four, maybe five, days to hike back to the chem lab," I say. "We should have enough water to get us home, if we're careful. We'll limit ourselves to one *very* small swallow an hour." I give my second canteen to Merry.

I dig my pedometer out of my backpack, set it to zero, and hook it to my belt. I want to know how far we travel. I check my compass, but the twins and the saddle are almost due west.

We hike until it's nearly dark. There isn't much vegetation on this side of the mountains, but even so, an hour of gathering nets us a little pile of firewood. We don't need a fire for the heat, but since there's a waning sliver moon tonight, the fire gives us some night vision. It'll also keep the animals away.

"I'll take the first watch," says Kenny.

Tyler volunteers for the second watch. Merry will take the third, and I'll take the last. I'm an early riser anyway.

We talk our way into the night, mostly about the terrors of our balloon ride. At midnight, I punch my backpack into pillow shape and fall asleep instantly.

I wake and feel intensely cold. *That's funny*, I think. We're never cold in this scorching desert. I wrap my arms tightly around my chest and drift off to sleep.

I wake in the half-light of early morning. Why didn't Merry wake me for my watch? The fire has gone out, and this alarms me. I sit up rapidly and see Merry slumped over sideways. I look at her closely. Her face is deathly pale, her expression one of abject terror. Whatever she saw was horrible. There's a single black rose in her right hand.

\* \* \* \* \*

I grab my rifle and survey the area around our camp. There's nobody in sight. I rouse Kenny and Tyler. The shock of finding Merry dead brings them awake instantly. We search around our campsite, looking for tracks or clues that might tell us something about the murderer. We find absolutely nothing. There are tracks leading in from the east, but we made those ourselves. We also scoured the area last night looking for firewood, but the only tracks we find are our own.

"Do you believe in the skinwalker now?" asks Kenny.

"I do," I reply. "But why would the skinwalker kill Merry alone? Once she'd knocked off our lookout, she could've killed us all. Why did she leave us alive?"

"She left us alive because she's playing with us," says Kenny.

This is a sobering thought. The skinwalker doesn't want to simply kill us. She wants to terrify us before we die. She's let us know she's here, and she's deadly. She's also told us she thinks she can kill us anytime she wants. If she wants to frighten us, she's succeeded.

The three of us turn around in circles, over and over. Where is she? Can she see us now? Is she watching? There's no sign of her.

We break camp quickly. Without a shovel, it's not possible to give Merry a proper burial. We find rocks and bury her beneath them. At least the vultures won't get her. We bow our heads when the last stone is place.

"Rest in peace, Merry," intones Kenny quietly.

We walk west with a new sense of urgency. I've decided to walk backward. I'll be no slower than Ty is going forward.

"Let me know if I'm about to trip over something," I ask. "I don't want this woman sneaking up behind us."

Despite being careful, less than an hour into our walk, I trip over a little rock and sit down hard.

"Ooof," I say as my butt makes contact with the ground.

"What did you trip over?" asks Kenny.

I point at the small rock.

"How'd you trip over that?" asks Ty. "It's tiny."

"No, I'm not hurt," I say stiffly. "Thanks for your concern."

Ty and Kenny smile.

"Nothing hurt but my pride." I make a note to be even more careful of my footing. I learn that walking backward is not easy, and find myself on my duff several more times.

After my latest fall, I look back along our trail, my heart skips several beats, and my blood turns cold.

Standing behind us is a woman. She's about 150 yards away. I quickly grab my binoculars and train them on her. Her hair is black as coal, as are her eyes. She's dressed in black from shoulder to toe. Her eyes are expressionless, like a shark's eyes, and they frame a prominent nose shaped like a hawk's beak. Her smile frightens me most of all. Her lips are curled in a grin that reminds me of the way a corpse smiles after a particularly painful death. Cold radiates from the skinwalker, and I can feel it here, 150 yards away. I shiver.

"Come here," I holler. "We'd like to meet you." In point of fact, I don't want her anywhere near me.

She stands, not moving, not even blinking.

I've been carrying my rifle so I wouldn't need any time to unsling it in the event of an attack. I lift the AK and take very careful aim. I breathe deep, release my breath, and squeeze the trigger gently. I miss her. At 150 yards, she's out of range. Tyler and Kenny take shots as well, with no more success than mine.

The skinwalker remains unmoving. She doesn't even flinch at the sound of the AKs barking. She stares at us, expressionless.

"All right, that's enough," I snarl. I sprint right at her. Surprised, Kenny and Tyler follow, although Tyler, on his gimpy knee, is quickly left behind. When I reach a range of seventy-five yards, I stop and shoulder my rifle again.

Just as I line her up in my sights, she disappears. She doesn't turn around and run. She doesn't fall to the ground. She simply…disappears. I walk to where she was standing. I'm absolutely certain I'm on the exact spot. But there's no sign of her. No tracks. Nothing.

"This is crazy," I say. "Nobody can disappear like that without leaving a trace."

115

We spend the next half hour exploring the desert in expanding circles around the place where the skinwalker disappeared. We find nothing. No prints. No caves. No arroyos. Not a single place for her to hide.

Without any other options, we walk west again. Once again, I walk backward. We break late for a quick lunch, and just as we're finishing, the skinwalker appears again. Once again, she's just out of AK range. I'd sell half my teeth for a sniper's rifle.

This time, when we resume walking, she stalks us. The blacksuits are evil, and Oskar Salieri is a fiend, but this woman radiates pure malevolence. I keep my eyes glued on her all afternoon. As the afternoon stretches on, she disappears. A few moments later, she appears, as if from thin air, to our left. She disappears once more, and a few minutes later, she appears on our right. Then she's behind us again, following, never getting closer than 150 yards.

"I've had it. She can't follow us if we split into two groups," I say. "I'm going to run as fast as I can to see if I can put some distance between us. I'll set up an ambush ahead. You two stay here. Give me an hour, and then follow me."

I take off at a sprint. I don't think the skinwalker is a sprinter, and I still don't buy the turning-into-an-eagle nonsense. She's quiet, and she's deadly, but I simply don't believe in shape-shifting. I look over my shoulder several times. Every time I look, I see Ty and Kenny standing back-to-back with the skinwalker patiently waiting. At least she's not coming after me.

I keep running until they're out of sight, and then I run for another fifteen minutes for good measure. I see an ideal ambush sight ahead. Two large rocks lie about fifty yards north of the heading we've been following. I break off a large shrub and use it to cover my tracks as I walk backward toward the rocks. I position myself behind the rocks and use the brush to camouflage my position. There's no way she'll be able to see me from the trail. I raise the barrel of the AK, being careful to keep it concealed behind the brush.

Forty-five minutes later, I see Ty and Kenny walk past, back-to-back. Both swivel their heads nervously from side to side. I wait for the skinwalker to follow them. Five minutes. Ten minutes. Fifteen minutes. Finally I give up and peer over the rocks. The skinwalker is nowhere to be seen.

I hear a shrieking sound behind me, and a chill runs down my spine. I swing around, my AK firing on automatic. The shriek I heard was the skinwalker's laughter. And there she stands, 150 yards to the north of me. She's been behind me for God knows how long. The sound of her laugh is like the sound of fingers scraping across a chalkboard, only worse. I'll hear that horrible screeching laugh in my nightmares for months. Assuming I live that long.

＊ ＊ ＊ ＊ ＊

Ty and Kenny come rushing back to me after they hear the sound of my AK.

"Did you get her?" Kenny asks anxiously.

"No," I say.

I'm still shaken by the way she was not only able to find my ambush, but how she got around behind me without me noticing. Once again I have the feeling of terror that comes with knowing she could have killed me, but chose not to. Her arrogance enrages and terrifies me at the same time.

"She did it again." I spit out the words, frustrated. "She was right behind me. It was *impossible* for her to sniff out my ambush. How does she *do* that?"

"I don't know," says Kenny. "But she's starting to make me mad."

As I maneuvered into my ambush position and waited for the skinwalker to walk into my trap, time passed, and the sun has begun to sink toward the mountains to the west. We have no more than an hour or so of daylight left. I check my pedometer. We've only walked twelve miles today. At this rate, we'll run out of water before we get home.

I briefly consider walking all night. But there will be little or no moonlight tonight, so we won't be able to see past the noses on our faces. At the very least, the skinwalker has a remarkable sense of sight and probably a powerful sense of smell as well. Stumbling around in the dark, we'd be sitting ducks for her. So we stop for the night.

"We sit back-to-back tonight. Three fires," I say, "one fire in front of each of us. We need enough brush to keep three fires burning all night. No watch schedule tonight. All three of us stay awake all night long."

Ty and Kenny nod in agreement.

One of us scans the desert around us while the other two gather kindling. Knowing the skinwalker may reappear at any moment, we work quickly. When we've stocked enough brush to burn all night, we sit down, back-to-back-to-back. There's no approaching us without at least one of us seeing. I settle in for a long night. If we can stay awake, there's no way she can sneak up on us.

"What's the skinwalker doing way out here?" I ask, knowing the question is rhetorical. "I can see why she'd hang around the chem lab, because there are people there. But why is she way out here in the middle of nowhere? She had no way of knowing we'd land our balloon here. *We* didn't know we'd land our balloon here."

"Dunno," says Tyler. "Maybe this isn't the middle of nowhere. Maybe there's something else out here that's drawn her attention, and we just blundered into her."

That's worth thinking about. Maybe there *is* something out here. We didn't see anything from the balloon, but then we weren't really looking for anything other than firm ground to land on.

I read my watch frequently. Every fifteen minutes I say, "Sound off."

Tyler says, "Right here, boss."

Kenny says, in her best scary movie voice, "Nobody here but the skinwalker."

"Not funny," I say. But it is, in a dark, Kenny-ish way.

I'm so frightened I have no trouble staying awake. I'm vaguely aware that my body is tired, but I never come anywhere near nodding off. Periodically, I begin to tremble with fear. I force myself to remain as calm as I can, considering a witch as wicked as the devil himself is stalking us in the darkness. When I do my fifteen-minute checks, my friends respond with voices alert and clear. They're not going to sleep either.

The night seems to last forever. My heart leaps into my throat every time I hear the slightest sound, and the desert is far from silent at night. I watch the sky to the east and finally see the false light that comes just before dawn. I take a deep breath and let it out slowly.

Suddenly, I'm cold. Not chilly, but *cold*. Deep, shivering, teeth-chattering cold.

"Sound off," I say, fear and near panic in my voice.

"Here," says Kenny. "Do you feel the cold?"

I wait for Tyler's voice, but he doesn't speak.

"Ty?" I say. "*Ty?*"

Ty's back feels cold where it presses against mine.

I jump to my feet in panic. Tyler falls over on his side. His face is locked in a horrible grimace. In his right hand is a black rose.

# 8

"Noooooo!" I scream.

Kenny begins to wail as well.

We hear the screeching laughter of the skinwalker, carried on the morning air, seeming to come from all directions at once. She shrieks again and again, mirthful, taunting.

I realize I'm hysterical, and I can't stop myself from sobbing. Enormous, gut-wrenching sobs, sobs that leave me breathless and gasping for air. Ty dead? He can't be. The thought is too terrible to imagine.

The skinwalker could walk right up to us and kill us both, because neither Kenny nor I are capable of doing anything but cry. We hold each other as we weep, crying hard, hot, bitter tears.

Very slowly, my rational mind begins to exert control. I have to get a grip on myself. We can't stay here all day. We need a plan. Kenny and I release the tight clutch we have on each other. I sit down, feeling as weak as a newborn kitten. I'm faintly aware that my nose is running, but I don't care.

I hear Kenny blow her nose.

"Here," she says, handing me a slightly used rag.

I find a dry patch and blow my nose as well.

"How did she *do* that?" I ask rhetorically. "We were wide awake. We had fires burning. How could she walk up without Ty seeing her or saying anything?"

"That witch is supernatural. What are we gonna do now?" Kenny asks, voice quivering.

*OK*, I think to myself. *It's time to be the Daughter of Gaia.* I take a deep breath.

"First, we're gonna bury Tyler," I say. I know I'm speaking, but my voice sounds distant and removed. My mind is miles away from my body. I rise slowly and begin shuffling around, gathering rocks. I put them next to Tyler. I can't bear to put them on top of him yet. Kenny begins to gather rocks, too.

Within half an hour, we've collected enough rocks. I force myself to lift a rock, and I gently place it on Tyler's chest. Kenny and I begin to cover Ty, slowly, gently, and carefully. Putting rocks on Tyler's face is the hardest part of all. I place one last rock, covering the last hint of Tyler's face, and I begin to cry again. I can't stop crying. *Tyler, who wrote songs for me. Tyler who could always make me laugh. How can he be gone?*

When we're done crying, we stand over Tyler's grave. "Please God…" I pray, but I don't know what to pray for. I want Tyler back. That's all I want. But I know it's not going to happen.

I numbly shrug into my backpack and sling Tyler's pack over my left shoulder. Kenny takes Ty's AK. We walk side by side today, shuffling our feet, moving slowly and awkwardly. I glance back once in a while, but there's no sign of the skinwalker. If she wants to sneak up behind me and cut my throat, let her.

We don't stop for lunch because we're not hungry. As the day wears on, my grief begins to slip away. Slowly, steadily, anger replaces pain. At first, it's a cold, weak anger. But it builds all afternoon. By evening, anger burns white hot. Neither Kenny nor I say a word, but I can see in her face a mirror of my own, teeth clenched, face stony with determination.

"We're gonna kill the hag," I say.

Kenny and I stop and watch the sun set. When darkness falls, we wait until we can't see beyond the ends of our noses. Without saying a word, I open Tyler's backpack and remove the part of the balloon he was carrying. I lay it out flat on the ground. It makes a loud crinkling sound, but that can't be helped. Kenny helps me spread out my piece of the balloon, and then we spread hers. We work by sense of feel alone, because we can't see a thing.

When we finish, we sit back-to-back in the exact center of the unfolded balloon, or as close to the middle as we can, given that we can't see. I unsling my AK and thumb it to rapid-fire. I hear a click as Kenny does the same. With her keen senses, the skinwalker may well see the trap we've laid. My hope is that, since we've been such easy targets, she may become a little careless. And a little carelessness is all we need.

We didn't sleep a wink last night, but I'm not tired at all. I'm too furious to be tired. Kenny and I struggle to remain perfectly still, because the slightest movement sets the balloon fiber crinkling. There's no moon tonight, and that's perfect for us. In the near-starless nights of this world, vision fails altogether on nights when there is no moon. I find it impossible to sit perfectly still for hours on end. One by one, nerves fire of their own accord, and I twitch.

Near dawn, the air turns bitter cold. My heart begins to hammer in my chest. I hear a tiny, almost imperceptible, crinkling sound to my left. My mouth is dry, and fear races up and down my spine. I swing my AK in the direction of the sound and burn off an entire clip, spraying the area from which the sound came. I swivel the barrel left and then right, down and then up. Kenny does the same. With the clip exhausted, I eject it and quickly load another. I stop and listen. Nothing. I crawl carefully over to the origin of the sound, poking the barrel of the AK in front of me. I hear a soft *thunk* as the tip of the barrel touches something. I reach out, shaking fingers extended. By sense of touch, I make out a face. Long hair. Sharp nose. Teeth. Rictus grin, even in death. As the sky begins to lighten, we confirm our kill visually. The skinwalker exudes cold and malevolence, even in death. I can't stop myself from shuddering. Her corpse has been riddled by AK fire.

Kenny crawls over and sits next to me. We lean against each other. As we sit, the tears come again.

We're still sitting next to the dead skinwalker when the Daughter's Guard finds us near midmorning. Margaret takes one look at us and knows not to speak.

"We found the skinwalker," I say, my voice toneless. "That's her, right there." I kick her with my toe.

"And the others?" Margaret asks quietly.

"Dead," I say. "Both dead."

"I'm sorry," says Margaret. She knows there's nothing else to say.

Finally, Kenny and I stand and stretch. Two nights of sitting and tension have left my muscles tight and sore.

"Let's go home," says Margaret softly. She stands on tiptoe, reaches up, and puts her hand on my shoulder. She squeezes my shoulder gently.

We follow Margaret as she turns to the west. Kenny and I hold hands as we walk, just like we did when we were little girls. Two sleepless nights and two days of unrelenting fear have left me numb. I stumble frequently, as does Kenny.

Margaret walks with us and explains that the Daughter's Guard began searching for us the minute our balloon blew out of sight. They had no way of knowing where we landed, of course, but they knew the direction we were moving.

Through the fog of my emotions, I see a fighter in front of me disappear in a burst of smoke and fire. Pebbles from the explosion fall across the desert floor. I stand still, trying to make sense of what I'm seeing. It finally dawns on me: we're under attack.

# 9

I look around the desert and don't see a thing.

"Drone!" shouts Margaret.

I look up and see the drone high above us. I instinctively drop to the ground, as do the others. Lying down is no defense, I realize, as three more warriors vanish in the midst of explosions.

"What do we do now?" I holler.

"Die," says Margaret. "You can't get away from drones when you're out in the open." We are surrounded by featureless desert. No vegetation except heat-blasted little shrubs and cacti.

*Nuts to that*, I think. I'm on my feet and running in an instant. The Daughter's Guard follows me, but two more go down.

And then, without discernible reason, the attack stops.

"Why's it stopping?" I ask Margaret.

"I don't know," Margaret says, puzzled.

I watch as the drone flies away to the north. After a few minutes, it stops, hovers, and slowly descends toward the ground. We lose sight of it. *What's it doing?* I wonder. The explanation comes to me in a flash.

"I think the drone ran out of ammunition. That's why it stopped its attack! And I'll bet it just set itself down at the place where it reloads."

Tired and emotionally drained as I am, I want to see where that drone landed.

"Follow me!" I shout, and I begin walking north toward the place the drone disappeared. The slowness of the Daughter's Guard frustrates me once again, but they take their mission seriously, so it would be rude to leave them behind.

Within an hour, we find a dilapidated-looking building surrounded by what used to be a barbed wire fence. A faded sign reads:


Property of the United States Army

Danger!

Keep Out!


The Daughter's Guardsman on point brushes what's left of the fence out of her way and walks cautiously toward the building. Her bow is strung, and she carries it in front of herself, ready to loose an arrow within milliseconds. The warriors are spread out in a skirmish line, six feet apart. Margaret has trained these men and women well.

I watch in horror as the guardsman on point disappears in a terrible explosion. She is lost in a cloud of smoke and fire. We hit the ground. I look up at the sky, expecting to see a drone overhead. There's nothing up there.

"Land mine?" suggests Kenny.

"That would make sense," I say.

A noise emanates from a round structure on the right side of the dilapidated building. The round structure is moving, rotating. As it swings around, I see a very large gun barrel swivel in our direction. It stops moving and begins firing. Even though we're flat on the ground, the gunfire hits one of the guardsmen. It swivels around and hits another.

It moves for a third time, and I shout, "Fall back!"

We are instantly on our feet and running. The gun brings down two more guardsmen before we manage to retreat beyond its range.

"Let's get out of here before that drone rearms," I shout.

"You heard the Daughter," hollers Margaret. "Let's get out of here on the double." The Daughter's Guard forms up and begins to trot away from the dilapidated building.

"There can't be anybody inside that base back there after all these centuries," I exclaim. "How did the gun swivel around and find us? How do the drones find us?"

"Infrared imaging, I imagine," answers Kenny.

"What's that?" I ask.

"The drones read the heat signature of our bodies," explains Kenny. "They had that technology in our own day. They're programmed to fire at heat images of a certain magnitude. If the heat signature's too small, it won't fire, or it'd wipe out every squirrel and bunny in Arizona."

"Is there a way we can make ourselves look like squirrels and bunnies?" I ask. "I'd like to get into that building and look around."

"Hmm," says Kenny, considering. "You know, I just might be able to do that. There's a closet full of cold-weather gear in the chem lab. It's made of a shiny reflective material. You put it on, and it seals your body heat inside. It's very efficient. Great stuff if you're camping outside in the cold."

"That's great, Kenny!"

"Of course," Kenny continues, "there's also the problem of the land mines that blew up one of our guys."

"But we can clear the minefield." I remember overhearing a program the twins were watching on the History Channel. The program dealt with clearing old minefields in Afghanistan, left behind by the Russians."

"You can do it," says Kenny skeptically, "but the life expectancy for amateurs is gonna be pretty low."

"But still, if you were careful…"

"Oh boy," Kenny groans, "ET's got another project."

I grin, and Kenny smiles dryly in return

We make camp early that night because Kenny and I are exhausted after two nights spent awake and terrified. I fall asleep at once and sleep surprisingly well, but wake just before dawn drenched in sweat from a nightmare involving Tyler and the skinwalker. I see Kenny awake, sitting at camp's edge, staring into the distance. I sit next to her.

"Do you think we'll ever get a night's sleep without nightmares again?" she asks.

"It'll take a while," I say.

\* \* \* \* \*

We reach the chem lab two days later. I've had a lot of solitary time during the walk home to process my feelings about Ty's death. I know I'll be grieving for a long time, but I have to keep functioning. There are too many things going on for me to throw myself a pity party. Kenny also seems to be doing well, considering.

My first job at the chem lab is to break the news to Eva. She's devastated. She and Ty had seemed so happy, which makes his death even worse. Her life as a slave before we found her had been one of constant misery. After everything she endured at the hands of the Sons of 1776, having happiness wrenched from her is cruel. Kenny spends lots of time with Eva, holding her, comforting her. I do so as well.

My next job is to announce Ty's death over the radio net. Chase calls back almost instantly.

"What happened?" he asks, and I can tell by his voice he's crushed.

I explain as best I can, but I can't make the facts any less painful. Grizz doesn't call, but he's probably off on a raid with the militia. I envy the few days he'll have without the knowledge of Ty's death.

The worst thing about Ty's death is how senseless it was. He wasn't fighting a noble battle; he was murdered by something malign and evil, for no imaginable reason. We weren't a threat to the skinwalker; we had no business with her at all. At least when the blacksuits kill, they kill for a reason.

Shortly after my conversation with Chase, Bree comes on the radio network, and I go through the whole story again.

Kenny, Margaret, and I plan for our return to the drone's munitions center. Any facility capable of keeping a drone aloft and armed for many centuries must possess some terrific automation. Perhaps we can find something we can use for our own purposes. Kenny has cut down the heat-reflective cloaks to fit members of the Guard. Since we have a limited number of cloaks, we'll take only Margaret and a dozen hand-chosen warriors.

The day before we leave, Grizz comes on the radio net and announces several successful raids against the blacksuits. Our forces chased the blacksuits away from two of the forts they had started to rebuild. The militia destroyed what little building they'd accomplished and appropriated the blacksuits' construction tools for our own use. Another raid had torched the Court's prime vineyards. There'll be a wine shortage in New Washington.

Grizz is as shocked at the news of Ty's death as the rest of us. I feel sorry for Grizz, Bree, and Chase, because Kenny and I have one another and can share our grief. The others must mourn alone. Grief shared always seems more manageable.

\* \* \* \* \*

Knowing there are drones in the vicinity, we have four fighters constantly scanning the sky. Each is guided by another warrior assigned to hold them by the arm and maneuver them around obstacles so they don't trip. We look a bit silly walking this way, but we've previously learned of a drone's presence only after one of our people was blown up, and that's an unacceptable price for an early warning system. We consider wearing our heat-reflecting cloaks as we walk, but reject the idea. With our body heat trapped on the inside of the cloaks, we'd broil.

When it comes time to pitch camp for the night, Kenny and I drive four ten-foot-tall poles into the ground arranged in a square ten yards to a side. We use the poles to mount two large sheets of canvas above our heads, one canvas sheet three feet higher than the other. The canvas over our heads should mask our body heat and make us invisible to drones.

"*We* may not see well on a dark night," Kenny explains, "but a thermal imaging drone can spot a heat signature as well at night as in the day."

When we arrive at the drone munitions center, I decide to survey the entire site before we try to work our way through the minefield. The old building has seen much better days, but the turrets containing the heat-imaging guns shine like brand new. As we walk around the east side of the building, I stop, and my jaw drops in amazement. The ground has been excavated to a depth of about four feet. The excavated area covers at least a hundred acres. Mounted in this shallow cavity are thousands and thousands of solar collectors, aimed toward the south, gleaming in the sun. We find another array of solar collectors on the west side of the building.

"They must have wanted to mount the solar collectors below ground level so they wouldn't be scoured by the odd dust storm," Kenny says.

"Those collectors are pristine!" I say in awe. "They look as though they've been cleaned this morning. There's not a hint of dust on any of them."

"That many solar panels must produce enormous amounts of energy."

"Is it possible there are people alive inside that building?" Margaret asks.

"I doubt it," I say. "Unless they have underground hydroponic farms, how would they get food? And if they were going to use hydroponics, why not build a greenhouse and use natural sunlight?"

"I'd say it's time to check out the minefield," says Kenny. "We don't know what kind of triggers the mines are using. If they use a pressure plate, the mine goes off only if you step on it, so the mines will be easier to clear. If they're using some kind of proximity motion sensor, things will be a lot trickier."

Before we enter the minefield, we erect the canvas roof so those of us not actually clearing mines can relax without worrying about a drone raining down fire. Those of us who are working in the minefields don our heat-reflective cloaks. The desert is hot enough when you're wearing cloth. Wearing a cloak that traps body heat, the temperature soon becomes scalding.

Kenny has assembled four heavy balls to help clear the mines. Standing well back from the edge of the minefield, she takes one and rolls it into the field like a bowling ball. There is no explosion. She repeats the process with the other three balls. Careful to walk only where the balls have gone, she works her way up to where the balls stopped rolling. I erect little flags to mark the safe path. I cast a wary glance at the turrets housing the thermal-imaging guns mounted near the corners of the old building. They don't budge.

When Kenny rolls the balls again, the third one sets off a mine.

"Pressure plate trigger!" Kenny grins. "This job just got easier. Powerful explosion, though. It blew my bowling ball to smithereens."

After the mine explodes, the gun turret swings in our direction. The turret seems to be activated when a mine detonates. Kenny and I drop to the ground. The gun doesn't fire. Our heat-reflective cloaks are working!

Sweat drenches my body from head to toe. I start to feel faint and realize there will be a limit to how long we can remain in the sun wearing our wraps. Kenny and I head back to the canvas shelter.

Kenny explains her mine-clearing strategy to us. "Crawl on your hands and knees. Brush the sand in front of you away *very* gently. Get an inch deep. If you find something buried there, use your knives to pry it out of the ground. Never, *ever* put any weight on the top of the mine, or it'll be the last thing you do. Clear a path three feet wide, and plant flags to mark the safe path. The mines probably need at least twenty or thirty pounds of pressure to detonate, or they'd have blown up every scorpion that crossed them."

I decide to try the strategy myself. I walk slowly through the small area that has already been cleared. I get down on my hands and knees and unsheathe my knife. Using the lightest touch possible, I scrape away the top layer of sand and work my way down. In minutes, sweat is pouring off my body. The temperature inside my suit is incredibly hot. If I stay in the sun long, I'll be baked like a potato.

I slowly work my way forward. I stop when my knife makes a scraping sound. I can see a fraction of a metallic object. Using my fingers and brushing very lightly, I uncover a circular device about twelve inches in diameter, buried about two inches deep. Taking my knife, I carefully insert it, point straight down, into the ground, touching the side of the mine. I pull the handle of the knife toward myself, and the mine is lifted slightly. I move the knife and repeat the operation all the way around the mine. Sweat is running into my eyes, and I wipe it away with the back of my hand. Finally, after several minutes of careful work, I can slip my fingers under the mine. I lift it cautiously, being careful to touch the sides and bottom only.

"Be careful!" Kenny shouts. "If you drop that thing, we'll need the rest of the afternoon to find all your pieces."

*Thanks, Kenny*, I think, but I don't want to say anything that might break my concentration. Taking little baby steps, I walk out of the minefield. Then, I slowly set the mine down. I hurry to the canvas shelter and instantly strip off my thermal cloak. My tunic is drenched in sweat, but the desert air around me seems downright cool. I gulp air. I didn't realize it, but I've been holding my breath for a long time.

"Nice job, ET," says Kenny.

"Your turn," I counter.

By nightfall, we've worked our way only twenty yards into the minefield. The work is slow, hot, and tedious, but it must be done if we're to explore the munitions setup. At this pace, it'll take us five days to clear a path.

My sleep this night is troubled by nightmares of Tyler and the skinwalker. Again.

We wake the next morning to a curious whirring sound coming from the west side of the old building. We arm ourselves and walk around the side to investigate the noise and are surprised to see thousands of little machines working their way through the solar collectors, burnishing them until they gleam. They also seem to be excavating underground wires, checking them, and reburying them.

"Checking to see if the wiring needs replacement," I mumble in wonder. Before civilization collapsed, it had evidently made great strides in robotics. This makes me more determined than ever to get into the munitions center and see what other surprises may be waiting there.

On the third day, one of the Guard gets careless and pays the price. The rest of us work more carefully than ever before. On the evening of the fifth day, we reach the munitions building. I stand in front of a huge doorway that looks as though it will roll up like a garage door.

"It's nearly dark," I observe. "We've cleared our way in. Let's wait till tomorrow morning to explore. I want to be fresh before we move in. There may be more booby traps inside."

I'm excited about tomorrow, so it takes me a while to fall asleep. I have a pleasant thought before sleep comes: no more back-breaking, sweat-drenching work is needed to clear the minefield.

* * * * *

Over breakfast, Kenny observes, "The door into that place may be rigged to explode if we open it."

"Don't even think about opening the door yourself," Margaret commands, looking back and forth between Kenny and me. "If someone is going to be blown up, it'll be one of the Daughter's Guards. We'll draw straws."

"That won't be necessary," says Kenny. She sorts through her backpack and removes a small block of Semtex. "We'll open the door the safe way."

After breakfast, Kenny rigs the door and sets off a very small explosion. We watch appreciatively as the door collapses in a cloud of smoke.

I pause before entering the old building. I can't help but be disappointed when all we find are deep piles of dust. The sun peeps in through holes in the roof and illuminates dust motes as they drift about. The walls are made of gray metal and have been badly worn over the centuries. The desert on this side of the mountains is almost totally dry, which explains why the building hasn't disappeared altogether. Dry, stable air is great for preserving things.

"Wait a second!" shouts one of our warriors. "Look at this!"

She points excitedly at a hatch that had been buried in dust.

We all work hastily to clear the dust from the hatch. Off to one side is a small box built into the floor. Kenny tugs on the recessed handle, and the box's small door swings up. Inside are two buttons, one red and one green.

"Hmm," mutters Kenny. "I'm guessing the green button is the one that opens the hatch."

"Stand back," says Margaret. The guardsmen look as though they will physically carry Kenny and I away if we don't back up, so we oblige.

Margaret herself pushes the green button. We hear a hydraulic *whoosh*, and the hatch in the floor slowly opens, revealing a broad ramp leading down. Next to the ramp is a set of stairs. While the floor of the building above ground is covered in dust, the ramp and stairs are spotless.

"OK," says Margaret. "Let's see what's down there."

As I peer down the ramp, all I see is inky darkness. There's another control box on the wall at the top of the stairs. When Margaret opens it, we see a red button, a green button, and a yellow button.

Kenny examines the buttons. "Red will close the hatch, green will open the hatch. I'll betcha yellow turns on the lights!" She reaches out and presses the yellow button before Margaret can react.

Margaret sputters, but Kenny was correct. The lights are on, and we can see a vast, cavernous room below us.

Descending the stairs, our eyes grow wide with wonder. The workshop and the chem lab are huge structures, but this room dwarfs them both. I estimate the room to be five hundred yards long and perhaps three hundred yards wide. The floor is covered with vehicles and electronic equipment. Vast banks of fluorescent lights cover the ceiling, making the huge cavern as bright as day. Rather than heading off helter-skelter, we move as a group through the warehouse. There are dozens of little cars with big balloon tires. There are tanks that stand fifteen feet tall from tread to turret. These explain the huge ramp leading down from the floor above.

We find several little machines with propellers and elaborate control panels. "Single-seat airplanes," Kenny murmurs. "This place is *awesome!*"

Our next discovery is shelving stacked high with what appear to be radios. "Those are real radios," Kenny exclaims. "We won't need relay towers to communicate anymore. And look how many there are! We'll have enough radios for every village to have its own."

On another set of shelves, we find banks of computers. There are hundreds of them. Whirring little robots are performing maintenance. The little robots busily pop the covers off some of the computers and inspect the insides. One machine pulls a wire from a connection inside a computer and replaces it with another. Another pulls out a circuit board, examines it carefully, and plugs it back in.

Next we find vast shelving units laden with complex-looking electronic equipment. I have no idea what it's for, but Kenny finds it fascinating.

"Books," I cry. I've located a large shelf laden with books. I open one and am only mildly disappointed to find that it is a technical manual. The laminated pages are covered with circuit diagrams and obtuse mathematical formulas.

As we pore over the books, we hear a thunderous sound. I unstrap my AK and look around warily, trying to locate a target. Looking up, a massive hole appears in the ceiling on the far side of the warehouse. Sunlight streams down through the opening. A drone descends and comes to rest on an elevated platform. With a busy whirring sound, dozens of robots open the drone and examine its innards. We also hear a clunking sound and see what appear to be very large shells being loaded into a chamber inside the body of the drone.

We see millions of these huge bullets loaded into clips stacked from floor to ceiling near the drone's launch pad. There is also a vast section where the clips have been removed. Less than half of the clips remain.

An hour after it appeared, the ceiling opens once again, and the drone launches itself. The hole in the ceiling closes behind it.

"Would you look at that," says Kenny. "The folks who built this place had automation down to a fine science. I'm guessing that drone's been flying for centuries!"

"There must have been huge technological breakthroughs before civilization collapsed," I say in amazement.

Later, I find Kenny poring over technical manuals. "I need to check with Bree to be certain," she says thoughtfully, "but I think those drones were designed to be guided by humans using these computers. In fact, I think the drones reverted to default programming when the last human operators disappeared, default mode being to zap anything with a human heat signature within a three-hundred-mile radius of the warehouse."

"You mean we can control the flights of the drones ourselves?" I ask. "We can use them to bomb New Washington? We can control the guns so we shoot blacksuits and not slaves?"

"I think so," replies Kenny. "But there's a problem. If I'm reading this right, New Washington will be on the very edge of the drone's range capability. We can fly it there, but it can only stay for a few minutes before we'll have to turn it around and fly it back here for recharging. In fact, we're gonna have the same problem with *all* this equipment. Everything in here is powered by electric motors. And the only place to recharge them is right here where the solar cells are located."

\* \* \* \* \*

My disappointment is visceral. "You mean we won't be able to use any of this stuff on the other side of the saddle?"

"I didn't say that," says Kenny. "But we *will* have to move some of the solar collectors over to our side of the mountains so we can do the recharging over there."

I stop and consider what Kenny is proposing. Moving this whole operation over the saddle is a daunting prospect. But we wouldn't have to move everything at once. We can start small, move just a small fraction of the solar collectors, just enough to get us started. Of course, we'll have to be careful to get our priorities right. What do we need first? The little rover cars? They'd be handy for moving supplies from village to village. Radios? We need better communication with the villages. Drones? Yes, we definitely want the drones. Tanks? Wouldn't it be fun to drive one of those tanks into New Washington? But how on earth can we get a tank over the saddle?

The trail is almost vertical in places. I'll leave that question for Bree and Chase.

And where are we going to get the labor we'll need to move things to our side of the mountains? We're already stretched thin. We have to grow more food so we can feed more liberated slaves. But to grow more food, we need to liberate more slaves. Catch-22. My head begins to spin with the difficult logistics involved in moving equipment from here to our home base.

"The fact that everything is being powered by electric engines makes sense," Kenny says. "Helen told us that the world had run out of fossil fuels and that's one of the reasons civilization collapsed."

"True," I agree. "And where better to build a solar energy plant than right here in the sunny Southwest? I wonder what happened to the last soldiers to man this site."

"They probably starved or ran out of water," Kenny suggests.

This question is answered moments later when Bardolph, one of Margaret's officers, finds a door leading into a room that was clearly a dormitory. We find dozens of skeletons lying on bunk beds.

"Do you figure they just lay down and died?" asks Kenny.

"Either that or they committed some sort of mass suicide," I say "Poisoned Kool-Aid or something like that."

"Whatever they did, let's take them upstairs and give them a decent burial," suggests Margaret.

"Excellent idea," I agree.

Margaret issues the orders.

I can't help but feel compassion for the poor soldiers stuck here in the middle of the desert watching their food and water supplies dwindle to nothing. What a horrible way to die. I'd much prefer a death in battle.

\* \* \* \* \*

Before we leave the warehouse, we carefully rebury the mines we cleared. I don't want the Sons of 1776 getting their hands on any of the goodies here. I make a map, detailed to the centimeter, with the location of each mine. We'll clear them much more quickly next time.

We spend the next few days making an inventory of everything stored in the warehouse. We'll take the inventory home so we can work out our priorities with Helen, Falstaff, and my friends.

We break speed records marching back to the chem lab. The moment we're back, Kenny gets on the net and tells Bree what we've found. Bree's excited, of course. She'll turn over all her projects to her assistants and join Kenny at the chem lab. From there, they'll take a dozen of Kenny's guards from the chem lab fort, now known as Fort Carlson, in honor of Kenny, and hike back to the warehouse. They'll figure out how to start breaking down and moving the solar collectors.

The Daughter's Guard and I work our way back to Fort Kennedy to find Chase has added to the fortifications. He now has a pit filled with sharpened stakes surrounding the fort. Together with its high walls, bartizans, turrets, and murder holes, this fort will be nearly impregnable.

Chase has been listening to our chatter over the net and says, "I'm done with the construction crew here at Fort Kennedy. You can send half of them to help Kenny and Bree when they're ready to start moving things. I'll have the other half start working on a new fort at the armory you just found."

After dinner, Chase shows me to my quarters. He has arranged a tidy little room for me. There is a large single bed with a fresh-smelling mattress. There's a blanket on the bed because nights at this altitude can be chilly. A roughly hewn chest of drawers with a pitcher of water and a small basin sits along the wall opposite the bed. The walls have been painted pale blue. Chase, bless his heart, has even left a small bouquet of wildflowers on my pillow. Tired from a busy flurry of days, and emotionally drained from the ongoing process of grieving for Ty, I go to bed early and fall asleep instantly.

Next morning, I lie in bed and watch the sunlight pouring through two small windows on the wall opposite the door. I stretch, and permit myself the luxury of lying in bed, doing nothing. I'm looking forward to an easy day walking the walls and halls of Fort Kennedy, introducing myself to the garrison.

I hear the sentry's horn. One blast means "friends are approaching," two blasts means "officers on deck," and three means "enemy approaching, everyone man battle stations."

I listen with trepidation as I hear the second blast. On the third, I'm on my feet running, shrugging into my tunic as I go.

# 10

I'm breathing heavily as I sprint up the last few steps and onto the deck at the top of the observation tower in the center of the fort. I watch as column after column of soldiers emerge from the rocks and trees of the saddle above us. Their shaved heads and tattoos mark them as the Sons of 1776. We knew they were coming. What we didn't know is how many there would be.

I stand quietly next to Chase as we watch. There are thousands and thousands of them, and they're still coming down from the tree line. The lead elements pass us by, but turn to their right and advance toward the northern twin. They've cut us off from Fort Taylor at the western foot of the saddle.

"Get on the radio to Fort Taylor," I instruct Anne, one of Margaret's junior officers. "Let Falstaff know what's happening. Warn him to be ready in case the Sons decide to bypass us and pay him a visit."

Falstaff has been steadily improving our fortifications around the farms and mines, so I know he can put up a terrific fight if the Sons decide to test him.

"They won't attack Falstaff until they take Fort Kennedy," predicts Chase. "They can't leave a thousand of us to harass their supply columns. Unless they're stupid, they'll take this fort before they move on."

"*Can* they take this fort?"

"Not if I can help it," says Chase with determination. "If they want to take it, we'll make sure they pay a high price."

All morning we watch as more and more Sons pour out of the tree line above us. They do not wear uniforms, nor do they march in military style. Most of the Sons wear sleeveless jerkins, but they are cast in a variety of colors, black being the clear favorite. Some wear shirts with sleeves. Footwear ranges from bare feet to shiny leather boots. The only way we can tell the officers from the soldiers is by watching to see who barks out commands. The two things they all have in common are shaved heads and arms covered with tattoos. The Sons look like formidable fighters, but they will lack the discipline of the blacksuits, or our own militia trained by Falstaff. That's a small advantage given their superior numbers, but it could be important.

The sun rises to its apex, and the Sons continue to pour out of the tree line. Some are carrying planks that look to be forty yards long and five yards wide.

"What are those for?" I ask.

"They're ramps," explains Chase. "I suspect the Sons will use them to scale the walls. They'll plant one end on the ground and push the other forward till it comes to rest at the top of our wall. Then they'll climb up the ramp and get into the fort. That's their plan, but we'll try to foil it." He raises his voice to the others. "Deploy Kenny Gas!"

Several of his soldiers at the foot of the observation deck scurry away toward the armory. They emerge carrying large jars, which presumably hold Kenny Gas. They climb the steps to the walkway near the top of the walls, and distribute it. Our defense against ramps will be to burn them as soon as the Sons deploy them.

Finally, by early afternoon, the parade stops. The last thing to emerge from the tree line is a large wooden catapult. We listen as their officers shout out commands. The Sons have surrounded the fort, but are staying out of range for the moment.

"I don't like the looks of that catapult," I say.

"Nor do I," says Chase. "We'll have to deal with it sooner or later. These walls are thick and sturdy, but if they hit them hard enough and long enough, the walls will come down. ET, let's talk to Falstaff and work out a plan." He turns to his bugler. "Sound three times if they start moving against the walls."

Chase and I descend the steps from the observation deck and head for the radio room. When we arrive, Falstaff is already on the line.

"How many are there?" Falstaff's voice can be heard above the static.

"I think there are about twenty thousand of them." Chase looks at me, eyebrows raised.

I nod in agreement. Twenty thousand sounds about right.

"Unless they're idiots," says Falstaff, "they'll position a thousand troops above the path up the saddle where it narrows and becomes steep. If we try to force our way up through that pass, they'll kill thousands of us. That means I can't send the militia up the saddle to help you."

I know the place he's talking about. I've taken to calling it "the Ladder."

"Without help," says Chase, "they can mount a siege and starve us out."

"How much food do you have?" asks Falstaff.

Food has always been our weak spot. It's the one thing we have in very short supply.

"We have enough food for two weeks," replies Chase. "We can make it last a month if we ration it."

"That's terrible," says Falstaff. "I should have sent you more food!"

"I should have asked for more," says Chase.

"Look, guys," I say, taking the microphone from Chase. "We don't have enough food to keep as much of it as we'd like anywhere. So this is nobody's fault. The question is, where do we go from here?"

"I have five thousand troops here at Fort Taylor," says Falstaff.

"Keep them there," I say. "If the Sons take our farms, we're finished."

"The rest of the militia is out raiding blacksuits. We'll need weeks to bring them all back."

I ponder this. "You'll have to cross the mountains somewhere other than the saddle. If you can do that, you can come up the saddle behind the Sons."

"We'll be outnumbered even so," Falstaff says pensively. "But if we can surprise them, we'll knock the stuffing out of them."

"The Sons will have sentries watching the foot of the saddle on the east side," Chase says. "You'll have to take them out, or the Sons will have time to turn and face you. They won't have the Ladder, on that side, but they *will* have the high ground."

"I have just the people I'll need," says Falstaff. "We've taken some village-born trackers prisoner in our battles with the blacksuits. They've been with us long enough that I trust them. They know how to move quietly and lay an ambush."

"Even so," I say, "you'll be hard-pressed to gather our warriors, cross the mountains, and surprise the Sons with an attack from behind before we run out of food."

"We'll just have to make the food last," says Chase grimly.

After talking to Falstaff, we radio Bree and Kenny. With the saddle blocked, they won't be receiving supplies either. The garrisons at the workshop and the chem lab will go on half-rations as well.

Shortly after we sign off, we hear the bugle sound three times. The Sons are on the move.

\* \* \* \* \*

Chase and I are back on the observation deck in moments. We watch as several Sons approach to a range of 150 yards, farther than we can shoot. The Sons raise their crossbows, arm them, and light their tips. They loose, and the bolts strike our walls. Since Chase's construction crew has just treated the wooden walls of the fort with Kenny's flame retardant, the Sons' flaming bolts gutter and die.

The bowmen retreat, and I hear cheers from our warriors inside the fort. But we've uncovered a problem. With their crossbows, the Sons have a weapon with greater range than our wooden bows. Our people can manage a range of fifty yards maximum.

Chase and I are armed with Kalashnikovs, but our effective range is only about one hundred yards.

Emboldened, the Sons send several thousand archers who begin to pepper us with crossbow bolts. Our defenders are behind walls, so the best the Sons can hope for are a few lucky shots. After an hour of battle, the Sons have succeeded in wounding two of our people, neither one seriously.

"Crossbows have greater range and more power behind their bolts," Chase explains, "but they're a slow weapon. They'll get off two or three bolts in a minute, whereas our best archers can get off ten or even twelve arrows in the same period."

The Sons' next scheme is to send their archers closer, about one hundred yards from the walls. They begin lobbing arrows over the walls, hoping to catch someone out in the open. Our people scurry for cover, so once again, the Sons use many bolts and achieve very little.

Even better is the fact that at one hundred yards, Chase and I can use our AKs. I carefully aim at an officer who is gesturing with his arms and shouting at his men and carefully squeeze off a round. The officer falls. I choose another target and fire again. Another officer goes down. We continue firing until the Sons have had enough. They retreat to a safe distance.

I wish for the thousandth time that we had a way to shorten the stock of our AKs so our militia could use them. But AKs cannot be shortened, and our villagers' arms are too small to wield them. So Chase and I will be the only ones with modern weaponry.

I watch as the Sons' officers gather and confer two hundred yards from our northern wall. They're obviously discussing their next gambit. We watch as they send out runners to communicate their plans. As the afternoon winds on, several thousand Sons move from positions along the east and west walls to mass opposite our north wall.

Chase has a garrison of one thousand fighters to work with. He has stationed two hundred warriors on each wall, leaving a force of two hundred men and women in reserve. In addition, the Daughter's Guard, nearly one hundred strong, is also held in reserve. Chase orders his reserves to the north wall, but we hold back the Daughter's Guard in case the Sons' maneuver is a feint to draw our reserves to one wall while they attack another.

This is no feint. With an earsplitting roar, ten thousand Sons charge toward our northern wall. In the front are three ramps, but the ramps are heavy, and the men who carry them are slowed by the weight. Our archers pick them to pieces. But for every Son who goes down, another takes his place. The Sons move the ramps ever closer to our walls.

Our militia in the turrets watches for the Sons to approach the rock piles marking our mines, and set them off, ripping huge holes in the Sons' lines. The places of those who fall are quickly filled by others. Still our archers take a heavy toll. Within ten minutes, there are at least five hundred Sons lying still on the ground.

Our fort is constructed with bartizans at the corners. These structures extend out beyond the walls. Any Son who nears the walls will take fire from three directions at once. Since our archers are firing from behind embrasures and murder holes, they present little target for return fire.

With four hundred of our men and women on the north wall, each loosing at least half a dozen arrows a minute, the Sons are taking staggering losses. At least a thousand are down when the first ramp is positioned. The Sons begin to charge up the ramp, and we counter by hurling jars of Kenny Gas to drench it. Our officers atop the wall order our fighters to delay igniting the Kenny Gas until the ramp is laden with Sons charging for the top.

"Fire!" shouts our officer, and the Kenny Gas ignites with a *whoosh*. Sons leap off the ramp to avoid the fire, but are caught on the sharpened stakes below.

The Sons place a second ramp, and this time we are a moment late igniting the Kenny Gas. Two dozen Sons have breached the wall. They draw swords and engage our fighters nearest to them. They overwhelm a few of our warriors, but the rest go down under a volley of arrows and well-placed shots from Chase's AK and mine.

The second ramp is ablaze when the third ramp is deployed. Once again we drench the ramp in Kenny Gas and ignite it as soon as the Sons approach the top. With all three ramps in flames, the Sons retreat, running as fast as they can for safety.

We've lost a dozen men and women, but the Sons' losses exceed twenty-five hundred. The battle for Fort Kennedy has just begun, but we've won the first skirmish resoundingly. Our fighters raise a vigorous cheer.

\* \* \* \* \*

The following morning, as I'm eating my half-ration breakfast, I remember my conversation with Snake, a member of the Sons we captured long ago. We'd asked Snake why the Sons hadn't already sent an army to attack us. His response was, it would take half the Sons' army to haul water over the long distance between the place the Sons call HQ and our positions on the saddle.

I discuss this recollection with Chase and Margaret.

"We have garrisons at the workshop and the chem lab," Chase muses. "Perhaps we can ask them to harass the Sons' supply lines. If they can't get food and water to their army, they'll have to go home."

We rush to the radio room and contact Bree and Kenny.

"I'm too far away from the saddle to offer much help. How about I send most of my garrison to the workshop?" asks Kenny. "I'll send food with them as well."

"Great idea, Kenny," I say. "Bree, can you supervise the raids on the Sons' supply columns?"

Bree's voice comes through the static a moment later. "Will do, ET. If the Sons can't eat, they can't fight."

Shortly after our conversation with Kenny and Bree, we hear three bugle blasts from the sentry tower. The Sons are on the move again.

\* \* \* \* \*

We climb the tower and find the sentries pointing to the north. We look in that direction and find the Sons have dragged their catapult toward the fort. It lies 150 yards north of the fort's north wall, too far for us to reach it with arrows or AK fire.

We watch as the Sons drag up huge rocks and pile them near the catapult. They load a rock into the catapult's firing bucket and crank the catapult's arm down, then sever the rope, releasing the firing arm. The rock bounces once, and strikes the north wall of the fort. Little damage is done.

Realizing they need to shorten the range, the Sons haul the catapult twenty yards closer. They're still out of our range, so we have no way of stopping their bombardment. They load and fire again, and this time, the rock strikes our wall. The timbers of the north wall shudder perceptibly.

The Sons' catapult doesn't possess the hydraulic sophistication of Bree's trebuchets. It takes them a good fifteen minutes to load and launch each rock. Still, by afternoon, the north wall begins to sag, and small cracks appear in some of the logs. We can't let the Sons continue to bombard our walls. Within a few days, they will come down.

I call for a meeting with Chase, Margaret, and her officers.

"We're gonna have to do something about that catapult," I say. "Does anybody have any ideas?"

"We can't touch it from here," says Chase. "The range is too great."

"And if we send a raiding party out to destroy it, they won't last five minutes. With their crossbows, the Sons can hit us at a range of a hundred fifty yards. Our bows have a range of about fifty yards," adds Margaret. "We'd never get close to the catapult."

"OK, then," I say. "We'll have to destroy it at night. Maybe we can sneak a party over the walls and get close enough to torch it."

"That's gonna be tough," says Chase. "The Sons will have posted sentries."

"That's where these come in." I paw through my backpack until I find what I'm looking for. I proudly display them. "Night-vision goggles."

"Where did you get those?" asks Chase.

"Kenny found them on a back shelf at the chem lab." I recall Chase leaving the Sanctuary before Kenny broke out the goggles.

"Do they work?" asks Margaret suspiciously. "They let you see in the dark?"

"Yep," I reply. "I've tried them myself. They work."

"What's your plan?" asks Chase.

"Chase and I will go over the wall around two a.m. By then, the Sons will be sleeping soundly, and their sentries will be bored and groggy. They don't know we have night vision, so they won't be looking for anything much beyond the ring of light cast by their fires and torches."

"Piece of cake," says Chase, sounding more confident than I feel.

"Daughter of Gaia, you surely don't think the Daughter's Guard is going to let you go out there alone," says Margaret in a matter-of-fact tone.

"Just this once," I return. "With only two of us, Chase and I won't make much noise. And when the time comes to run for cover, we'll be able to move a lot faster without you."

Margaret disagrees strenuously, but I'm the boss.

# 11

Chase and I rappel down the outer wall in the dead of night. We're wearing black clothing and have darkened our faces and arms with charred wood. We've slung our AKs over our shoulders, but the weapon of choice tonight is the bow. We need to work silently. I have a jar of Kenny Gas, and Chase has his Zippo lighter.

The night is still, and the moon is a waning crescent. There's very little light, and that's to our advantage. Chase and I need to get within about forty yards of the catapult. We advance slowly, eyes focused on the ground, careful to place our feet where they will make no noise. The sound of a twig breaking will surely attract the attention of the sentries.

At a range of one hundred yards, we see the sentries clearly. They're distributed evenly around the catapult, three of them to the left of the catapult and three to the right, walking back and forth. They don't look sleepy or bored.

We advance another twenty yards hunched over and then go flat on our bellies. We drag ourselves forward using our elbows. When we're within range, I study the sentries carefully through my goggles. They're alert, but have no hint we're near. I look at Chase. With my hands, I indicate he should target the three sentries on the left while I take out the ones on the right. I haven't used my bow much lately, but I have to trust in my training.

Chase and I string arrows and loose simultaneously. My target falls. I quickly loose two more arrows, but miss with my third. The last sentry is startled and has raised his horn to his lips when I hit him on my second attempt. No more than twenty seconds have elapsed since we loosed our first arrows. With the sentries down, we move in quickly. I break the jar of Kenny Gas on the catapult, and Chase uses his lighter to set it on fire.

With this bonfire burning, the whole world will know we're here now, so we turn to dash back to the safety of the fort. Before we've taken two steps, we're brought up short by four men with arrows notched and aimed right at our chests. From their dun-colored clothing and long black hair, we know they're Apaches. The Sons have brought their scouts along as well.

\* \* \* \* \*

"Drop your weapons," says the tallest of the four. The Apaches stand only a few yards away. If they choose to kill us, they can't miss at this range.

With my heart thundering and knees weak with fear, I drop my bow and shrug the AK from my shoulder. I have no choice. If we make one wrong move, we'll be dead.

"Take those funny things off your eyes and drop them as well," orders their leader.

We comply. The night, which had seemed so light, turns dark again.

"Walk that way." He gestures toward our left.

Chase and I do as we're told. One look over my shoulder reveals two Apaches right behind us, bows at the ready, while the other two Apaches sweep up our AKs, bows, and goggles.

Our walk is a brief one. We're in the Apache's camp. Four tents surround a fire burning low.

"Fetch the Leader," says the Apache in charge. A young man with red hair runs off to the east.

Apaches emerge from their tents, awakened by the noise we've made.

"Sit," says the Apache leader.

Chase and I sit.

"Bind them."

Two Apaches tie my hands behind my back, and one kneels in front to bind my feet. I lash out with my feet at the Apache in front. I catch him square in the chest, and he falls backward with an "Ooof." But with my hands bound and without a weapon, I can't do any more. One of the Apaches pulls my hair, hard, from behind while my ankles are bound. In pain and unable to see in front, I can offer no more resistance.

"I am Faithful Eagle," says the Apache leader as he looks at us with contempt in his eyes. "You are the One Who Got Away. No one escapes the Apaches. Those of us who chased you have lived in shame, derided by our people. Killing you will give me great pleasure."

That's a moot point. I don't want to die, but I'm prepared to do so. I knew what I was getting myself into when I took the oath of the Daughter of Gaia. Worse, by far, is my memory of Snake telling me,

*"Apaches got a million ways to make a man talk."* Our situation, then, is desperate. Chase and I both know the secret to opening the hatches on the workshop and the chem lab, and I have to believe Snake was not exaggerating. Chase and I will talk, sooner or later. If the Sons take the workshop and the chem lab from our people, everything we've worked for will be destroyed.

"You thought you could sneak around at night without the Apache seeing you," says Faithful Eagle contemptuously. "The N'de see everything, you little fool."

"You didn't see us soon enough to keep us from burning the catapult," I say, echoing his tone of contempt. "Perhaps I'll escape from you weak women this time as well."

Chase looks at me as if I've gone crazy. *Why are you making him angry?* his eyes ask.

I want them angry. If they're angry enough, they may make a mistake.

The Apaches surrounding me are outraged. "Cut her now," they jeer. I've drawn their eyes to me; their faces are masks of anger and loathing. Faithful Eagle raises his fist to strike me.

"Don't do that, Faithful Eagle. Not yet."

The speaker emerges from the darkness outside the Apache camp. I study him as he approaches. He's a big man for this world, standing well over five feet tall. He sports a dapper little brush mustache. Dressed in creased gray slacks and a natty black shirt, he radiates urbanity.

I'm very surprised by his appearance. He's definitely not cut from the same cloth as his short, shaven-headed, tattooed disciples.

"I'm guessing you're the one they call the Leader," I say.

"Very perceptive," he answers. "And I suspect you're the one they call the Daughter of Gaia."

"We know each other by reputation, then. You don't look much like a Son of 1776," I observe. "No shaved head, no tattoos."

"Did you think we were all crass and ignorant?" he asks.

I look around. How can he talk this way about his people? Won't they be angered at being called "crass and ignorant?" Scanning the area, I understand. The only people nearby are the Leader and his Apaches.

"My ancestors were intelligent men," the Leader continues. "They were determined to carve out a place of power for themselves after the collapse of civilization. They found a following in the ranks of the various antigovernment militias. There were dozens of isolated militias, each with a stash of high-powered weapons and hearts filled with hatred. We simply brought them together and told them what they wanted to hear."

"But things didn't work out for you," I say, prompting him, hoping for more information, playing for time.

"No," he admits. "We were overrun by gangs moving north from Central America. They greatly outnumbered us and drove us away. We were forced to abandon our home territory. Many centuries later, we returned. Plague had weakened the Salvadorans, and we slaughtered every one of them, men, women, and children. Regrettably, during the centuries we spent in the wilderness, we lost the capacity to open the hatches of the workshop and the chem lab. And that's where you come in," he says with a wicked grin. "But enough talk. What do you have there, Faithful Eagle?"

Faithful Eagle displays the weapons the Apaches took from us. The Leader ignores the bows, but hefts the AK experimentally. "You'll show us how to use this," he says flatly.

He examines the goggles curiously.

"They wore those over their eyes," explains Faithful Eagle.

The Leader fastens the goggles and leaps back in surprise. He tries them again and grins. "These will be very, very useful."

The Leader looks around the campsite through the goggles. Satisfied he knows how to use them, he removes them, turns to me, and smiles.

"You will tell us how to enter the workshop and the chem lab. Of that, there is no doubt," he says in a matter-of-fact voice. "You will die within the hour. Of that, there is no doubt. We'll keep your friend here alive until we've determined you've told us the truth and we can open the hatches. And I warn you, if you lie, your friend will die a very painful death. Of that, there is no doubt. The only question is, will *you* die quickly or slowly? Which will it be?"

* * * * *

I struggle with my emotions, determined to show no fear. "I won't tell you a thing. Of that, there is no doubt." I strive for a tone of arrogance.

The Leader smiles sadly. "Faithful Eagle, please convince the Daughter of Gaia to tell us what we want to know."

There is a look of brutal hatred on Faithful Eagle's face. He draws his knife from its sheath and kneels in front of me. He holds the point of his knife near my left eye, then pulls it back. He looks at me, studying me, trying to decide where to use his knife. He is so close I can smell his stinking breath. I hurl myself forward, catching his nose with my forehead. His nose spouts blood, and he sits back on his heels, trying to stanch the flow of blood with the heel of his left hand.

He looks me in the eye and says, "You will die very, very slowly. The Leader said you would die within the hour. You will not be that fortunate."

I sneer. "What a great warrior you are, nose broken by a little girl."

Chase begins to understand my strategy. I'm making the Apaches furious, and their attention is focused on me. He looks around for something to cut the vines binding his hands and feet.

I struggle to keep a mask of defiance on my face. I'm startled when the tip of an arrow appears from Faithful Eagle's neck. He grabs his throat and falls over, making gurgling sounds. Within seconds, the Apaches are all down. The Leader has an arrow lodged in his shoulder, but is still on his feet. He disappears into the darkness, pursued by several arrows. He hollers, "Raise the guard. Don't let these people get away," as he runs.

Given the bonfire we've made of the catapult, numerous Sons must already be awake. From all around us come the sounds of men readying themselves for battle.

Margaret steps into the clearing, surrounded by the Daughter's Guard. They quickly cut through the vines binding our hands and feet.

"But how —" I begin, but Margaret interrupts me.

"There's no time. Follow me," she hisses.

Startled as I am, I have the presence of mind to gather up my goggles and my AK. Then, Chase and I follow Margaret.

"Use your speed, Daughter of Gaia. Get back to the fort. The Guard and I will be right behind you."

"You'd better run fast," I reply flatly. "I'm not leaving the Daughter's Guard behind."

Margaret's face displays her frustration as we run together. "You're stubborn, Daughter of Gaia."

We reach the walls, but instead of the single rope Chase and I used to rappel down, there are now at least twenty ropes. When it becomes clear no member of the Guard is going to start climbing before I do, I grab a rope and pull myself up and over the wall. Chase is right behind me.

The night is still dark, but with my night-vision goggles, I can see several hundred Sons in pursuit. A brief, sharp fight ensues, pitting our warriors on the walls, and the Daughter's Guard on the ground, against the Sons, who are rushing toward us. Several of my guardsmen fall before the last one pulls herself over the top of the wall. But the Sons pay a heavy toll as well.

\* \* \* \* \*

"You disobeyed my instructions," I note.

"Fortunate for you we did," counters Margaret.

I throw my arms around her. "Bless you!" I whisper in her ear. "But how did you manage to sneak up on the Apaches?"

"With the right motivation, the Daughter's Guard is capable of being *very* sneaky. We saw the Apaches take you prisoner. I followed you alone. Motivated or not, I don't think one hundred guards could've followed you without making some noise. When I saw where they were holding you, I brought up the rest of the Guard. Besides, most of the Apaches were watching you."

"She wasn't making friends with them," Chase comments. "She made them so mad they were practically spitting."

Chase is right, of course. I worry about the future, however. Having escaped the Apaches twice, I'm bound to be enemy number one.

Chase and I grab a few hours of sleep. After breakfast, we climb the tower and look at the still-smoking wreck of the Sons' catapult.

The Sons settle in to starve us out. After their first costly assault on our walls, they're not anxious to attack us again. And with their catapult in ruins, they don't have a lot of options.

Our attempts to ambush their supply columns have not met with much success. We set up ambushes to catch their supply train and wind up being ambushed ourselves by Apaches. We catch a couple of supply columns, but not enough to have any impact on the siege of Fort Kennedy.

After three weeks, we call off the effort to attack the Sons' supply trains. We're losing too many of our people to the Apaches. In the fort, we cut our half rations to quarter rations. Our people are beginning to weaken. By the end of the month, our fighters are gaunt and listless.

Falstaff is terribly frustrated. He wants to help us, but can't move until our militia returns to Fort Taylor. Given his need to recall the militia from far-away raids, and the necessity for finding a new way to cross the mountains, I don't expect any help from him for at least one more month. With the Sons holding the Ladder, there's no way for Falstaff to climb this side of the saddle. And so, we wait.

At dinnertime, I reflect that the one blessing of being stuck up the saddle is that we aren't subjected to the blistering heat of the lowlands. Because of its altitude, Fort Kennedy has warm days and cool nights. As I'm contemplating working my way through my meal for the day (two carrots and a dried tomato) a runner bursts into the dining hall.

"Kenny is on the net," he says. "She wants to talk to you. She says it's urgent."

I follow the runner back to the radio room.

"Hey, Kenny," I say, pushing the talk button. "What's up?"

"Hey, ET," Kenny says. "Whatever happened to 'This is Fort Taylor calling the chem lab'?"

"I'm too hungry to say all those words," I counter. "So what's happening?"

"My long-lost, beloved son has returned."

"I assume you're talking about Garganto?" I ask.

"How many long-lost, beloved sons do I have?" says Kenny. "Yes, Garganto."

"Your reunion must have been touching," I say.

"Yeah, our eyes were all misty. How would you feel about Garganto squashing the Sons' supply columns?" she asks.

166

My spirits rise. "Great idea! Can you figure out how to tell him what to do?"

"Of course I can," says Kenny. "I'm his daddy, and he *loves* his daddy. He'll do handstands if I ask him to. Well, maybe not, seeing as his arms don't work. But you know what I mean."

"You bet I do! Get him on it right away."

This could work. I doubt the Apaches will slow down Garganto. I doubt the Apaches will go anywhere near Garganto.

# 12

We're getting weaker. Several weeks of half rations and many more weeks of quarter rations have left us emaciated. I can see my ribs. I'm in the observation tower watching the Sons do nothing, which is precisely what they've done since we burned their catapult.

There is good news from the workshop and the chem lab. Bree and Kenny have found an edible cactus, so they're not as hungry as we are in Fort Kennedy.

"The cactus is vile tasting," Kenny reports. "It's so bitter my taste buds seize up every time I even *think* about eating it. We grind it up into mush, add a little water, swallow it down fast, and hope we don't barf it back up. Beats starving, I guess."

Most of our fighters who were raiding blacksuit positions around the ring of villages have finally made it back to Fort Taylor. Falstaff isn't waiting for the rest. He's coming to relieve us with a force of ten thousand warriors, but with the saddle in the hands of the Sons of 1776, he must find another way to cross the mountains. It may be weeks before he finally arrives.

Kenny gives us regular updates on Garganto. She's relocated from the chem lab to the workshop, so she can supervise him more directly. Garganto stomps his way home from the saddle every night and reports on the things he's been squashing, and then turns around and stomps back again. If his reports are accurate, he's wreaking havoc on the Sons' supply lines. My greatest hope is that Garganto will disrupt their supply columns to the point they'll give up and go home.

Margaret wants me to take a handful of chosen guards and attempt to escape at night. On a dark night, this might be possible. But I'm not going to abandon my friends. Margaret understands this, but is frustrated nonetheless.

The next day dawns crisp and pleasant. At midmorning, we see signs of movement in the Sons' lines. I ask our sentry to sound the horn three times. Something's up. Our people scurry to their battle stations, although "scurry" is a relative term when people are starving. We're moving as fast as we can.

Chase joins me in the tower.

"They're on the move?" he asks. I simply nod toward the evidence.

The Sons are moving on all four sides of the fort. Even without binoculars, I can see they've replaced the assault ramps we torched during their first assault. They form lines 150 yards from our positions. I worry about what will happen if the Sons breach our walls. How much fight is left in our starving warriors?

"Do you think they're finally gonna attack?" asks Chase.

"If they're not, they're putting on a pretty good charade," I reply.

\* \* \* \* \*

The early morning sun glints on their crossbows and swords. The clanking sound of metal on metal carries through the still morning air. We watch their officers bark out orders, forming them into assault lines. They have dozens of ramps. I doubt we have enough Kenny Gas to burn them all.

"I wonder what got them all riled up," I say.

"Maybe Garganto's been cutting them off from their supplies. Maybe they have to move before they end up in the same shape we're in," Chase says.

A careful look through my binoculars shows the Sons are hardly as emaciated as we are, but they do look a little leaner. Beefy arms look a bit more slender. Either that or I'm seeing what I want to see.

Watching the Sons form up, it's clear they're not a trained militia. They mill around, and their lines are thicker in some places than others. They're a collection of roughnecks and brigands, not a disciplined military force. Perhaps our training will see us through. Since we're outnumbered by more than ten to one, we'll need every advantage we can find.

"I think they're gonna come at us from all four sides at once," says Chase. "They learned their lesson the first time. When they come from just one direction, we can position all our forces on that side. Let's keep the Daughter's Guard and a couple hundred of the garrison here in reserve. We can send them where they're needed most."

By late morning, the Sons are ready. One long blast on a trumpet sends them charging toward our walls.

Our warriors may be starving, but they're still deadly accurate with a bow and arrow. In the thirty seconds or so it takes the Sons to reach our walls, dozens and dozens have fallen. We detonate Bree's mines once there's a mass of Sons in range. The mines tear gaping holes in their lines. Once the Sons reach the pit surrounding the fort, they come under fire from three directions: from two turrets and from the walls themselves. Weak as they are, our archers still loose a minimum of eight or ten arrows a minute, and at such close range, they can't miss. The Sons lose over a thousand fighters in the first few minutes of battle.

The Sons learned a lesson from the first battle. They throw up a dozen ramps at once along each wall. On the north and south walls, it does them no good. Shouting commands, our officers direct our fighters and they douse every ramp with Kenny Gas, wait until the ramp is laden with charging Sons, and set the ramps on fire.

On the east and west walls, we're unable to destroy all the ramps. The Sons have two intact ramps on the west wall and three on the east wall. They come pouring over both. Chase splits his reserve in two; one heads for the west wall and one for the east.

"Push them off the walls, and burn those ramps!" Chase yells. He looks at me. "We'll keep the Daughter's Guard in reserve as long as we can."

I nod in agreement.

Chase and I will stay in the tower. From here, we use our AKs most effectively. Set on continuous fire, Chase and I are able to mow down dozens of Sons as they appear at the tops of the ramps. We eject clips and reload, firing until the barrels of the rifles are too hot to touch. Where the Sons have crossed the wall and are slowly pushing our warriors back, we look for the Sons' officers. Without uniforms, they're hard to find, but we target anyone who waves his arms and shouts instructions. When their officers go down, it takes some of the fight out of the Sons. But they can't retreat because the pressure from wave after wave of Sons behind them charging up the ramps pushes them forward.

The Sons who were attacking the north and south walls see that ramps are up on the other walls, so they shift their attack to the east and west. Our officers on the walls observe the Sons' move, and they direct our defenders to move to the east and west walls as well. Only a skeleton force remains on the north and south walls. Although dozens and dozens of Sons have come over the wall, our people are fighting bravely. They give ground haltingly. As more Sons surmount the wall, they become jammed up, with the back rows pushing forward, but the front rows unable to advance more than a few feet at a time.

The traffic jam gives us the perfect opportunity to employ Kenny's "flashbangs." These are miniature bombs that go off with a deafening roar and an intense burst of light. People within a radius of several yards are temporarily blinded and deafened. Chase loads a launcher with a flashbang and fires it into the middle of the massed and immobile Sons. The effect of the flashbangs is stunning. Sons push blindly, trying to retreat. As they retreat, they knock their comrades off the ramp and onto the stakes below. Sons still outside the fort are unaware of what's happening and continue to push their comrades up the ramps. Chase is alternating flashbangs between the east wall and the west walls. He continues firing until our supply of flashbangs is exhausted. The carnage is terrible to watch. Thousands of Sons perish.

Our people on the walls make excellent use of the confusion in the Sons' ranks. They keep pressure on the Sons inside the fort and slowly but surely push them back, regaining lost ground. Unfortunately, we're unable to clear all the Sons from the fort. Their ramps are still up, and they have a toehold on both walls.

"Margaret, let's see if the Daughter's Guard can force the last of the Sons from our walls," I say.

Margaret divides her fighters into two groups and sends one to the west wall and one to the east. From my perch, I watch anxiously as the Daughter's Guard advances at a run. They collide with the fighting

173

groups on the east wall, and the impact of their charge forces the Sons back. I see Margaret in the lead, sword drawn, hacking and slashing so fast I can scarcely see her arm. Encouraged by the Guard's charge, our warriors on the walls push the Sons back. Within twenty minutes, they've cleared the east wall. With the last of the Kenny Gas, our fighters burn the remaining ramps.

Unfortunately, our forces can't dislodge the Sons on the west wall. As their attack on the east wall collapses, the Sons move around the fort and join their forces on the west side. Our own forces rush to the endangered wall as well. The battle has come down to this desperate fight for the west wall.

Despite our best efforts, Chase and I are unable to stanch the flow of enemy fighters coming over the walls with AK fire. Our starving militia is rapidly tiring. The Sons slowly and inexorably push our militia back. The Sons pour over the west wall and into the fort itself. They set fire to our barracks, storage buildings, and dining hall. Red and orange flames hungrily devour the vulnerable wood. The time has come for our last stand.

"Sound the trumpet four times," I order the sentry. This is the prearranged signal to abandon the fight on the walls and retreat into our seven strong points. We have six turrets and a final fastness beneath the tower in the center of the fort. These strong points provide cover for our archers as we reach the battle's endgame. They are elevated, so our warriors have the advantage of firing down on the enemy.

Throughout the battle on the walls, our warriors in the turrets have kept up a withering fire directed at the Sons outside the walls. Dozens of archers releasing eight to ten arrows a minute at close range has taken a terrible toll. Thousands of Sons have fallen before ever reaching a ramp. Still, there are thousands of Sons left. They still greatly outnumber us.

Chase and I descend from the tower into the central fastness. This is a miniature fort in the center of the fort, designed to accommodate one hundred warriors. The remnants of the Daughter's Guard and a contingent of Chase's most skilled archers join us in the there. The Sons are concentrating on capturing the turrets before they turn their attention on us. With the Sons at close range, they fire more accurately into the murder holes. Hitting such a small target takes an excellent shot, and some luck as well, and the Sons take massive losses as they reduce our forces in the turrets.

One by one, we watch the turrets fall. The flaming buildings inside the fort make it difficult for those of us in the fastness to provide support for our brothers and sisters in the turrets, but we do what we can. Finally, the last turret falls.

The Sons pause to reorganize. The roar of battle is replaced by silence, broken only by the cries of the wounded. The fires set by the Sons are burning low, so we can see them as they mass on the west side of the fort. I'm amazed to find no more than three or four thousand Sons left. Still, with less than a hundred fighters ourselves, we're hopelessly outnumbered.

The Sons try to form into rows for an assault. Every archer in the fastness, as well as Chase and I, pick off the officers as soon as we can identify them. This strategy is successful. The Sons look disorganized. They mill around aimlessly.

I pull Chase and Margaret aside.

"If we stay in here," I say, "they'll pick us off sooner or later. They'll find cover, and at close range, they'll knock us off one by one, even through the murder holes. We'll take a lot of them with us, but in the end, we'll lose. I say we go down with our banners flying. Let's go right after them."

"They outnumber us thirty or forty to one," Margaret points out.

"But we have AKs and the finest fighters in the world," says Chase. "I agree with ET. Let's go down swinging."

We study the Sons' positions. They're still wandering around, disorganized. Our archers continue to bring them down.

"Everybody listen!" I holler. "We're gonna go down fighting. We're gonna charge right into the center of the Sons' lines, and we're gonna take a lot of them with us. A hundred years from now, people will still be talking about our last charge!"

The room is filled with the roars of our warriors.

"When we open the gate, come out running, and make some noise!" I say. "The fighting will be hand to hand, so watch each other's backs."

I look at our half-starved, weary warriors and find they still have fight in their eyes. We may be badly outnumbered, but we'll make a ferocious last stand.

"Form up!" orders Margaret. "Draw your swords, and prepare your shields."

Our men and women form four ranks, the gate being just wide enough to accommodate four people abreast. I step in front of one rank, and Chase steps into the lead of another. Margaret, seeing me in the lead, heaves a huge sigh, but says nothing. Margaret herself leads a third column, and her young officer, Bardolph, heads up the last. The door bursts open, and we emerge running, hollering loud enough to be heard up and down the saddle.

We catch the Sons by surprise. We reach them and attack with swords. The sight of a howling enemy in their midst, hacking and slashing with abandon, unnerves them. They've lost most of their officers. They're bullies and thieves, not trained militia. At least three-fourths of their brothers have perished today. Our determined charge disheartens them. A few of them drop their weapons, turn, and run. The trickle of runners turns into a river as we continue to wade into their disorganized lines. Finally, even the bravest of them turns tail and runs.

They jam up as they try to escape through our front gates. We could easily take down hundreds more of them while their backs are turned to us.

"Let them go," I order. There's been enough death today. Besides, as they retreat down the eastern side of the saddle, they'll run into Garganto at the bottom.

The Sons of 1776 are broken. After the initial euphoria of seeing the Sons retreating, I find I'm feeling curiously numb. I should be exhilarated, shouldn't I?

\* \* \* \*

We go on the radio net and announce our victory. Congratulations pour in from every station. The one I enjoy most of all is the one from Gretchen, who is in charge of Fort Taylor in the absence of Falstaff.

"I'll have food brought up to you right away," she says.

My mouth waters at the thought of food only hours away.

"Thanks for that," I reply. "We're a little hungry up here. Have you sent someone out to find Falstaff and tell him to come back?"

"We're on it," assures Gretchen. "The last we heard, he'd found a way to get over the mountains, so he's probably only a few days away from you."

"That's great news, Gretchen!" And then I have a terrible thought. "Gotta go," I say abruptly.

I immediately call the workshop and ask for Kenny. When she's on the line, I blurt, "Tell Garganto not to squash Falstaff when he comes. He's on your side of the mountains and only a few days from the saddle."

"Roger that," says Kenny. "If you don't have any other use for Garganto, I'd like to send him south, to see if he can find a way around the mountains in that direction. I'll give him strict instructions to avoid squashing anyone."

"Sounds like a good plan to me," I agree. "But have Garganto hang around long enough to squash a few Sons retreating down from the saddle before he goes."

"Oh," adds Kenny, "more good news. Bree and I have installed a propulsion system on the balloon. We can steer the sucker now."

"Kenny, that's great news! Can you bring the balloon to Phoenix?"

"I think so. I'm pretty sure I can get enough lift to clear the saddle."

"I have some plans, and I'm gonna need the balloon," I say.

"Great," sighs Kenny. "The Mad Hatter's been planning again."

# 13

When Gretchen's fighters show up just before dark, our ragged little company raises a cheer. We eat under the stars, because the Sons burned all our buildings except for the fastness. Vegetables never tasted better. We're careful not to gorge ourselves, though. As much as I want to eat everything in sight, I know that my stomach has shrunk and can handle only so much food. There are only about ninety of us left, out of a force of well over a thousand. Still, our losses, though terribly painful, are small compared with the Sons'.

I dream all night about the screams of the Sons as they died. I awake when it's still dark and rush to the latrine and vomit. While I was caught up in the fight, I had no time for feelings. Now, afterward, I'm sickened by what we've done. I give up all further thoughts of sleep—I want no more nightmares of dying Sons. I decide to climb the observation tower, the place where I did most of my killing.

When I reach the top, I'm only mildly surprised to find Chase there. Chase is a big kid, but his slumping body leaves him looking much smaller. From his expression, it's obvious he is feeling the same thing I am. We talk about the demons that haunt us, the gut-wrenching sickness we feel when we think about the horrible things we've done. I guess talking is a form of mutual therapy.

"How did this happen?" I ask plaintively. "How did we become killers?" I can't stop the tears from falling.

Chase, seeing my tears, begins to cry as well. "I don't know," he sobs. "But I think the fact we're sitting here crying is a good thing. If I ever lose my sense of grief over killing people, I'll worry about what I've become."

For a long time, we hold each other, both of us racked by sobs.

"We're fighting for a good cause," I say finally. "We had to do what we did. Funny, isn't it, how that doesn't make it any easier?"

In a way, I can see the Sons' point. The workshop and the chem lab were built by their ancestors, so, from their perspective, we stole them. On the other hand, we know a lot about the Sons, having spoken with both Eva, who was their slave from the day she was born, and from the Sons we captured after the skirmish in the old town. They live by enslaving anyone weaker. They have no respect for human life. They kill without remorse. They're evil people by any standard. If they held the workshop and the chem lab, they'd use the technology to expand their reach and enslave more people. So I think we hold the moral high ground. Or, at least, that's what I tell myself when I wake up in a cold sweat, or after I've heaved everything in my stomach into the latrine. In Tucson, I thought I'd become a doctor and save lives. Now I find myself taking them.

We spend the day after the battle digging a mass grave for the Sons' fallen. Weak from lack of food, the work is slow going. Gretchen's fighters who brought our food tell us they'll take care of the digging, but I want to help. The least we can do for the people we've slaughtered is to give them a burial. I tell the survivors of the fight they don't have to help, because I know how weak they are. Still, they continue to dig.

It takes all that day and the next to finish the graves and haul the dead to the burial site. Standing near the graves afterward, my eyes tear up, and I start to cry again. Chase puts his arm around me, but I hear him sniffling too. Many weeks will pass before I can sleep without nightmares, and I frequently visit the latrine to throw up.

\* \* \* \* \*

The next day, Kenny and Bree arrive. Their arrival in the balloon is an awesome thing to see.

Once on the ground, Kenny describes their arrival. "We descended from the heavens like the goddesses we are."

"Oh, please," I groan.

"Jeez, ET," says Kenny, "you're nothing but skin and bones!"

"I never dreamed how terrible hunger could be," I reply. "Hunger is *physically* painful. You ache day and night. It's hard to believe that even in our twenty-first-century world, millions of people went to bed hungry every night."

"I wish we could take you to the Shake 'n' Burger and fatten you up on greasy burgers and French fries," says Bree.

"Oh my God," I say, mouth watering, "I swear I'd do almost anything for a burger and fries right now."

Kenny changes the subject slightly. "I will never eat another cactus as long as I live. Not only do they taste awful, harvesting the things is impossible. They have these tiny little spines you can hardly see, but every time you harvest one, you wind up with a thousand of those little suckers buried in your hands and arms. I felt like a pincushion! I never thought I'd look forward to eating veggies, but I can't wait to tear into a big plate of cauliflower."

Kenny and Bree have lost weight as well, but their cactus diet has kept them from the worst of what we've experienced up here on the saddle.

I watch as a column of villagers emerges from the tree line above us. There are over a thousand of them, and they're heavily laden with solar panel equipment.

"We couldn't get anything over the saddle, of course," says Bree, "so we spent our time stockpiling equipment from the solar farm. Chase sent us his construction crews just before the Sons showed up, and we used some of our garrison troops to disassemble and move as much equipment as we could. We have enough solar panels to start our own little solar farm. We won't be ready to power drones yet, but we'll have a good start."

"If only we had enough workers to move equipment more quickly," I comment wistfully.

"We made another invention as well," says Kenny.

I look at her expectantly.

"I figured out a way to make the groundwater drinkable," says Kenny. "The water is toxic because it has a massive acid content, and some feisty little bacteria that make you hurl when you try to swallow it. The acid content is weaker now because over the centuries, rainwater has diluted the acid in the groundwater to the point where we can actually neutralize it. I've found if you dump in enough borax, it neutralizes the acid, and the water pH goes back to about seven, right where it should be. And there's plenty of borax near the chem lab. Then, if you boil what's left, the heat kills the bacteria, and you're in business. We can't make a whole lake drinkable, but we can take a liter or two and fix it up."

"Kenny, that's awesome! You two are geniuses," I say as I embrace both of them.

"Aw, shucks, ET. You're getting me all choked up," says Kenny with a smile.

At dinnertime, all three of us dig into our plates of vegetables with gusto.

Around a mouthful of asparagus, Bree says, "Helen has called a grand meeting of all the village elders. We're on our way to join her. Would you guys like to travel with us?"

I look at Chase. "Personally, I'd like to take another couple days to regain my strength," I say.

Chase nods in agreement. "I'm as weak as a newborn babe."

Chase and I take the next few days off, along with the rest of the garrison. We slowly begin to regain the weight we've lost. It's funny how we take important things like food for granted until we don't have them.

On the sixth day after the battle, Falstaff and his force arrive. Seeing them come out of the tree line above us is a deliriously happy sight. I catch sight of Grizz's unruly mane of hair and fly down the steps of the tower and out the gate. He sees me coming and begins running as well. We wrap our arms around one another.

"I was so worried," Grizz whispers in my ear. "I was afraid I was going to lose you. I've been so upset I couldn't eat or sleep."

"All the way through the siege I knew I was likely to die, and the worst part of it was that I'd be dying alone, without you," I say, tears in my eyes.

"I want to hold you and never let you go," says Grizz. We hold each other fiercely. Even the sound of familiar voices isn't sufficient reason to let go.

"Gosh, would you look at them!" I'd know that voice anywhere: Luke.

"Do you think he's gonna kiss her?" Han speaking.

"Why would he wanna do that?" asks Luke.

"Cause she's a girl, dummy," counters Han.

"ET's not a *girl*," objects Luke.

"What do you mean? ET *is* a girl. Look at her. She has *girl* stuff." I hear the sound of a *thwack*. That'll be Han whacking Luke on the back of his head.

"Of course she has girl stuff. But she's our sister, and *sisters aren't girls!*" Luke this time, with another *thwack*, meaning he's repaid Han.

Grizz and I remain locked in each other's arms until we hear the unmistakable sound of Falstaff clearing his throat.

"Sooner or later, you two have to come up for air," he points out.

We break our embrace, but I hold on to Grizz's hand. I'm not ready to let go just yet.

Han and Luke embrace me, arms so strong I can scarcely draw breath.

When they let go, I look them over. How could they have grown so big, so fast? They're over six feet tall now, and still growing. What happened to the little urchins who used to think the height of humor was putting pepper in the saltshaker?

"You look skinny," says Luke.

"Of course she looks skinny. She's been eating shoe leather and stuff," counters Han.

"I never got to the point where I ate shoes," I say. "But I was getting close."

"Hey, Uncle Grizz," says Luke, "are you and ET gonna get married or somethin'?"

Grizz looks perplexed. He's saved by Falstaff, who clears his throat again. "You two report to your brigade commander," he orders.

"Yes, sir!" they say in unison. "Bye, ET! Bye, Uncle Grizz!" And they're off and running.

"You're gonna have to teach me the secret for making those two knuckleheads obey like that," I say.

"I just take their swords away and make them peel potatoes and wash dishes for hours on end," explains Falstaff.

"Hmmm," I say. "They didn't have swords back in Tucson. And we had a dishwasher."

"I am deeply sorry, Daughter of Gaia, that we couldn't rescue you," says Falstaff, head hanging down.

I put my hands on his shoulders. He raises his head, and I look him in the eye. "I'll hear no more of that," I say sternly. "You moved as fast as you could. It's not your fault our militia was spread all over

185

the place. And it's not your fault you couldn't come up the saddle. We both know the Sons would've cut you to pieces if you'd tried. I'm amazed you got here as soon as you did. I didn't expect you for at least two or three more weeks."

Falstaff nods his head.

Grizz says, "We marched fast, ET. We couldn't have gotten here any sooner. And the passage we found through the mountains was downright scary. It took a lot of rock climbing and rope work to get through. We lost over a hundred warriors making the passage. But our men and women knew the Daughter of Gaia was in trouble, so they did some pretty incredible things."

Kremke has been standing quietly, observing. Grizz puts his arm around him. "This guy is one of us," he says. "He's led raids against the blacksuits. He's a real warrior. And when we crossed the mountains, he spent a lot of his time breaking trail. I trust him."

I can't read Kremke's face. I'd think he'd appreciate the praise, but his expression is neutral. I'm still not sure *I* trust him, but I'll give Grizz the benefit of the doubt.

"I'll recall the guardsmen who've been following you," I say to Kremke.

Kremke grunts. I guess I didn't expect a thank-you.

I change the subject. "I should thank the militia for their efforts."

Grizz, Falstaff, Kremke, and I walk through the militia's camp. As always, I'm swamped everywhere I go, surrounded by crowds. I say over and over again, "Thank you. Thank you for marching so fast and working so hard."

186

Later in the afternoon, Chase and I decide to accompany Falstaff and his warriors down the saddle. From there, Falstaff will turn over command of the army to Gretchen, and he'll accompany us to the Sanctuary for the grand meeting of village elders.

\* \* \* \* \*

Before we begin our march the next morning, Falstaff once again reassigns some of his fighters to bring the Daughter's Guard back up to one hundred strong. I find this a painful process, because I had known each member of the Guard personally. I introduce myself to the new guardsmen, and I can't help but think of the ones I lost as I shake hands with their replacements. I console myself with the knowledge that, with all the advances we've been making, the time for killing will end.

I warmly greet Gretchen, Falstaff's second-in-command. "It's been a while since we drove the Sons away from the workshop together, my friend."

"I'm glad to see you, as well, Daughter of Gaia. And yes, it's been too long since I marched with you. If you'll pardon me, ma'am, we need to fatten you up a bit."

"I'm working on it," I reply with a smile.

Dinner that evening includes peaches.

"We liberated the fruit from the blacksuits during a raid," explains Gretchen. "We had them badly outnumbered, so they ran away. My fighters spent an hour in the grove. I had to work hard to keep them from eating so many peaches their bellies would explode. None of our people has ever eaten a peach before, you see. We knew

187

from messages we heard over the net that you'd be joining us soon, so we saved some for you."

I take a bite and close my eyes as I relish the taste of peach on my tongue. I've forgotten what fruit tastes like. I open my eyes to see Grizz with his eyes closed, savoring the sensation as well. Chase and Falstaff also wear expressions of profound delight.

"May the Mother bless you, Gretchen," I say. "See if you can liberate a few more."

\* \* \* \* \*

When we arrive at the Sanctuary, we're ushered into the Great Cavern, where the village elders are gathered with Mother Helen. They raise a cheer as I enter the room. I reply with my official Daughter of Gaia response: I smile from ear to ear, raise my right arm, and wave. I've done this so many times, I don't even think about it; I just do it. There are well over a hundred people in the cavern. I see their faces, bright with hope, and the old feelings of doubt begin to surface. How can I avoid disappointing these good people? I choke off the negative thought and remind myself that I'll do my best, and that will have to suffice. Benches are arranged in a great circle. I like the dynamic it creates. No one sits at the head of the table. We're all equals in this room.

The cheering finally stops. When my small group is seated, Helen stands and says, "We're so glad you came today! The village elders were determined to stay in session until you could come and approve our plans. We know how weak you must have been after being starved up on the saddle."

I'm deeply uncomfortable being called on to approve plans made by a roomful of wise men and women more than twice my age, but I say, "Please, tell me what you've been thinking."

"Before we begin," says Helen, "we must bring you up-to-date on some developments you may have missed while battling the Sons on the saddle. Let me turn the floor over to Falstaff, who can explain our first problem."

Falstaff stands. "The blacksuits have taken to using our people as human shields. As you know, the blacksuits are trying to rebuild their outer-ring forts, and we're doing everything in our power to slow them down. When we started, we launched raids at night. We didn't need to discriminate among our targets. If it moved, we hit it. But the blacksuits now force their slaves to sleep with them in their camps. We're finding it harder and harder to pick out blacksuits, especially on dark nights. During the daytime, it's even worse. The slaves work on construction, and blacksuits stand among them. The slaves tell us to go ahead and fire, they're willing to die. But it's difficult for our archers to loose their arrows when they know they'll hit their brothers and sisters."

"The blacksuits have become cowards," I say, "hiding behind civilians. This is bad news, but there's a positive side. We have them scared. They're afraid to meet us in open battle. Tell me, Falstaff, is there a way we can raid the quarry where they mine their stone?"

"Yes, of course," says Falstaff. "We've identified three quarries, and we were planning a raid to hit all three on the same night when we received word that the Daughter of Gaia had been captured. We put our plans on hold until we could resolve the greater threat."

"Please continue with your plans to raid the quarries. When the day of final reckoning arrives, our job will be much easier if we don't have to fight our way through an outer ring of strong forts," I say.

Falstaff sits, and Helen stands. "The second problem we've found," she begins, "is that the blacksuits are now clear-cutting trees, moving toward the mines. We launch raids to slow them down, but they still make good progress. At the current rate, it'll take them well over a year to clear a path all the way to the mines. But they've committed massive numbers of slaves to the project."

"This may provide us with a golden opportunity," I say. I see a sea of confused faces staring at me. "In one great battle, we may be able to deal the blacksuits a fatal blow. Think how much easier it will be to take New Washington if the greatest part of their army is destroyed in battle at the mines. We gotta do everything we can to delay the blacksuits. We'll need time to prepare our militia so they'll be able to weather the best punch the blacksuits can throw."

I see slowly spreading smiles and nods of affirmation.

"Given a year to prepare," says Falstaff, "we'll be ready!"

The room is filled with cheers.

When the room is quiet, Helen continues. "Those are our problems, but now for our plan. We want to speed the defeat of the Court. The single biggest obstacle we face is the shortage of food. We are subsistence farmers. We must work all day every day to keep food on our tables. And yet, we need more people to grow our militia and to move the solar panels and wonder weapons from the place we now call the armory. Our council has decided that every village will place its people on three-quarter rations. Doing this will free fifty thousand workers to clear land for planting more crops, and fifty thousand workers to bring the technology of the armory to our side of the mountains. We will also provide Falstaff with twenty thousand new recruits for our militia."

Helen sits, and the room falls silent. I feel every eye in the room on me.

"Surely, this is too great a price to pay," I object. "Living with hunger day and night is an incredible sacrifice!"

My old friend Bertram, the first villager we met after coming through the brane, rises to speak. "Before you came, Daughter of Gaia, our people lived with hunger because the courtsmen are greedy. So we're no strangers to hunger. Our hunger to defeat the Court is far greater than the hunger of our bodies. We make this sacrifice willingly and with joy."

I hear a chorus of agreement from all parts of the circle of elders.

"May the Mother bless you all," I say finally. "Your willingness to sacrifice strengthens my own commitment to bring you victory, and to bring it soon." I'm really raising hopes here. I wish I were as certain as I sound.

Once again, the Great Cavern is filled with cheers.

When the meeting concludes, I circulate among the elders, learning their names and thanking them for their commitment to our cause. They reply that it is they who should thank me for my commitment.

We share a light meal with the elders that evening. There is an unmistakable current of joy and hope in the air that makes our meager meal seem more filling. We listen as musicians perform, and the elders ignore their aches and pains to dance like dervishes.

Grizz asks me to dance, and we join them. I watch Chase and Kenny dance, and work hard to keep from laughing. Chase is a magnificent athlete, but he lacks all sense of rhythm. Still, he makes up for his lack of skill with energy and enthusiasm. Kenny, on the other hand, is a daughter of Terpsichore. Eyes closed, her lithe body moves in perfect harmony with the music. For the millionth time, I see why she was so popular with every boy at Sierra Vista High School.

\* \* \* \* \*

We say good-bye to the elders the following morning. Some of them face journeys of over thirty days to return home. Bertram remains behind.

I'm standing near the entrance to the Sanctuary when I'm pleasantly surprised to find Bree directing villagers laden with the equipment necessary to produce wolf bane. By producing wolf bane at the Sanctuary, we won't have to spend so much time hauling it from the other side of the mountains. The manpower saved will be significant.

"Sister Juliet will supervise the production of wolf bane here at the Sanctuary," says Bree.

I go in search of Sister Juliet. My meeting with her is disturbing. I greet her warmly, but her response is cold.

"Are you upset with me?" I ask.

"You know," she says, "I was once the person who would be replacing Mother Helen when she died. But now, all I hear is how wonderful the Daughter of Gaia is. I guess I'm a little bitter. And now they have me making wolf bane, and believe me, the ingredients for wolf bane smell putrid."

"I have no intention of ever replacing Mother Helen," I say earnestly.

"Of course not," says Sister Juliet, and she turns on her heel and walks away.

Later, we meet with Helen and Bertram, and Kenny explains she'd like to train Bertram to make fertilizer from the recipe she's created. Bertram can then take his knowledge and train people from every village. Within a couple months, every village should be fertilizing their fields.

"The key ingredients are pee and poo, so they're readily available," says Kenny.

Helen, seeing the confused look on Bertram's face, translates. "Feces and urine," she says. Bertram nods.

"You'll also need to extract ammonia from decaying plants, and a few other little things, but the fertilizer is easy to make, and it should really increase crop yields," Kenny concludes.

Helen asks what my plans are for the future, and I tell her about my new project.

"I want to pay a visit to New Washington," I say. I watch as everyone's mouth goes agape. "I want to get the blacksuits' military plans. I know where they keep their maps and their records from when I was captured. Salieri, bless his heart, gave me a tour of their command center. With Kenny's balloon, we can drop down in the middle of the night, steal their plans, and be gone before they even know we've been there."

"I don't suppose you'd consider letting somebody else lead this mission?" asks Helen.

"I'm the only one who knows exactly where the command center is," I point out.

Falstaff looks at the floor and grumbles.

"Oh boy," says Kenny. "Here we go again."

We spend the next two hours working out our plans. We decide that Kenny, Grizz, Chase, Kremke, and I will go. Bree will stay behind and continue work on our nascent solar farm.

"The balloon will easily carry us," says Kenny thoughtfully. "We don't want to carry much else because the more we carry, the slower we travel. And the longer it takes to get the balloon up in the air."

We decide to leave the following evening at sunset. The plan is to get to New Washington well after dark, bring the balloon down until it hovers over the palace, rappel down, steal the plans, climb back up the ropes, and be gone well before dawn. There'll be a new moon, so the balloon should be pretty much invisible from the ground.

"Oooh," says Bree. "I have something you might find useful." She leaves and returns a minute later with four small electrical devices. "We have enough juice in our solar farm to charge some small objects. These two are little two-way radios. And these two are electric lanterns. They have enough charge to last for days."

"That's great," I say. "Those of us on the ground can communicate with Kenny in the balloon. And the light from the little flashlight I brought with me from Tucson is looking pretty feeble."

As the sun sinks slowly toward the western horizon, we prepare to leave. We'll travel light. We bring bows for the silent work we'll need to do, and I see everybody is also carrying a sword. Even though we plan to do our killing silently, we take our AKs and several spare clips. If we have to use them, it'll mean we're in big trouble. Remembering my disastrous first balloon ride, I decide to take an extra canteen and a five-day supply of food. Kenny has a little munitions locker built into the side of the gondola.

"What's in there?" I ask.

"All sorts of mayhem," Kenny replies breezily.

We're in the midst of casting off, so I don't pursue the matter.

Kenny begins heating gas to inflate the balloon. She shows us how the propulsion system works. It involves pushing foot pedals like crazy to fill up a bladder of air. When the bladder is full, the air is released through a narrow channel, and the balloon moves in the opposite direction.

Kenny proudly explains. "It's like filling a party balloon with air and then letting it go. Only we travel in a straight line. Then, we refill the bladder, and off we go again."

"So, our chemistry genius and her friend the mechanical genius have come up with a motor that any kindergartener could've invented?" I ask, flummoxed.

Kenny looks hurt. "It works," she says defensively. "We spent days and days fine-tuning the pedals and the bladder. You won't believe how fast we go."

I smile and sigh. But Kenny is right. We cover ground at an incredible pace.

The worst part of Kenny's propulsion system is the noise it makes. Each time we release the air stored in the bladder, we fly quickly through the air, but a person on the ground would conclude he was watching a balloon with a severe case of flatulence. With all six of us working the pedals energetically, we fart our way across the darkened land below.

"How are we gonna sneak into New Washington when we sound like an elephant who's just eaten a mountain of beans?" I ask.

"Easy," says Kenny. "When we get near New Washington, we take the balloon up a few thousand feet. They'll never hear us from the ground. When we're directly over the palace, we descend. When we're done with the raid, we shoot straight up again and head home."

Five hours later, I see bright lights on the ground in the distance. We've reached New Washington.

# 14

"The palace is the building over there," I point to a well-lit building.

Kenny takes the balloon up to a height of three thousand feet. We fill the bladder half full by pedaling furiously.

"Don't overfill the bladder or we'll overshoot the palace," Kenny warns.

We release the bladder and wind up just short of the palace. We pump a little more air into the bladder and release it. The ripping sound of air released seems incredibly loud, but Kenny's probably right. We are so high, people on the ground won't hear a thing.

The balloon is directly over the palace, so Kenny closes the burner. We sink rapidly, but once we're practically on top of the palace, she opens the burner slightly, and we stabilize about ten feet over the cistern that covers the roof.

We have a straight shot from the side of the gondola to the ground on the north side of the building, so we'll rappel down on that side. There's no moon tonight, but in the muted light cast by torches on the walls of the palace, we can make out three guards on the north side below us. We string our bows. They make difficult targets because all we can see are heads and shoulders.

"I'll take the one on the left," I whisper. "Grizz, you get the guy in the center, and Chase, you take out the one on the right."

We're out of practice with our bows, so I'm happily surprised when all three guards go down on our first volley. I wasn't worried about missing the first shot or two because the guards would have had a hard time figuring out where the arrows were coming from. They would never suspect the arrows were coming from above them. But with no misses, we're home free.

We lower a long rope over the side. I'm relieved to see it reaches the ground with rope to spare. I was pretty sure I remembered the height of the palace, but you never know. I rappel down followed by Grizz, Chase, and Kremke. We reach the ground without incident. I had wanted to use four ropes so we could slide down more quickly, but Kenny nixed the plan because with all our weight on one side, the balloon would be overbalanced. Kenny pulls the rope back up into the gondola. We don't want blacksuits passing by wondering what the rope is all about.

The windows on the ground floor are about eight feet above the ground, so Grizz interlaces his fingers to form a stirrup. He holds his cupped hands a couple feet above the ground. I plant my right foot in the stirrup, and Grizz boosts me up. I catch the ledge of the window and pull myself over it and into the room. Kremke and Chase follow. Chase leans out the window so Grizz can catch his arms and pull himself up and through the window as well.

No sooner is Grizz in the room than we hear the chilling blast of a blacksuit bugle sounding in the night. I peer out the window and see a passing blacksuit patrol that must have seen Grizz's legs disappear through the window. A burst of AK fire takes down four of the patrolling blacksuits, but the remaining two hit the ground and take cover behind their fallen comrades.

There are loud sounds from the barracks that surround the palace. Within moments, we're surrounded by hundreds of blacksuits.

\* \* \* \* \*

Blacksuits on the north side advance toward the palace, but we cut them to ribbons with our AKs. We have a standoff on the north side. The blacksuits can't advance on us, but there's absolutely no way for us to climb the rope back to the balloon.

Thinking about the balloon causes a momentary burst of fear. Have the blacksuits seen it? I anxiously watch the blacksuits opposite us, but none are looking up. The flat black color of the balloon combined with a moonless night make it almost invisible. Nonetheless, there's enough ambient light from torches set on the sides of the palace and the surrounding barracks to enable a careful observer to see the outline of the balloon.

"We can't stay here," I say. The blacksuits will be in the building from the other three sides anytime now. "Follow me."

I locate the stairs, and we climb. The light cast by Bree's electric lanterns is very bright, so we easily find our way. The military offices are located on the third floor. There's a huge room along the west wall that serves as the blacksuits' command and control center. I find it quickly. Fortunately, there are only three ways into the room.

"We need to hold the blacksuits off for a few minutes so we can get what we came for. Chase," I say, "can you cover the door over there? Grizz, will you take the door on the south side? Officer Kremke, please cover the stairs."

Within a matter of seconds, I hear the bark of AK fire coming from all three locations. The room is filled with highly polished, beautifully crafted desks and huge tables where maps are laid out flat. In a minute, I locate Salieri's desk. It's the largest desk in the room, and there's a name plaque on the wall above it. By the light cast by the electric lantern, I examine the desk and find a folder with the following title:

Strategic Plan for the Defeat of the Rebellion

Top Secret – Eyes Only

I pick it up. Beneath the folder are maps showing the location of all the blacksuits' defensive positions and troop deployments. I've hit the gold mine. A wise foe would keep this information under lock and key. But the blacksuits have consistently underestimated our capabilities. Their arrogance will be their undoing. Hearing the sound of blacksuits all around us, I stop reading and sweep everything on the top of Salieri's desk into my backpack, and then shoulder it.

"I can't hold them off much longer," shouts Kremke. "They're massing for an attack down below. There'll be hundreds of them coming up these stairs in any minute!"

"Time to give them something else to worry about," I holler.

I begin emptying file cabinets, creating a huge pile of paper near Kremke's position by the stairs. I throw wooden chairs on the stack as well.

"OK, everybody," I shout. "Break off, and climb the stairs to the next floor up."

When I see everybody in motion, I set the papers on fire. Within seconds there's a huge fire raging. *They won't come up those stairs*, I think. *And they'll need to put that out soon, or they'll lose everything in the command center.*

As we dash up the stairs, I thumb the transmit button on my two-way. "Kenny, can you position the balloon so you can drop the rope down the south wall?"

"Can do, ET. I'll need to give a little blast of the bladder to gain steerage, but with all the commotion down there, the blacksuits will never hear."

"OK," I say. "When I give the word, drop the rope down smack-dab in the middle of the south wall."

We reach the fifth floor to find blacksuits on the stairs above us. Fortunately there aren't many, and a brief firefight brings them down. Nonetheless, we need to move quickly because I can hear more blacksuits coming down the corridor just outside. We sprint to the top floor and down the hall to the suite in which I was kept during my captivity. I try the door, but it's locked. Chase kicks the door and breaks the lock. We dash into the room to find a man and a woman cowering in the corner.

"If you don't move, we won't shoot you," I say.

Killing people who are trying to kill you is one thing. Killing people who pose no threat is another thing entirely. I look out the doors leading to the balcony and see hundreds of blacksuits in the courtyard below. I duck back under cover. The blacksuits think they have us trapped. Even from a height of sixty feet, I can see the eager expressions on their faces. From their perspective, there's no way we can get out of the palace without running straight into their assembled masses.

"Kenny," I say into my radio, "can you lower the rope about twenty feet? The minute we start climbing, we're gonna be like ducks in a shooting gallery, but I can't think of anything else to do."

"Give me one minute before you start climbing," says Kenny.

In less than ten seconds, a flashbang detonates in the midst of the blacksuits in the courtyard below. All of the blacksuits within twenty yards of the flashbang are rendered momentarily blind and deaf. Shortly after the first, a second, third, and fourth flashbang detonate. Kenny has been very busy. Bless her for the foresight of building a munitions locker into the gondola. To create even more confusion, Kenny lobs three canisters of tear gas into the panic-stricken crowd below.

Most of the blacksuits below are totally disabled and blindly trying to retreat. The ones not blinded are disorganized.

"Up you go," Kenny says over the radio.

The rope appears instantly, but it's a good three yards to the left of the balcony. *Well,* I think, *there's no time to readjust. The blacksuits below will be recovered and ready to fight in a minute or two. Gotta jump.*

I climb onto the top rail of the balcony and leap toward the rope. For a second I'm convinced I'll never reach it, but with my arms stretched to their full extent, I'm able to get my fingers around the rope. I lock on with a death grip. I wrap my knees around the rope and take a moment to catch my breath. Then, I bring up my knees until I look like a U-shaped inchworm. A few more feet and I'm clambering over the edge of the gondola. Chase, Grizz, and Kremke are soon aboard. Kenny turns the burner up to maximum and releases the gas stored under extreme pressure in her pressure chamber. The balloon shoots up like a rocket.

Below us, the blacksuits have regained their hearing and vision and finally realize that we have escaped in a direction none of them could have guessed: straight up. By the time they come to this realization, we're well out of range.

Flames are shooting from multiple windows on the third floor, so my fire has spread. I'm ecstatic. We've penetrated the innermost sanctum of the blacksuits and stolen their most secret plans. High on adrenalin, I throw my arms around Grizz's neck and kiss him passionately. Initially surprised, it takes him a second to kiss me back. The kiss lingers, and when I finally back away, I'm infused with the familiar feelings of love and joy, but also a crying desire for something more. I now know I want to spend my life with Grizz, but my vows make that impossible.

"Can't you two do that in private?" grumbles Kremke. Chase and Kenny have big, goofy grins on their faces.

\* \* \* \* \*

Once we're back at the Sanctuary, we spend hours poring over the intelligence we've stolen. By midafternoon, we've had a chance to digest what we've read and ask Helen and Falstaff to join us. Like all the villagers, they are illiterate.

"Here's what we've found," I say. "First of all, the blacksuits are recalling retired soldiers and pressing teenagers into service, so their army will be larger than we thought."

"But old men and children won't make crack troops," Falstaff notes.

"Second," I continue, "they're doubling down on their efforts to clear the forest from the outer ring to the mines. Let me read what they say: 'The rebels are harrying our loggers every day, but they don't slow us down significantly because they're hesitant to kill their own people. We should be through the woods in a little more than a year. We may or may not actually attack the mines. We assume the rebels must be building defensive positions there, so a direct attack on the mines may prove costly. But knowing that we *can* attack the mines will force the rebels to keep a large body of troops there to defend them. With a large force pinned down at the mines, the rebel forces will be spread thin on every other front.'"

"You have to hand it to the blighters," growls Falstaff, "they're not dumb. We must defend the mines at all costs, but that will leave us weaker on every other front."

"But the worst news," I continue, "is this: 'We will convert the land we control from production of luxuries to the production of basic foodstuffs. Within a year, we'll have our own source of food, so we can burn every village to the ground and destroy their crops. The rebels won't know which village we'll be attacking next, and they don't have nearly enough militia to defend every village. We'll surprise them with every strike. We'll starve the rebels to death.'"

"I never thought the blacksuits would be willing to abandon their luxuries," murmurs Grizz.

"They'll only have to do without for a couple years," I say. "Once they've starved us into submission, they can go back to business as usual. And the worst thing is, we can attack them anywhere we please today, but once they start growing subsistence crops, we won't be able to burn their crops in the fields. If we destroy their food, the first ones to starve will be their slaves."

"The bottom line," says Helen "is that we must defeat the blacksuits and take New Washington within a year."

"That's the way I see it, too," I agree. "We need our wonder weapons. And we need them soon."

"But the villages are already on three-quarter rations," says Chase. "Our resources are stretched as thin as they'll go."

The room falls silent as we let the new facts sink in. We could lose this war.

"We'll have to fortify our village forts," says Helen. "They'll have to defend themselves until we can send help. I have no idea how they'll find the time to do all things they need to do."

The Sanctuary's radio operator breaks the silence when he rushes into the room.

"Begging your pardon, Daughter of Gaia," the man says, "but Eva is on the radio from the chem lab. She says it's very urgent."

I drop what I'm doing and rush to the radio room.

"Hi, Eva," I say. "What's up?"

"There's a man here you might want to talk to," Eva replies. "He stumbled in yesterday, more dead than alive. He's from a community that's reaching out to other surviving humans who share his community's values. He says his people kept alive a strain of wheat that produces enormous crops of grain. If he's right about the yield per acre, we'll easily double or triple our food production."

During the wars that ended civilization, one of the enemies of the United States developed a virus that killed every member of the grass family, which, of course, includes wheat, oats, and rye. The virus starved billions of people around the globe. If there's a prolific strain of wheat alive that can be grown today, we can go a long way in solving our problems with hunger.

"Put him on so I can speak with him," I say.

"I can't do that," says Eva. "He's fallen into a coma. We're trying to revive him, but we've been unsuccessful so far."

"Did he tell you where he came from?" I ask urgently.

"Yes," says Eva. "He's from a place called Los Alamos."

"And what's this deal about sharing his community's values?" I ask.

"Their values sound like our own," says Eva. "They value human life, care for one another, live in peace, democracy. All that stuff."

"We're on our way! Do everything you can to keep him alive. This may be the breakthrough we need. If we double our food production, we free a hundred thousand villagers to move the solar cells and the weapons we need to this side of the mountains. With drones and tanks along with Garganto, we'll crush the blacksuits."

\* \* \* \* \*

We decide the "giants" will all go to the chem lab and determine what to do next. If we decide to launch an expedition to bring back seed stock for the new grain, Grizz, Chase, Kenny, Kremke, and I will go. Bree will stay behind to supervise the movement of the solar farm.

Margaret is extremely unhappy. "How can we guard the Daughter of Gaia when she travels without us?"

"We need to move fast," I explain. "I'd love to take you along, but I want to get there and back as quickly as we can. The sooner we get that grain back here and planted, the sooner we'll double our food supply."

"That's assuming the misfortune you run into doesn't kill you," Margaret counters.

"We'll keep our eyes open," I assure her. "Don't worry, Margaret, we'll be careful."

"'Careful' is one word I'd never use to describe the Daughter of Gaia," Margaret objects.

My only response is to smile. Margaret is partly correct. I've never been reckless and have been as careful as circumstances allowed. But I have a penchant for attracting trouble.

* * * * *

We travel fast and light to the chem lab. When we arrive, we find the traveler is still alive, but in a deep coma.

I watch the stranger as he sleeps. He's a big man, probably five feet ten inches tall. His breathing is steady, but large blood-soaked bandages on his head and neck show the seriousness of his injuries. He is near death. I sit next to his bed as the others depart the room, leaving the stranger and me alone. I cup one of his hands with both of mine. We sit in silence. *Please wake up*, I think. *We need that grain.*

Out of nowhere, Jules appears, floating above the ground, head nearly touching the ceiling. She is looking at the stranger, her expression serious, as though she is pondering some extremely difficult question. Her hands rise slowly until they are in front of her, palms down. She closes her eyes, and her forehead creases as she concentrates.

The stranger's eyelids flicker, and Jules disappears. The stranger's eyes come all the way open and look at me curiously.

"Hello," I say. "I'm Erin."

The stranger speaks in a croaking whisper. He's clearly near death. "I'm pleased to meet you, Erin. My name is Johnny. Johnny Grainseed."

I smile at him warmly, waiting for him to continue.

"I come from a place called Los Alamos," he whispers. I move my ear closer to his mouth because his voice is so weak. "We're sending out expeditions in all directions looking for other groups that have survived Armageddon. We want to see if we can connect several groups and work to restore civilization. I've spoken with Eva and seen the operation you run here. You're obviously civilized."

"We try." I smile.

"And you're able to use technology," Johnny continues. He closes his eyes, and I worry he has fallen back into a coma. But his eyes open again. "I hope you will become an important node in a network of communities that will restore society."

"I hope you're right," I say.

"Wherever we've traveled, we've found people struggling to scratch enough food from the earth to survive. The scientists at Los Alamos have bred a variety of grain that has withstood the plague that killed the other grasses. This strain yields massive stalks so full of seed that the plants cannot stand up. The stalks literally bend over until they touch the ground. And the crops grow from seedling to harvest in a period of only ninety days."

Even though Johnny is close to death, his excitement is unmistakable.

"So," he whispers, "you can harvest four crops a year. A hundred acres of our grain will feed thousands of people."

Johnny coughs, and a trickle of blood runs from the corner of his mouth. I dab at it with a clean cotton cloth.

"Can you tell me how we can find Los Alamos?" I ask.

"Can you draw a map?" he asks.

"Yes." I poke around in my backpack until I find a small pencil and a piece of paper. "I'm ready."

"You must travel east across the desert. The desert slowly gives way to a scrub forest. The ground in the forest is broken and difficult to cross. Once you are in the scrub, walk three or four days to the northeast and then swing to the north. You will travel at least two weeks through this forest, and the land will begin to rise. You will come upon a river running from west to east. Build a raft and cross this river. Next, you will enter a pine forest. Continue north for another week, and you will come to the blasted lands. Nothing but small wind-burned tumbleweed grows there. It will take you another four or five days to cross the blasted lands. You will see a mountain range to the north. Find the black mountain, black because fire has burned all vegetation from its flanks. You must cross the black mountain on its western side. On the other side, you will find Los Alamos."

I scramble to record each detail. Johnny's voice weakens. He has to pause and rest a bit before he continues. I place my ear right next to his mouth in order to make out what he is saying.

"In the scrub forest, you must beware of the zealots. They were the ones who gave me these injuries. And in the blasted lands, you'll encounter fierce storms. We're not certain why, but there's a narrow corridor that seems to channel high winds through those desolate lands. You will need a code word to be accepted at Los Alamos." He wheezes. "The code word is 'Oppenheimer.'"

All the talking has exhausted Johnny. His eyes flutter and close. They never open again. By sunset, he is gone.

I solemnly relate Johnny's words to my friends shortly after he passes away. "What do you think?" I ask.

"Let's start as soon as we can," says Grizz. Kenny and Chase nod in agreement.

In the morning, we bury Johnny. He was a brave man pursuing a noble cause. If we can find Los Alamos and return with his grain cultivar, we will transform the New United States.

\* \* \* \* \*

I spend the next day inspecting the operations at the lab. The chem lab is running smoothly. Eva has a group working on sewing softbark to produce more balloons. Parties scour the desert each day and bring back borax for water purification. We'll soon begin carting borax over the saddle so the villages can take advantage of our new technology. I hope we'll soon reach the point where late monsoon rains won't force our people to ration water.

I ask Eva if she'd consider working with Bree on moving and assembling solar panels. Eva has proven to be intelligent and a quick study. She'll be a real asset for Bree. Bree says that by the time we return, we'll have a small working solar farm at the Sanctuary, and another at Fort Taylor.

"Kenny," I ask, "can we use the balloon to fly across the desert instead of walking?"

"The load will be pretty heavy if we carry the five of us and all the equipment we'll need. That means we'll go through propane pretty fast," Kenny replies pensively. "We don't need to go up more than a hundred feet or so, and I can lash several cylinders of propane to the sides of the basket. I'd guess we can make it across most of the desert on half the fuel we carry. We'll use the other half to get home on the return journey."

I remember seeing green fields far to the east during our ill-fated first balloon voyage. But I estimate it'd take us over ten days to cross the desert on foot. We can stash the balloon on the far side of the desert and use it again to get home. We won't need to cross the desert on foot at all.

We leave the following morning. We're heavily burdened with supplies. We're each taking an AK and dozens of spare clips, but we've decided to take swords and bows as well. In one extended firefight, we could easily burn through several clips of ammunition. We need to take a healthy supply of borax to purify water, and as much dried food as we can manage. I throw in two hundred yards of Bree's light but sturdy vine fiber rope. The mountains on the stranger's map may make some rock climbing equipment necessary.

Johnny made it all the way from Los Alamos to the chem lab, so he must have foraged for food along the way. Even so, we decide to take as much food as we can carry. It's been a couple weeks since the siege of Fort Kennedy, and I'm still a bit thin. So at every meal, my friends hector me to eat more. Kenny threatens to hold me down so

Grizz can force-feed me. They insist on taking a lot of food so they can fatten me up.

"You could always save weight by leaving that huge barrette behind," teases Chase, referring to the pink barrette Kenny has worn ever since my escape from the Apaches.

"You never can tell when you might run into a good-looking guy," Kenny sniffs. "A girl has to take care of her appearance."

I can't help but laugh. The clunky barrette doesn't improve her appearance at all.

"*Et tu, Brute?*" says Kenny, scowling at me.

Our first day of flight is uneventful. We bring the balloon down at sunset and camp for the night.

On the second day, I ask Kenny if she can take us up higher so we can scout the land in front of us.

"We definitely don't want to get caught in the jet stream again," she answers. "But I'd guess we can safely go up a couple thousand feet."

She adjusts her burner, and the balloon begins a slow and steady rise. The land below falls away, and details become smaller and smaller. I study the terrain in the distance. I can easily make out the green fields I saw on our earlier journey, near both the eastern and northern horizons. Thin ribbons of blue show us rivers. One runs north and south and the other east and west. They must intersect at some point, but we are too far away to see their junction. Between us and the green fields lies nothing but the dun-colored desert, flat land broken by nothing but an occasional low-lying hill. And to the south, the desert stretches as far as the eye can see.

"I've seen what I need to see," I say.

Kenny reduces altitude to conserve fuel. As nightfall nears, we take the balloon up for another look and see we're only a few miles from the green fields to the east.

"Good thing," says Kenny. "We've burned nearly half our fuel. Tomorrow we walk."

We land and deflate the balloon. We find a shallow, dusty arroyo and stash the basket and the balloon. We're still in the desert, so plants are scarce. It takes us a couple hours to gather enough foliage to conceal the balloon. Anybody standing on the edge of the arroyo would see it instantly, but from a distance, the balloon is invisible. The arroyo is a shallow one, so it's unlikely a flash flood will wash the balloon miles away.

Before we leave in the morning, we take care to get our bearings and look for landmarks. I'll be staying oriented with my compass and pedometer every step of our journey, but even so, we could easily be off by a few miles when we return. We take careful note of the hills nearby and the mountains behind us to the west. When I'm certain we'll be able to find the balloon again, we set off.

By noon, the landscape around us begins to change. Plants are taller, more numerous, and closer together. We're moving through a transition zone—not desert and not forest, but something in between.

By late afternoon we begin to see scrubby trees, similar to the ones in the forest we left behind, and by sunset, we're in a forest. There's a brook burbling away to the north. We've gone through about a third of the water we brought with us, so the brook will give us the opportunity to top off our canteens.

Kenny takes a beaker out of her backpack, and I walk with her to the stream. When we find the brook, she fills her beaker with water. Back in camp, she measures out a small amount of her borax mixture and dumps it in the beaker with the water. I've never seen Kenny's water purification system before, and I have to say, I'm impressed. The water in the beaker froths and bubbles the minute the borax is added.

"Fundamental acid-base reaction." When the frothing subsides, Kenny says, "Now we boil the water for a while, and it'll be ready to drink." Once the water is boiled, we let it cool and top off our canteens.

When darkness falls, we set our watch schedule for the night. With five of us sharing shifts, we'll each get a good six hours of sleep. I fluff my backpack pillow and prepare to turn in when I see a man and woman standing just inside the ring of light cast by our campfire. They have weapons slung over their shoulders.

# 15

My first reaction is to reach for my AK, and I have it in hand when the man says, "Relax, please. We're not dangerous. We saw your campfire and decided to investigate. We've been watching you for the last hour. You look like friendly folk, so we decided to introduce ourselves."

I make a mental note to put out our fire the minute we've purified our water in the future.

"Please," I say, "join us. Are you hungry? Our food is dried, so it's not very tasty, but it'll fill an empty belly."

"No thanks," says the man. "We just finished a dinner of roasted rabbit an hour or so ago."

The two strangers sit down by the fire. I see that what I had taken for "weapons" are actually musical instruments, quite similar to guitars.

"You're musicians," I observe.

"Of a sort," says the man. "I'm Steve, and this is Edie."

We introduce ourselves.

"I'm very surprised to see two people traveling alone armed with nothing more than bows," I say. "The world's a dangerous place."

"The secret to staying healthy," Steve says, "is to be the ones who find other folks and not the ones who get found."

"But aren't there lots of bad people roaming the wilderness?" I ask.

"The legends speak of huge roving bands of evil folk, and I guess it was true back then. But now, most of the survivors have built walled cities or found mesas or islands to live on. There are still bad people out here, but we don't see too many of them," Steve explains.

"And we're minstrels," says Edie. "Most folks are happy to spend an evening with us. Like Steve says, the secret to staying healthy is to find the other guy before he finds you. We're pretty good at it."

"Minstrels," says Grizz. "Will you play something for us?"

"We'll be glad to," Steve says, "if you'll spot us a swallow of water. Our canteens are almost empty, and it doesn't look like rain."

Kenny gets out her beaker and heads back to the stream. "We'll have water for you in just a minute," she says over her shoulder as she disappears into the darkness.

"Where are you from?" I ask.

"We don't have a home," says Steve. "I guess you could say we're from somewhere, everywhere, and nowhere."

"You just travel?" asks Chase. "That sounds like a hard life."

"No," says Edie, "it's not hard at all. We enjoy meeting new people. So, where are *you* folks from?"

I'm hesitant to answer, but realize it's safe to tell them if I leave out the details.

"We come from a nation of several hundred thousand people," I say. "We're mostly subsistence farmers, and we've heard of another group of people who have grown a kind of wheat that's immune to plague. We're going to visit them. If the grain is as fruitful as they claim, we can go a long way toward solving our problems with hunger."

"You're on a grand quest," says Edie.

"I suppose you could look at it that way." I smile.

Kenny returns and impresses Steve and Edie with her borax trick. She brings the water to a boil and offers it to them.

Steve and Edie look at the water with undisguised suspicion. After waiting for the water to cool, Kenny takes a swig of it herself.

"The water's safe," she says. "Please. Fill your canteens."

Our new friends treat us to a concert. Edie's soaring soprano blends beautifully with Steve's mellow tenor. The songs they sing are ballads. Most are love songs with an occasional tune about the joys of life on the road. The songs are lovely, and we reward the singers with applause after each one. I haven't heard anything so beautiful since we left Tucson.

Steve and Edie lay down their instruments and perform two short plays. In the first play, Steve plays the role of a stiff and not-very-intelligent king, while Edie plays the role of his clever wife. The witty wife prevents the king from making disastrous decisions while making him believe that her ideas are really his own. The play leaves us laughing so hard I struggle to catch my breath.

They perform a second play in which Edie is a beautiful girl, coveted by all the boys for miles around, and Steve plays a humble boy who outmaneuvers rivals who are richer and more attractive, slowly wooing Edie into marriage. This play is funny as well, but also has a serious side. It offers a message about our values and the way we lose sight of the things in life that are *really* important.

When they're done performing, I ask if Steve and his wife would like to travel with us.

"Oh," says Steve. "Edie's not my wife. She's my wife's sister."

I look confused, so Steve clarifies. "My wife's name was Laura. She died not long ago. Laura, Edie, and I performed as a trio for years. But we ran into a group of travelers who said they were heading home. They said their people were very wealthy. Their community was a strong one, so they were never bothered by wandering bands of thieves. They said they never went hungry, and their people worked hard to help one another out. They made their home sound like paradise. When they asked us if we'd like to live with them, we couldn't say no. You see, life on the road has its advantages, but we couldn't resist the prospect of security, steady meals, and companionship.

"Unfortunately, the people turned out to be phonies. No sooner did we arrive at their village than it became obvious that what they really wanted from us was our labor. We tended their crops, washed their clothes, cooked their meals, and cleaned up after them. At night, they demanded we entertain them. We weren't alone. They'd lured others with the same promise.

"They kept their 'guests' in a cluster of wooden shacks and guarded us closely so none of us could escape. One night, Laura managed to steal a log that had an end still burning from the cooking fire. She smuggled it into our hut and started a fire. We ran out of our shack and since there was a strong breeze blowing, the fire soon spread to other huts and then to the masters' homes. In the chaos that followed, we escaped.

"We ran for hours, until Laura collapsed. One of the masters had shot her in the back with an arrow as we were running away. Laura never said a word about it until she couldn't run any longer. The arrow had pierced her back and lodged in her lung. We removed it and stanched the bleeding, but we couldn't stop to rest so she could heal because we knew the masters would send out posses to recapture us. So we rigged a travois, and I lay Laura in it and pulled her for days. For a while, she didn't seem so bad, and we thought she'd recover. But then she began coughing up blood. We wanted to stop and nurse her, but Laura wouldn't hear of it. 'Keep moving,' she said. 'I'll be just fine.' During the daytime, we could hear the masters pursuing us, so if we stopped, we'd be in danger of being recaptured. 'Keep moving,' Laura said. 'I'm as strong as a horse.'

"One morning, we woke and found Laura dead. I loaded her in the travois and kept pulling her for hours. I couldn't bring myself to leave her behind, you see. She'd been the only woman I'd ever loved, the only woman I'd ever wanted. I'd known her since we were children, and I couldn't remember a time I'd been without her. Later that day, Edie finally convinced me to let Laura go. We buried her. I cried. I never knew eyes could cry so many tears."

When he finishes speaking, we're all silent. I can't help but reflect on the similarities of his relationship with Laura and mine with Grizz, because he's the one I love, the only one I'll ever love. The parallels make the story all the more poignant for me. I just hope our story has a happier ending.

"I'm sorry," is all I can think to say. "I can't imagine how painful it must have been to lose your wife."

"I guess I've taken a long time to explain why we won't take you up on that offer to travel with you."

Steve and Edie spend the night with us in our camp. One or the other stays awake all night long.

In the morning I tell them, "I can only promise you that if you'd travel with us, we'd never take advantage of you. But I understand why you can't believe me."

Even Kremke joins us in wishing Steve and Edie good luck when they leave.

We part company, but we're destined to run across them again.

\* \* \* \* \*

We make a turn to the north, following Johnny's map. There's no scale on it, so the only clues as to the distance we must travel are Johnny's rough estimates. From what he said, it'll take us at least forty or fifty days to make the trip.

A couple months ago, Kenny began running on a daily basis. Back in Tucson, she was not a fan of exercise. But in this dangerous world, the ability to move quickly over long distances is sometimes the difference between life and death. Kremke is a runner. He says he enjoyed the runner's high back in the corps, and he runs almost every day. As a result, since Chase, Grizz, and I are all runners from way back, the five of us are in great shape.

It's hard to move quickly through this forest. Unlike our forests on the other side of the mountains, the ground here is extremely treacherous. This forest is cut by numerous ravines and rushing streams. Huge boulders block our way at times, and there are numerous thickets we must avoid, or the thorns would tear our skin into bloody jerky. We have to watch our foot placement very carefully. But, even moving through the broken ground of this treacherous forest, we cover fifteen or twenty miles a day.

Ten days into our walk, we begin to compare blisters. The shoes we wore when we crossed through the brane are beginning to look shabby, and we'll soon have to trade them in for the crude sandals the villagers wear.

The good news we find as we travel is that there's game in this forest. We're able to dine on roast rabbit or grilled squirrel every evening. We make our fire before sunset every night and burn only dry wood to minimize the smoke. We're careful to extinguish the fire the minute we're done cooking and purifying our drinking water.

On our fifteenth day out, we hear the noise of a crowd coming from our right.

"Do we investigate or keep on walking?" I ask softly.

"Let's see if we can get a look," replies Kenny. Chase and Grizz shrug with expressions that say "Why not?"

We move slowly and carefully toward the noise. When we see movement through the trees, we drop to our stomachs and pull ourselves forward, elbow in front of elbow. We come to the edge of a clearing and see a large crowd of perhaps a hundred people, standing in a circle, loudly cheering. They're all small people, dressed in an oddly colored assortment of homespun wool jerkins.

"What are they looking at?" Kenny whispers.

It takes a moment for us to realize that there are two men in the middle of the circle, fighting each other bare-handed. Every time one strikes a blow, the crowd erupts in cheers.

The sound of voices in front of me and to the right stops me cold. Two women stand less than ten yards from us. Fortunately, they're engrossed in the fight, and haven't heard our approach. I touch my friends and point in the direction of the women with one hand and press the index finger of my other hand to my lips.

"I say it's a waste of a slave," says the taller woman.

"When they try to escape, you gotta teach 'em a hard lesson," says the other.

"I still say we ought to just whip 'em both," says the tall woman.

"Nah. Makin' 'em fight till one or the other's dead sends a better lesson. Makes 'em think real hard about runnin' off in the first place."

"I thought those two were never gonna start fightin'."

"You knew if Garth gave 'em a bitter enough taste of the lash it'd encourage 'em to go at it sooner or later."

The conversation ceases as one of the men knocks the other to the ground. The one on the ground is obviously badly hurt. The man still standing has tears running down his face. His voice carries to us: "Sorry, Fen. You know I don't want to hurt you."

The man on the ground, also in tears, says, "Do it, Rafe. Just make it fast."

I want to do something to help. With our AKs, we could probably take down the hundred people in the clearing. But we'd also alert anyone within five miles of our presence. And killing one hundred people to save one is morally problematic. There's nothing to be done.

We crawl away from the clearing as quickly as we can without making noise. When we're out of earshot, we run as fast as the trees and broken ground will allow. We don't let up until we're miles away. We keep moving until darkness falls, making further travel impossible.

"There are some twisted people in this world," says Grizz. "Were they the zealots?"

"According to Johnny, we're too far south to have run into the zealots," I say. "Those people must be a different bunch of creeps."

"Seeing that stuff back there motivates me to move as quietly as I possibly can," says Kenny.

That's a good thing, because you can usually hear Kenny coming a mile away. I'm not optimistic about her chances of being quieter. "Quiet" and "Kenny" are two words that don't naturally fit together.

"I guess the Court isn't the only government that enslaves its people," says Chase.

"The law of the jungle seems to be the rule," says Grizz. "But there have to be *some* good people."

"I'm hoping the folks at Los Alamos are good ones," I reply. "If they're not, we're gonna be in a lot of trouble once we get there."

Three days later, in the early afternoon, Chase, who is in the lead, raises his right hand, gesturing for us to stop. I soon see why. A pole has been driven into the ground, and atop it is a human skull.

# 16

"That's a *very* unfriendly welcome mat," says Kenny. "I think they might be telling us to go away."

"We can't go away," I mutter.

"Do you think we've found the place that says 'Beware of Zealots' on the map?" asks Grizz.

"I don't know if the people who put that skull up there are zealots or not. But I'm thinking we should avoid *anybody* who uses a skull as a calling card," I reply.

"Maybe we can travel *around* the zealots' land," suggests Chase.

"That's worth a try," I agree.

We turn to the east and walk a course perpendicular to the one we've been following. We find skulls every hundred yards or so.

That night, we decide to forgo the fire to purify our water even though there's a pond near our camp. We want to attract as little attention as possible.

The following day we come to a broad river near sunset. The water is rushing by in a torrent, with the current flowing to the south.

"If we had a raft, we could do some serious white-water traveling," Chase points out.

"Without a raft, it'd be suicide to go into the water," I observe. "We can't go east any more. I guess tomorrow we head north again."

"Into the land of the zealots," says Kenny.

\* \* \* \*

We sacrifice speed for silence as we walk. We pick the placement of our feet carefully. Even with the roaring of the river to our right dampening sound, we don't want to snap twigs or do anything else that might alert the zealots to our presence. We pause at dark and sleep without lighting a fire to purify water. Our water supply is down to about a third of a canteen each, so we'll have to make some hard choices tomorrow night.

We travel until, at midday, we come to a large clearing. We smell woodsmoke, so we must be near a zealot village. From the tree line, we scan the clearing in front of us. Crops are being cultivated, although I can see no one in the fields. The tree line on the other side is a good three hundred yards away. If we sprint, laden as we are with supplies, we'll be in the open for about a minute.

"We don't have much choice," I whisper. "We're gonna have to cross that field."

We rise and sprint from the tree line. Just as we start, we see a party of ten small people emerge from the opposite tree line. Do we run? Do we fight? There's a village nearby, so we'll draw a crowd no matter what we do.

"Welcome, strangers," says a rotund man with a smile.

The others smile as well. "Welcome," they say.

The people aren't armed. And they look very friendly. Can these be the zealots? I walk toward them with a smile of my own. "Pleased to meet you," I say.

We meet them halfway across the clearing.

"What brings you here?" says the fat man pleasantly.

"We're looking for some people who sent a messenger to us a while ago," I say. "They have some crops we'd like to look at."

"We haven't sent out any messengers, and we don't have any fancy crops, but you've found another bunch of friendly people," the rotund man says. "Please, come into our village and join us for lunch."

I turn the proposal over in my mind. These people look friendly, and they don't appear to be armed. I'm just about to accept their offer when I see a skull mounted on a pole in the middle of the cleared field to our left. Despite their friendly demeanor, these people are zealots.

"We appreciate the offer," I say, "but we're in a bit of a hurry. I think we'll just be moving on." I struggle to keep my smile steady.

The heavy man and his friends lose their smiles immediately. They look at us coldly. "You four are mighty unfriendly," the man says. There's a look in his eyes I don't like. "Still, if you want to go, we won't stop you."

Looking over my shoulder as we go, I watch to see if the crowd behind us will draw weapons. They don't. They stand where they are and watch us until we enter the tree line on the opposite side of the clearing. The minute we're out of sight, hidden by the trees, we begin to run.

Within ten minutes of our parting, we hear the sound of drums behind us. A moment later, they're answered by drums ahead of us. We keep moving, trying to put distance between ourselves and the group behind. We stop after half an hour to catch our breath.

"Those must have been the zealots," Chase says. "Did you see the pole with the skull on top?"

"I saw it," I reply. "Best we get out of here as quickly as we can."

We travel as fast as we can, which is nowhere near as fast as I'd like. But it's difficult to move quickly in this forest. All day long we listen to the sinister sound of drumming. No matter where we are, the drumming comes from all sides but the river. The zealots obviously have us surrounded. During a rest stop, I walk to the river and eye it carefully.

"There's no way to cross it," says Grizz, who has followed me. "Those are class six rapids. We wouldn't last two minutes."

"That drumming is creepy," says Kenny, who has also joined us. "And half the time my skin crawls because it feels like we're being watched."

"I know," I say. "I get the same feeling."

We continue traveling north. We climb up hills and down into narrow ravines. Occasionally we find our path blocked by a rushing stream, clearly a tributary of the main river. We spend precious time looking for a good place to ford the stream. The drumming continues. The monotonous ostinato wears on my nerves. I begin to understand why the slow dripping of water on a man's forehead hour after hour is an effective form of torture. I want to plug my ears, but know it's not a good idea to travel deaf.

When darkness falls, we're forced to stop. With no moonlight, visibility is down to a few feet. We can't move on. Even with night-vision goggles, the forest footing is too treacherous. A broken ankle is the least of things that might happen if we stumble on in the dark. And a broken ankle would be deadly at this point. In the familiar forests on the other side of the mountains, we can move more freely after dark because we know where the trails are. Over here, we must stop. As the world turns dark, the drumming stops.

"Do you think they've given up?" Chase asks.

"Not likely," I reply. "I hated the drumming, but silence is almost worse."

We sit back-to-back. We agree we'll all stay awake. Memories of the night Kenny, Tyler, and I spent with our backs together haunt me.

Near dawn, we hear movement in the forest all around us. Twigs snap and dried leaves rustle when crushed underfoot. We still can't see, but since the noise comes from every direction, it's obvious we're being surrounded. We burn off AK clips firing into the gloom, and occasionally we're rewarded with the sound of someone crying out in pain. But without visible targets, most of our bullets are wasted.

The rising pink light of dawn finds us surrounded by well over a hundred zealots. Each zealot has an arrow trained on us. Before we could squeeze off more than two rounds, we'd look like porcupines.

"No need to be unfriendly about this," says a short man, stepping forward. "You folks just stand up and keep your hands in the air so we can see 'em." His no-nonsense manner reinforces my thought that trying to do something suddenly would be a bad idea.

We have no choice. We lay our AKs on the ground and stand, remove our swords, and slowly raise our hands.

\* \* \* \* \*

"Leave all your equipment on the ground," the man says. "If you make any sudden moves, you'll be dead."

We carefully shrug our packs, bows, and quivers from our shoulders. They fall to the ground with a thud. We stand still as our hands are bound behind our backs. Once we're securely tied, the zealots pat us down, looking for concealed weapons. Each of us carries a pocketknife of some sort. The zealots find them and throw them in a pile with our other belongings.

"Myra," says the short man, "pick some of your friends to help you carry their things back to the village."

A group of women quickly pick up our belongings.

"Follow Morton," says the short man, pointing at another man with a shock of blond hair.

We follow Blond Hair through the woods. I consider the odds of making a run for it and decide we'd have little chance of getting away. The zealots are all around us.

After a short time, we find ourselves on a narrow path. The path weaves its way around trees and cuts ravines sideways, making for easier climbs and descents. In less than an hour, we smell woodsmoke, and within moments, we emerge into a clearing and find the walls of a fort before us.

The gate swings open, and a crowd of curious villagers looks us up and down. Blond Hair leads us to a crude cage, about four feet high and six yards to a side. The joints of the cage are lashed together by thick vines. The zealots open the gate and unceremoniously shove us in.

The crowd around our cage parts, and a man dressed in a black robe walks toward us. When he reaches our cage, he studies us thoughtfully.

"I'm the deacon," he says. The deacon stands meter-stick straight. He wears the condescending expression of a self-important man. His nose is long and hooked, and his lips are thick and unpleasant.

"I'm Erin," I reply.

"My people tell me you killed some of us in the darkness with thunder. What witchcraft did you use to do that?"

"There was no witchcraft involved. We have weapons that make a loud noise when we use them."

"And which weapons would those be?" he asks.

The crowd parts again, and I see where the zealots have piled our belongings neatly, about ten yards from our cage.

"The long weapons make the noise," I explain.

"And what must you do to cause the weapon to make noise?" he asks as he picks up an AK.

"If you give it to me, I'll show you," I say.

"Don't take me for a fool!" he thunders, face red and pinched with anger.

"OK. You touch the little lever underneath, but be careful to keep the skinny end pointed away from everybody."

"This lever?" he asks, pointing at the trigger.

"Yes."

He presses the trigger. The AK is set to rapid-fire, so it discharges and literally jumps out of his hand. The people around us throw themselves to the ground. The deacon looks at the AK as though it were a coiled poisonous snake.

"That is the devil's work!" howls the deacon. "Throw those thunder makers in the river!"

A group of zealots approaches the AKs very cautiously. They tentatively touch them as if expecting them to begin roaring again. They carefully pick them up and hold them at arm's length. They disappear into the crowd, which separates, giving them wide berth.

"These five are witches," intones the deacon. "They must be purified in the fire of the lamb."

I don't like the sound of being purified in fire. "We are *not* witches," I object.

"If you are not witches," says the deacon, "then tell me the Three Commandments."

With my Methodist upbringing, I know there are Ten Commandments, not three. What should I say? If I disagree with him, it may make him even angrier. But since I don't know the Three Commandments, I opt for honesty.

"My people observe Ten Commandments," I counter.

The crowd begins to howl and hoot scathingly.

"I told you!" cries the deacon. He raises his right arm exultantly into the air. His eyes roll back in his head, and spittle sprays from his mouth as he roars. "The Ten Commandments are wickedness! Those who hold to the Ten Commandments must be eliminated so they can't spread their sinful, blasphemous beliefs."

"What *are* the Three Commandments?" I ask.

"It is well you learn them before you are purified in the fire of the lamb," says the deacon. "First, obey the deacon. Second, purify sinners in the fire of the lamb. Third, love thy neighbor."

"How do you purify the sinners and love your neighbor at the same time? Burning people isn't consistent with loving them," I object.

The crowd howls again. "Blasphemer!" they cry.

"If you weren't witches," says the deacon, "you would know that burning you in the fire of the lamb purifies you. The fire of the lamb burns all your sins away! You will awaken in heaven at the right side of the lamb with a clean soul. We purify you *because* we love you. You will burn in the fire at noon tomorrow. Prepare your filthy souls."

\* \* \* \* \*

Once the deacon has left, Kenny says, "I never did like Presbyterians."

I can't help but laugh.

I examine our cage for a way out, some shred of hope, but come up empty. The vines that bind the joints together could be cut with a knife, but the zealots took our knives away.

All day long, we watch helplessly as the zealots drive five heavy poles into the ground and pile firewood around the bases. My fear grows as the zealots pile the wood higher and higher.

"Great," says Kremke. "I'm gonna get burned at the stake with a bunch of juvenile delinquents."

"Maybe not," whispers Kenny. "Do you know my barrette that you all laughed at?"

"Yeah," I say. Good luck attracting boys with it now."

"ET," Kenny hisses, "it's got a little knife in it."

"A knife?" I say, stunned. My spirits soar.

"Yes. A knife," Kenny whispers. "Ever since we were chased by Apaches, I decided I'd like to have a hidden weapon on me in case they ever caught me. So I worked with Bree to make this barrette."

"We can't use it right now," I say, thinking aloud. "The zealots will see us. We'll wait until tonight."

We try to sleep, but the day is a hot one, and our cage sits in the sun. I nod off, but wake almost instantly as sweat runs in my eyes, making them sting. Grizz moves next to me. His shadow keeps my head out of the sun. I sleep for a while and then return the favor. Chase and Kremke snore, and Kenny sits with her back to the cage wall, chin resting on her chest.

A small boy walks slowly toward the cage. From behind his back, he reveals a stick. He pokes at us with the stick. I'm tempted to grab the stick and poke back, but decide it'd be senseless. A zealot adult chastises the young one.

"Love thy neighbor," she says.

"Even the blasphemers?" the child asks doubtfully.

"Love thy neighbor," the woman repeats.

The little scalawag throws his stick on the ground and stomps away.

At lunchtime, the zealots throw smoked meat and carrots into our cage. We divide them up and devour them. The meat is hard as frozen steel, but we gnaw away at it. I have no appetite, but force myself to eat.

All afternoon, zealots go about their business. Occasionally, one stares at us, but they turn their heads sharply if we make eye contact. The funeral pyres are finally finished.

"If we don't get out of here, these fiends are gonna toast us like marshmallows," Kenny mutters.

"Then we'll just have to escape," I reply.

The dinner menu is identical to lunch, and once again, I force myself to eat.

\* \* \* \* \*

At sunset, the zealots retire into their wooden houses. Their windows are made of thin animal skin coated with grease. You can't actually see through them, but they admit a filtered light. We watch as the windows go dark one by one. A lone sentry is posted to watch us, but he appears disinterested.

"ET," says Kenny, "I'm gonna lay down so my head is right by your hands. You turn so you're facing the sentry."

"I'll sit between the guard and you guys so he can't see what you're up to," volunteers Grizz.

I scoot around so I'm seated facing the guard. He won't be able to see what's going on behind my back. Kenny slides behind me and lies down on her side.

"The handle of the knife is the little round knob on top," she says.

Our hands are bound tightly behind us, but even so, we have use of our fingers. I fumble around and locate the barrette. I can't quite reach the knob, so I scoot to my right on my butt to get a better angle on it. I find it and lock the thumb and index finger of my right hand around the knob. With my hands bound, I can't move my wrists enough to pull the knife from its sheath, so I push my whole body to the right, careful to keep my hold on the knife firm.

I feel the knife come loose of its sheath, and two things happen at once.

Kenny growls, "Ouch! Leave some hair behind."

And I drop the knife.

"Oh jeez," I say. I squirm and wriggle around trying to find the knife.

The guard sees me moving around and decides to investigate. He walks up to the cage and peers in at us. The knife is behind my back, and as he moves around the cage, I do a little hop backward on my butt so the knife is beneath me.

"You're mighty wiggly," he says, looking directly at me.

# 17

"I'm just trying to scratch my leg," I say. "That's hard to do with your hands tied. I don't suppose you'd consider untying my hands so I can have a good scratch?"

"Nope," he says simply. He circles the cage one more time. Curiosity satisfied, he returns to his chair. He closes his eyes and appears to nap. Wondering if this is a trick to throw us off our guard, I decide to proceed very cautiously.

I scoot forward, but the knife, which I'm sitting on, scoots with me. I'm still sitting on it. I lift my rear and launch myself forward, pushing off with my fingertips. I'm certain the knife is behind me. I grope around with my fingers, trying to locate it.

"To your left, just a little," says Chase.

I butt-hop to my left, and my fingers make contact with the knife. As I struggle to pick it up, I shove the knife backward where I can touch it with only the very tips of my fingers. It's out of my reach. Scooting backward, I find the knife again, and this time I succeed in picking it up. I hold it by the handle, but the blade points down. I manipulate the knife awkwardly, but carefully, with my fingers until the blade is pointed backward, away from me.

I catch my breath. I don't think I can manipulate the knife well enough with my fingers to cut through my own bonds, but I'm reasonably certain I can cut through someone else's.

"This is a pretty small knife," I observe.

"Did you think I was carrying a meat clever on my head?" Kenny asks.

"Good point. Sit right behind me," I whisper to Kenny.

We squirm around until we're back-to-back. I hold the knife between the thumb and forefinger of my right hand, blade facing down. With the fingers on my left hand, I grope around, trying to find Kenny's hands.

"Quit tickling my butt," Kenny hisses.

"I'm trying to find your hands," I say.

"To the left," she says. "That'll be to your right."

I find her fingers and then the rope. I begin to saw away.

"Ouch!" gasps Kenny. "That's my wrist you're cutting."

"Sorry," I whisper and feel around with my fingers until I find rope again.

After fifteen minutes of sawing, my fingers are tired. Still, I know I have to keep going. I feel the vines beginning to fray.

"I can feel the vines getting looser," says Kenny. "Let's see if I can break them. She grunts softly as she tries. "No luck yet. Keep cutting."

The sentry snorts and wakes. We hold our breath until he falls asleep again.

After a half hour of cutting, I have to rest.

"Can you pass the knife to me?" asks Grizz.

"I'm afraid we'd drop it," I respond. "I just need to rest for a minute."

When my fingers stop aching, I resume cutting. This time we're successful. Kenny pulls her hands apart, and the last of the vines snap. She keeps her hands behind her back, watching the sentry carefully.

"Hand me the knife," she whispers. "With my hands untied, I have more freedom to move than you do." Despite the fact she's free, Kenny has to work with her hands behind her back, so if the sentry wakes, he'll think her hands are still tied. Nonetheless, within minutes, all four of us are unbound. We wrap what's left of the vines around our wrists and ankles, hoping the sentry won't examine them too closely.

Chase, Kremke, Grizz, and I sit between the guard and Kenny as she begins to saw through the thick vines holding the cage together.

The sentry issues a series of grunts and snorts. Fearful that he'll wake, Chase, Kremke, and Grizz feign sleep. Kenny swings around, keeping her body between the guard and the work she's been doing. The guard yawns and stretches. He's awake. He eyes us suspiciously. If he comes closer again, he'll surely see the fraying vines where Kenny is cutting. He rises and picks up his torch. He walks toward us. Kenny sits in front of the vines she's been cutting, but if the sentry walks around the cage again, he can't miss the frayed vines. He walks right up to the cage and peers in warily. I hold my breath.

"Mmmph," the sentry says. "You girls should get some sleep. You'll want to be wide awake for your purification tomorrow." He chortles, turns around, and walks back to his seat. We wait, motionless, until his head falls to his chest again.

"This side's loose!" Kenny whispers. She's cut through all the vines vertically from top to bottom. She moves two feet to her left and begins cutting again. She quickly finishes cutting through the vines from top to bottom again. All that's left is to cut the ones on top and on the bottom. Looking nervously at the guard, she shifts her attention to the vines on top, cutting horizontally between the two seams she's already severed. If the sentry wakes now, we're in desperate trouble. There's no way to hide what Kenny's doing. Going for broke, Kenny turns around and cuts the vines with her hands in front of herself. Each second seems like an hour. I nervously glance from Kenny to the sentry and back again.

Finally, Kenny finishes her cutting. With her foot, she kicks out a two-foot section of wall. There's just enough room to crawl through. The sentry stirs restlessly, and the four of us pause in terror. If he wakes up, we won't be able to silence him before he cries out for help.

"We can't move until we have a little more light," I say. "We don't want to go floundering around the forest in the dark."

Grizz glances at his watch. "The sun won't rise for four and a half hours."

Kenny puts the section of the wall she's removed back in place. There's no way to camouflage what we've done. But if the guard gives the wall a cursory look, he may not notice the loose vines. We settle in nervously and wait for the sky to lighten.

I jump when I hear the sound of another man approaching our cage. He walks up to the sentry and shakes his shoulder. The sentry wakes.

"Your shift is over, bright eyes," the new sentry says.

My heart begins to pound. The new man is going to relieve the old sentry. What if this one wants to take a good look around? If he looks carefully, even from his chair, he may be able to see the severed vines.

"They've been pretty quiet," the departing sentry says.

The new guard sits and looks at us. Grizz, Kenny, Kremke, and Chase fake sleep. I sit, blocking his view of the side of the cage as much as possible. Within fifteen minutes, the new guard begins to snore. I'm guessing the zealots have never had anyone escape from their cage. The guards have both been very careless. Clearly, they don't view us as a threat. I realize my whole body is tense. I breathe deeply and force myself to relax.

Minutes pass, but they seem like hours. Finally, the sky begins to brighten almost imperceptibly: the false light just before dawn.

"Time to go," I whisper.

* * * * *

"Let's hope the zealots aren't early risers," says Grizz.

I rip a thin piece of cloth from the bottom of my tunic.

"Get some of that twine," I say, nodding at the vines we've shredded. "We're gonna tie up the sentry."

Kenny kicks the side of the wall, and it falls. We squeeze through the small opening.

I walk softly until I reach the sentry's chair. I quickly cover the sentry's mouth with the strip of cloth I've cut and pull the ends around the back of his head where I tie it. He struggles, but Kenny holds him down as Chase and Grizz bind his hands and feet. In a moment, he's trussed up and can neither move nor cry out.

"Let's go!" I whisper. We reclaim our gear, which the zealots have left neatly piled no more than ten feet from the cage. I quickly strap on my sword belt, shrug into my backpack, and slip my bow and quiver over my shoulder. I'll miss my AK, which I assume is resting on the bottom of the river.

Taking care to stay out of the pool of light cast by torches mounted every ten yards or so, we quietly approach the gate. We find it closed, and from out of the shadows, we make out two guards posted in twin towers built on either side of the gate. Unlike the sentries posted to watch us, these guards are awake and paying attention.

"Do we take them out?" Chase asks softly.

"The walls are only about eight feet tall. Let's go over the wall instead,"

We move in silence, slipping from shadow to shadow until we reach the wall opposite the gate. I'm painfully aware of each lost second. The sky is beginning to brighten, and it's only a matter of time until the zealots begin their day.

We find a barrel sitting by the wall on the side opposite the entrance. I look carefully at the sentries on guard by the front gate. It's too dark to see them clearly. I step up on the barrel, grab the top of the eight-foot wall, and pull myself up and over. I land with a jaw-clamping thud. I wait on the far side until my friends have joined me. We sprint into the forest north of the village.

The sun has not risen, so the world is still very dark. We can see well enough to avoid pitfalls, but not well enough to run. We pick our way carefully through the forest, frustrated by the slow pace. Within minutes, the sun rises, and we can run, albeit carefully.

Behind us, the drumming begins. Another drummer ahead of us responds.

"Not those drums again!" moans Chase.

"I guess the fine people of the village have realized their guests are gone," says Grizz.

I scrutinize the forest floor as we run. Finally, I find what I'm looking for. I stop, and my friends look at me quizzically.

"The forest floor here has been eroded down to granite," I say. "If we stay on the granite, the zealots won't be able to track us. Kenny, Kremke, and Chase, leave a trail headed north for about ten minutes and then come back to this exact spot. Turn east and head for the river. That's where Grizz and I will be."

I draw my sword and blaze a tree.

"Just so you'll know where to turn," I say.

"What's the plan, ET?" asks Kenny.

"I can't explain now. Trust me on this one."

Kenny shrugs, and she, Kremke, and Chase head north.

Grizz follows me as I run toward the river, careful to keep our feet on the granite. The roar of the rapids grows louder. By the time we reach the river, we must shout to be heard.

"You're not gonna do what I think you're gonna do," hollers Grizz.

I throw all my gear on the ground. I open my backpack and extract the rope I packed back at the chem lab. Bree's rope, sturdy and light. I tie one end around my waist.

"ET, no!" says Grizz. "Just look at the river. These are class six rapids here. You won't stand a chance."

"No other choice." I yell to be heard over the thunder of the rapids. "If we keep on traveling through zealot country, they'll catch us again. We can't outrun them."

"Let me go," shouts Grizz.

"You know I'm a better swimmer," I point out.

Grizz simply nods, resigned.

My plan is a simple one. Get to the far side of the river, anchor my end of the rope up in a tree, and have Grizz tie the other end to a tree on this side. Presto, we have a hanging bridge. I have two hundred yards of rope, so I have to get across the river no more than two hundred yards downstream.

I survey the rapids carefully. The river is narrow here, no more than fifteen yards across. That's good, because there's less river to cross, but bad, because the water will be particularly rough where it's squeezed through the narrows. There's a strainer, two massive rocks close to one another, just a few feet from the near bank. There's no way to go around them, and there are worse hazards downstream, so I'll have to go through. I remove my shoes and dive in.

# 18

The foaming water is surprisingly warm. It immediately pins me to the left-hand rock of the strainer. It also pulls me down. I find a groove in the rock and grab it with both hands, struggling against the downward suction. I see another crease in the rock less than a yard to my right. I reach out with my right hand, and the river immediately sucks me under. With my left hand holding on, I feel frantically for the handhold with my right hand. I finally find it. With all my strength, I pull myself up, spluttering and gasping for breath.

I'm within a foot of the place where the torrent roars between the two boulders of the strainer. I have no idea where the current will take me, so all I can do is take a deep breath and throw myself into the churning foam. The river pulls me under immediately. I'm moving unbelievably fast. The current slams me sideways into a submerged rock. The pain in my left side is fierce, but worse, the power of the collision has driven the breath from my lungs.

I reach up, looking for anything to hold on to. The rock I'm pinned against is submerged. I can feel the top, and it's underwater. I get both my hands on top of the rock and pull myself up. I'm fighting the downward pull of the current, but I slowly pull myself toward the surface. With my lungs ready to burst, I break the surface and take a deep, gasping breath. No sooner have I drawn breath than the torrent dislodges me and carries me off again.

I see a downed tree lying in the water in front of me. If I can grab hold of it, I may be able to pull myself along the tree to the far side of the river. The raging river slams me into the tree, and once again, the force of impact drives the breath from my lungs. I struggle for breath. I throw my arms over the tree and hang on. The current has other ideas, and it sweeps my legs under the tree. For the moment, I'm U-shaped, with my arms thrown over the tree above water and my legs pulled beneath the tree and downstream. I'm able to pull myself toward the far shore. I'm within three yards of the bank.

There's an obstruction of some sort under the water, and the water courses over it with incredible strength. It tears my legs so fiercely that I lose my grip on the tree, and once more, I'm rocketing downstream underwater. I'm thrust upside down in the angry current. I thrash around trying to get myself right side up. I realize the rope I tied around my waist has wrapped itself around my legs, binding them together. I untangle myself and am right side up when the river slams me into yet another obstruction. I'm frantic with the need to breathe. If I can't get my head above water, I'm going to drown.

Feeling around desperately for a handhold, I find one and pull my head from the water. Once more, I gasp for breath. I drag myself to the right and find myself in a stable position. There's a huge rock just upstream from the boulder I cling to, and the upstream rock is channeling the water around me. To my left and right, the torrent rages furiously, but in my current position, the water is sheltered. I take a minute to rest. My body is throbbing with pain. The mighty collisions of flesh and bone on rock have left me bruised and battered.

On the west bank of the river, Grizz is slowly picking his way through the broken ground, trying to stay up with me. He's about a hundred yards upstream, so I still have plenty of rope to work with.

I assess my situation. I'm only two yards from the far shore. But the minute I leave my sheltered location, the rampaging tide will pull me downstream again. Immediately downriver is an enormous boulder, but it juts out from the riverbank, the bank I want to reach. If I can somehow manage to find a handhold on that rock, I may be able to pull myself to shore. Taking a deep breath, I leave my small safe haven, and the torrent drags me downstream once again.

This time there's no undertow, so I'm able to see what's coming. The current does its best to turn me around, but if I hit that downstream rock headfirst, I'm a goner. Flopping around, I'm able to orient myself, so I'm more or less on my back with my feet headed downstream. I strike the rock with incredible velocity and feel an excruciating shock in my knees and hips as they absorb the force of collision. My hopes of using the rock as a stable point from which I can cross the two yards between myself and the shore disappear when the current drags me under again. The rock has been undercut by the current, and I'm drawn into an underwater maelstrom. I struggle mightily, but I'm spun around and around by the swirling water. I can't hold my breath any longer, and I'm ready to give up and accept my fate, when the whirlpool spits me out and up against the shore. With the last of my strength, I pull the top half of my body up on the bank.

For five minutes, I don't even try to move. My ribs are in agony, my left wrist is either sprained or broken, and my feet first collision with the undercut rock has left my ankle, knees, and hips howling in pain. My tongue fetches up against a rough tooth. I've managed to chip a tooth somewhere along the line. Fortunately, it's just a canine, so I'll be able to smile without looking gap-toothed.

"ET!" Grizz roars from across the river. "Are you OK?"

I flip over on my back and drag my legs from the water. "I'm peachy!" I shout back.

247

I tentatively try to stand, and my entire body rebels. Nonetheless, I force myself to rise. On the west bank, Grizz is tying the rope to a sturdy-looking tree. He winds the rope around a branch and pulls it around the tree a couple times before tying a knot.

I reel in the excess rope. Since the river is only twenty yards wide, we're going to be able to salvage at least 150 yards of rope.

I find a stout-looking tree with nice solid branches. I untie the rope, which I'd fastened around my waist on the far shore, and reel in the excess from Grizz's side of the river. My body howling at me with every move, I shinny up the tree and tie the rope firmly around the tree and above a sturdy branch. I can hardly use my wounded left wrist, and this slows me down. It's hard to tie knots one-handed, but I use my left elbow to keep the knot in place while I pull it tight with my right hand. When I'm done, we have a nice taut rope reaching from the west side of the river to the east.

Kenny, Chase, and Kremke work their way downstream and join Grizz on the west shore. I can see them gesturing and talking, but I can't hear a thing they say over the thundering river. As I watch, Grizz distributes the gear I abandoned, dividing it among the three of them. He is the first to cross. The rope sags a little, but there's no doubt it will hold. The process of moving across a rope bridge hand by hand is time-consuming and physically demanding. It takes well over half an hour for all four of them to make the passage. When we're all safely across, Grizz severs the rope.

"You swam across the river?" asks Kenny with a note of disbelief in her voice.

"'Swim' is not the right word," I reply. "It's more like I crashed my way across. I think I hit every rock in the river."

"ET, you're a crazy woman," says Kenny.

I concede with a rueful grin. "We really didn't have much choice. The zealots would have caught us again tonight. At least now we have a raging river between us. I'd like to see the little wieners try to get across."

"How are you feeling?" asks Grizz.

I modestly lift my tunic a few inches and show my friends the welter of bruises that cover my ribs.

"I've been better," I admit. "I'm afraid I'm going to slow you down, 'cause my knees are in bad shape. And I can't bend my left wrist without seeing fireworks in my head."

"Let's look at that," says Kenny. The slightest movement is excruciatingly painful, so she finds a stick, fashions a splint, and ties it in place. Gentle as Kenny is, the pain is still agonizing.

"Would you like me to carry you?" Grizz asks with concern.

"No," I say. "Just walk slowly."

We leave the river behind and turn north once more. I shamble along as best I can, but it's clear we're not going to make a lot of progress. We stop for the night after traveling barely two miles.

\* \* \* \* \*

When I wake the following morning, my bruises are worse than they were the night before. After a light breakfast, we march north again. As my muscles loosen, the pain becomes a little more bearable. But the longer I walk, the worse I feel. My knees are the worst. The pain in them increases with every step. By midmorning, I'm barely able to move.

Grizz, who's been walking beside me, calls a halt.

"ET winces every time she takes a step," Grizz explains. "Let's stop for a couple days and give her a chance to heal."

"I can walk," I object. But even as I say it, I know Grizz is right. I'll never make it. I'm too badly hurt.

I sit and examine my injured wrist. My fingers have turned pasty white. My wrist has swollen to an enormous size, more than double its usual circumference. The wrapping around the splint retards the swelling and has cut off the flow of blood to my hand.

"I need your help for a second, Kenny," I call.

"Your wrist looks awful," she says.

"Gee, you think? We're gonna have to remove the splint," I say. "We'll let the wrist swell as much as it wants. We'll splint it again when the swelling is done."

Kenny carefully removes the tape binding the splint to my wrist. Even though Kenny is being as gentle as possible, I yelp in pain as each strip of tape comes off.

I cradle my injured wrist in my right hand. No matter what I do, the pain throbs. I start to rummage through my backpack.

"Wait," says Grizz. "What are you looking for? Let me get it for you."

"Thanks, Grizz. I think I still have a bottle of Excedrin in my first aid kit."

Grizz finds the bottle and removes the childproof cap. (The cap is also ET-proof at this point.) I shake out two Excedrin and swallow them with a drink from my canteen. I might as well have left the pills in the jar. My wounds continue to hurt like the dickens. I've already had the pinkie finger of my left hand broken in an old encounter with the Sons; it sticks out a strange angle. I wonder what my wrist is going to look like after it heals.

Grizz flops down beside me. "I didn't think you could make it across the river," he says. "White-water aces would've steered clear of that part of it. And near the end, you were underwater forever."

"There were times when I wasn't sure I was gonna make it, either. I hit a whirlpool, and it dragged me under. Just when I thought I couldn't hold my breath a second longer, it spit me out on the far shore. I was lucky."

"You know I love you, ET. I've nearly lost you so many times, I've lost count. In my next life, I'm gonna fall for a girly girl who looks both ways three times before crossing the street."

I smile. "I know what you were feeling, Grizz. You've been in danger a few times yourself. And every time, I felt like half of me would die along with you. When we finally beat the Court, we'll settle down into nice next-door cottages with little white fences. The most dangerous thing we'll do is harvest our vegetables."

Grizz grins. "I'll believe that when I see it."

I stroke Grizz's cheek with my fingertips and lose myself in his impossibly deep blue eyes. "You'll see it," I say, voice husky with emotion.

\* \* \* \* \*

When you're brought up in the Sonoran Desert, you learn to live with heat. In fact, I far prefer desert heat to the humid haze we found in Michigan when we drove up to visit my aunt Susan every year. The lone exception to my general heat ambivalence is the month of June. June is the most dreadful month of the year in Tucson. Daytime highs routinely top one hundred degrees, and there's no breeze. July and August bring the monsoons, which blow up in the afternoons, reliable as clockwork, and drop the temperature by a dozen degrees or more. But June is relentless, nonstop, oven-like heat.

On one such scorching June afternoon, Bree and I were playing rummy at her house when we heard the sound that brings instant bliss and an ear-to-ear grin to the face of every ten-year-old: the tinkling of the ice-cream truck. Thinking about that music, even today, makes me salivate. And I'm sure almost every parent has been inundated by little beggars pleading for money within seconds of hearing the truck.

We found Bree's mother in the backyard on her knees, weeding around the greens. "Please, Mama," Bree pleaded. "I'll dry dishes tonight!"

With a long-suffering sigh, Bree's mom stood up, went into the house for her purse, and dug out a dog-eared dollar bill. Bree snatched it, and we were out the door like rockets, with a cry of "Thanks, Mom!" (or, in my case, "Thanks, Mrs. Stone!").

We caught up to the ice-cream truck just as the driver was making a left turn by Veterans Park. The ice-cream man knew us by sight. We were steady customers.

"What'll it be today, girls? The usual?"

"I'd like a Drumstick, please," I said.

"Strawberry Shortcake bar for me, please," said Bree.

"Yep, the usual," confirmed the driver.

*We were sitting on the ground, backs against a huge eucalyptus tree, licking our ice cream bars and watching a lizard scampering up and down a wall, when trouble arrived. In this case, trouble's name was William H. Kremke Jr., Willy, as he was called, was a hulking big boy who had been in our fourth-grade class last year.*

*Big Willy was a bully. Slow-witted and disinterested in school, his name was constantly "on the board" for misbehavior, and his homework always came back from the teacher covered with red marks. I don't think he had a single friend. Given this background, I understood what made Willy a bully, but I steered well clear of him. Our friendship with Grizz, who was also a very big kid, probably helped to keep the Tucson Ramblers safe from Willy. Nothing frightens a bully more than the specter of an honest fight.*

*Unfortunately, on this particular afternoon, Willy was in a foul mood, Grizz was not around, and Bree and I looked like easy prey.*

*Bree was one of the few African-Americans in Bessie Mae Reynolds Elementary School. She was also very smart and very popular. And she was very small, short, and weighed no more than forty pounds. The combination of these characteristics made her very unpopular with Willy. He'd occasionally make snide remarks or slurs, but only when Grizz wasn't around. Bree chose to shrug them off. Unable to get a rise out of us, Willy would leave in pursuit of more responsive prey.*

*On this particular afternoon, though, Willy walked right up to where we were sitting and flopped down on the ground in front of us. Looking Bree straight in the eye, he puffed out his cheeks and made monkey sounds.*

*"Get lost, Willy," I said.*

*"I ain't talking to you, alien girl. You don't speak monkey, now, do you?"*

*"And neither do I," said Bree mildly.*

*"Of course you do," said Willy. "All you people speak monkey."*

*"Afraid not," countered Bree cheerfully.*

*Willy turned his attention to me. "Why don't you hang out with your own kind?"*

*"Bree is my own kind," I said. "She's smart, she's fun to be with, and she's a really good friend. So she* is *my kind. Now, why don't you stick to* your *kind?"*

*"Just what do you mean by that?" Willy asked, face growing red. Back talk is not something Willy had much experience with. Most of his victims cower.*

*"Take it any way you want to," I fired back.*

*"You think monkey girl is better than me?"*

*"She's more my kind than* you *are," I said evenly.*

*We had all risen to our feet as the exchange grew more hostile.*

*"You and your friends are a bunch of faggoty, monkey-loving, stuck-up snobs. You think you're too good for the likes of me!"*

*"Actually, I don't think I'm too good for anyone," I disagree. But I'm running out of patience with Willy. "And if you call my friend a monkey one more time, you're gonna be in trouble."*

*Willy's face grew redder than ever. We were not behaving like the easy marks he expected. "Oooh, I'm scared. And I'll call monkey girl a monkey whenever I feel like it." In his anger, he reached out and swatted Bree's Strawberry Shortcake bar, knocking it from her hand. It wound up stuck upside down in the grit on the ground. Bree was crushed. Being called names is no big thing, but losing your ice cream* is *serious.*

*Before I even realized what I was doing, I made a fist and punched Big Willy square on the nose. I didn't think about punching him; it just happened.*

*Willy's eyes began watering, and when he touched his nose, his fingers came away red with blood. Seeing the blood, he began bawling. He turned around and ran away across the park.*

*"You're a witch, Taylor! You'll be sorry for this!" he hollered back over his shoulder as he sobbed.*

*Several other kids from our school were in the park swinging on the swings. They laughed as they watched Big Willy run.*

*I instantly regretted hitting Willy. Not because I was worried about Big Willy getting even. I was ashamed of myself. I'd never hit anyone before. I'd always thought there was something wrong with people who solved their problems with their fists.*

*Bree looked at me, mouth hanging open in disbelief.*

*"You just punched Willy Kremke," she said, amazement in her voice.*

*"I didn't plan to," I explained. "I don't know why I did it. It just kind of happened. I actually feel a little bad about it."*

*"Why? He had it coming. Did you hear the way he started bawling? Some big tough guy!"*

*I shared my Drumstick with Bree. Her Strawberry Shortcake bar was a total write-off.*

*When I went home, I told my mother about the fight. My knuckles were swollen and tender, and I'm sure she would have noticed them sooner or later. Besides, I was feeling very bad about punching Willy, and confessing made me feel a little better.*

*Over dinner that night, my escapade was the subject of intense conversation. My father had only had a couple shots of bourbon after work, so he was still plenty lucid. He and my mother were very displeased, to say the least. But the twins were profoundly impressed.*

*"You punched Big Willy in the nose?" Han bubbled. "He's, like, the biggest bully in school!"*

"You gave him a bloody nose?" Luke asked, incredulous. "I wish I'd have been there to see it! Imagine, my sister beating up Big Willy Kremke!"

"ET, you rock!" said Han.

"Awesome!" added Luke.

Unaccustomed to hero worship from my siblings, I was at a loss for words.

My brothers' reaction annoyed my father. He locked two angry eyes on me. "You can't go around punching people, even if they are bullies," he said. "Look how your brothers are reacting. Do you want them to think violence is good? You have to set an example for them. A good example. ET, You're grounded for a month."

After dinner, I hissed at Han and Luke, "If you two knuckleheads would've kept quiet, I'd only be grounded for two weeks!"

* * * * *

Later that evening, my parents received a visit from Officer William H. Kremke Sr. and his son. Officer Kremke was livid. He called me a bully and demanded I apologize. According to Willy's story, I attacked an innocent, helpless Willy with no provocation.

I didn't mind apologizing. I felt bad about what I'd done.

"I'm sorry, Willy," I said. "I never should have punched you. I was wrong, and it'll never happen again."

But after apologizing, I insisted on telling my own side of the story and volunteered to call Bree and ask her to come over and verify it.

256

*"That gang of kids is nothing but trouble," Officer Kremke spat. "Of course they'll lie for each other."*

*"Officer Kremke," said my father, "ET is not a liar, and neither is Bree. My daughter would never have punched Willy without a reason. Now punching Willy was wrong, and ET is being punished. But don't call her a liar."*

*Officer Kremke scowled at my father, and I was afraid the incident would escalate. But with a snort, Officer Kremke turned around. He and Willy stormed off our porch and roared away in the city's Crown Vic.*

*My grounding was reduced to two weeks.*

\* \* \* \* \*

The zealots have no intention of following across the river. We wind up spending a week by the river. We make good use of the time. Or, rather, I should say my friends make good use of the time. I'm unable to do much of anything. My friends practice their bow skills. The first two days, they look awful. But by the end of the week, they're hitting the bull's-eye with regularity. With my wrist hurting, I can't join them.

Chase was able to do some hunting, and he brought home several squirrels and rabbits. He saw a deer, but says he got too nervous and missed his shot. More important than the deer, however, is the brace of plump little partridges he's downed. Not only do they taste much better than rabbit and squirrel, we can use their feathers to fletch more arrows. By the end of the week, our quivers are bulging. I was able to sharpen everybody's swords and knives, but that's the extent of my contribution. Not being able to help very much is extremely frustrating. I now know what my mom felt like when she broke an ankle and we had to wait on her for a couple weeks. She hated it. I always thought being waited on would be pretty nice. It's not.

By the end of the week, the color of most of my bruises turns from red and purple to green and yellow, and I can actually touch them without wincing. My ankles, knees, and hips are still stiff, but I can walk without too much pain. My wrist is another story. The swelling is down quite a bit, but I still can't use my left hand without setting off lightning bolts behind my eyes. Kenny splints it, and I can only hope it'll mend with time.

After Kenny splints my wrist, I hobble off into the forest, testing my knee. It's getting better. I'll soon be able to travel on it. Just as I decide I've tested it as much as is prudent, I hear a noise off to my left. I look quickly and see Kremke looking at me. His bow is drawn, an arrow knocked. I knew it. He hates me so much he's going to shoot me.

"So, you're gonna shoot me," I say as evenly as I can.

Kremke ignores my question. "Do you know what you did to Big Willy when you hit him in the nose that day?"

"Officer Kremke, I've already apologized for that. I didn't mean to hit Willy. It just happened. And I feel very bad about it."

"Do you know how kids laughed at him after that? Every day, day after day, kids taunted him. Did you know Willy didn't want to show his face in school? Do you know he cried every morning that month when I made him go?"

"I didn't know any of that. And I feel bad about it. But Willy knocked my friend's ice cream out of her hand, and it fell in the dirt, topside down. She started to cry, and something just snapped inside me. I didn't even know I was gonna punch Willy until after it happened."

"I know Willy was a bully. He still is. But I want you to think what his life was like. Willy was dumb. He never learned how to learn. He was always the one to get the worst grades. He never had any friends. So at some point, he just stopped trying. Willy had a choice between being a bad kid who didn't care about school and being a dumb kid who tried but just didn't get it. What choice would you make, Taylor? Would you be bad or dumb?"

"I guess I never really thought about it. But it sure explains how Willy got to be Willy."

"You always had it good, Taylor. You were smart, and you were popular. Kids just naturally gravitated to you. But imagine how different your life would be if you were living in Willy's shoes."

I sit down in a heap. I'm amazed at how imperceptive I was. Why didn't I see what Big Willy's life was like?

"I'm sorry," I murmur. "I was very insensitive. I wish I would have reached out to Willy. Maybe one good friend was all he needed to set him on the right path. Heaven knows the Tucson Ramblers had enough brainpower to tutor Willy through almost anything."

Kremke stands silently for a moment, and then looks at the bow in his hands. He lowers it. "I wasn't going to shoot you. I had the bow drawn because I saw a rabbit, and I was going to bring him back for dinner. But then I heard you."

Kremke and I walk back to camp together. Neither of us speaks. I think we've said everything that can be said. When we hear the sound of the others in camp, I turn to Kremke and say, "I really am sorry."

From that day forward, we never mention Big Willy again, but our relationship changes. We don't hate each other anymore.

# 19

On the eighth day, we leave our camp behind. We make decent time as we travel. I can't move as fast as I usually do, but the pain in my legs is tolerable. By the end of the week, the ground begins to rise. The gain in altitude is modest at first, but within two days, the path before us begins to rise steeply. We're going to do some rock climbing.

At first the slope is manageable, and I'm able to climb along with everybody else. By the end of the day, however, we run into a slope that's close to pure vertical. The river is still roaring to our west, so Chase scouts the ground to our east to see if there's an easier way up. There isn't.

"You're not gonna be able to climb that wall," Grizz notes matter-of-factly. "Without your left hand, there's no way you can maintain three points of contact."

Tears of frustration in my eyes, I agree.

"So," says Grizz, "we can either wait down here for you to heal, or we can rig a boson's chair out of the rope and winch you up there."

"I'm sorry," I say.

"Nothing to be sorry about," says Kenny. "You got us away from those vicious little zealots. The least we can do is haul you up the cliff. You'll feel like the Queen of Sheba once we rig your chair and start hoisting."

"We'd be dead now if we hadn't crossed the river," says Chase. "Leave the work to us for a change."

Next morning, Chase fashions a boson's chair from our rope. Grizz uses his machete to fashion a rough pulley. Kenny coils the remaining rope and throws it in her backpack. Then she climbs roughly two hundred feet up the cliff.

"Found a nice flat place," she calls down to us. She uncoils the rope and sends one end whipsawing down to us. "Tie the pulley to the rope, and I'll hoist it up here."

Chase does as Kenny requests, and five minutes later, we have a pulley on the platform two hundred feet above us. Chase cuts a couple short lengths of rope and ties one end to the boson's chair. The other ends he knots around the long rope. Then, he and Grizz climb up to join Kenny, with various pieces of wood strapped to their backs. They'll need the wood pieces to mount the pulley.

Fifteen minutes later, they call down to me, "Get in the chair, ET."

I step into the chair, one leg on either side of the "bottom." I tighten the slipknot around my waist and holler up, "Ready!"

The wall is not perfectly vertical, so I scrape against the face of the cliff as they raise me. They're very careful and pull very slowly. Well over halfway up the cliff, the pulling stops.

"What's up?" I ask.

"The rope is snagged," shouts Grizz. He comes scurrying down the cliff face until he reaches the place where the rope is hung up.

"Dang! I can't reach it. No worries, ET, I'll get a pole and free it that way."

Which is a fine thing for him to say, but I'm 150 feet off the ground in a makeshift rope chair. I don't like heights, and I force myself to avoid looking down. If I look, I'll panic for sure. I experimentally tug on every rope I can reach, and am relieved to find the boson's chair remains sturdy.

Ten minutes later, Grizz works his way down the cliff with a long branch strapped to his back. He reaches the place where the rope is snagged. After three or four attempts, he manages to free it.

"All set!" he hollers, and Kenny and Chase resume cranking the pulley. Within minutes, I'm on the ledge with them.

Above us is more cliff. My friends find another ledge and winch me up again. This time we run into serious trouble. The side of the boson's chair gets snarled up on a rock outcropping. Before I can react, I find myself looking straight down 350 feet to the forest far below. I'm beneath the rock outcropping, so my position is hidden from my friends above. They continue to turn the winch.

"Stop!" I scream. "Stop! You're gonna drop me out of the chair."

I'm well past horizontal. The rope of the boson's chair cuts right into my stomach. My left side is nearest to the cliff wall, and despite the pain in my left wrist, I use my left hand to grab a scrubby bush growing out of a tiny crack in the rock face of the cliff. The roots of the bush are not strong enough to support me. They give way, and the bush comes out of the ground. The momentum my body gains from the loosening bush pulls me even farther beyond horizontal. The rope of the boson's chair shifts, and I'm certain I'm going to fall. But the rope catches me again, this time in the chest. The pain is almost unbearable.

I hear small rocks plummeting down behind me. My first thought is the rock I'm caught upon is disintegrating, a thought that brings me close to panic. The truth is, the shower of rocks is caused by Grizz, who has climbed down the rock face to find me all but falling out of my boson's chair.

"Easy, ET," he says. "We're gonna get you out of this. I'm not sure what we're gonna do yet, but we're gonna get you up there, safe and sound."

"I'm a little uncomfortable right now," I say, trying to keep my voice from betraying the fear I'm feeling. "The rope is killing me."

"We can't just put slack in the rope from above, 'cause that'd probably dump you right out of the chair," says Grizz.

"Well," I say, "let's not do that." I hear sarcasm in my voice, and I regret it.

"If I can free the rope of your chair from the snag, you'll fall out, too. Your center of gravity is gonna pull you down. But if you throw your weight up and back the second we clear the snag, you should be able to right yourself."

"Peachy," I say.

Grizz is a good ten feet away from me. He examines the cliff, looking for a way to scramble over toward me. He finds a crevice to place his right foot and a small rock to grab with his right hand. He stretches to fit his right foot into the crevice. Then he grabs the other rock with his right hand, only to have it give way. For a second, Grizz is unbalanced, and it looks like he's going to fall. He throws himself at the rock wall, and since he's securely anchored, he stabilizes himself.

"Careful, Grizz! I don't want two of us dead on those rocks down below."

"Me neither," says Grizz, and I detect a note of sarcasm in *his* voice.

On his next attempt, he gets close enough to push the long stick to the place where the rope on the side of the boson's chair is caught on the snag.

"Can you see where the rope is caught?" he asks.

I twist my neck back as far as it will go.

"Just barely."

"The instant I clear the rope from the snag, throw your body up and back as hard as you can. If you don't, you're gonna wind up way down there," he says, gesturing with his chin. "And I'll probably land right on top of you."

Grizz slides the stick under the rope and uses the snag itself as his lever. He pushes down as hard as he can, given that he's holding on to a cliff face for dear life. I see sweat pouring down Grizz's face as he pushes down on his stick. The rope moves, and I throw myself up and back with as much force as I can muster. The only thing I accomplish is to overbalance. The rope does not come clear of the snag. The rope of the chair is now caught on my throat. I begin to gag.

"Hang on, ET. The rope is on the very last part of the snag. This time it'll come off for sure."

That's a good thing, because I can't breathe. The rope bites into my throat.

Several things happen simultaneously. Grizz gives one last push, and the rope comes free. My initial thought is that I'm falling.

But I throw my body up and backward. I have a panicked instant of weightlessness as the boson's chair rights itself. But gravity brings me down into the chair, which is now right side up. The sudden loss of tension in the rope causes Grizz to unbalance. For a terrifying moment, it looks as though he's going to fall. But he drops the pole, catches himself, and hugs the wall. The pole clatters against the rock as it falls.

"Can you turn yourself into a pendulum?" Grizz asks. "We need to start winching you up again, but if we do it now, you're gonna get hung up on the snag again."

Grizz looks up and hollers at Kenny and Chase, "Be ready to crank the minute I holler!"

Kenny's voice comes down the rock face. "Will do!"

I maneuver myself around so I can push myself away from the rock. I throw my weight forward and then backward. Nothing happens. I push away from the cliff with my feet again. I throw myself forward and backward again, time after time, pushing off from the cliff every time I start getting too close. Finally I begin to swing back and forth.

When I'm at the apex of my swing, Grizz shouts, "Winch!"

And just like that, I'm around the snag and then above it. Kenny and Chase continue turning the pulley. I smack into the wall again several times, but within moments, I'm on the ledge above with my friends. I lie down on my back and look at the beautiful blue sky above. I wait for my pulse to settle and my breathing to normalize. When I'm calm enough, I stand up.

Grizz wraps me in a tight hug. I can't help myself. I kiss him on the mouth, deeply, passionately, and he returns the kiss ardently. Within moments, I push myself away. Getting off the snag was child's play compared with the discipline it takes to break our embrace.

Chase and Kenny are looking at us, fascinated. "I've never seen *that* before," says Kenny. "Are you two becoming an item?"

"Yes," I say. "No. It's complicated."

"Ooh la la," teases Chase with a silly grin on his face.

"Give it a rest," I snarl.

Chase says nothing more, but the silly grin remains on his face.

"I'm sorry I kissed you," I say to Grizz.

"No need to be sorry. That's the most fun I've had in months." Grizz looks me in the eye. "Are you really sorry you kissed me?" he asks seriously.

"No," I reply, and feel my cheeks turning red.

"From now on, I'm gonna climb up the cliff face right beside you," insists Grizz. "I'll keep a lookout for gnarly rocks you might get hung up on."

"Besides which, you can smooch a little more during the upward journey," says Kenny with a mischievous smile.

"Oh jeez," I say. "Stop it."

They haul me up again. With Grizz by my side, nothing untoward happens, other than the occasional collision with the wall.

With the light failing, we decide to camp for the night on the ledge. It is barely four feet wide.

"I hope nobody does any sleepwalking," Kenny says.

"Or rolls around in their sleep," I add. "Let's keep a watch, just in case."

"I doubt anybody's going to bother us up here," says Kenny.

"Good point," I return. "And I know from personal experience that none of you are sleepwalkers or restless sleepers."

With no firewood nearby, we eat a cold dinner. I fall asleep thinking about the kiss Grizz and I shared. The memory fills me with warmth and contentment, which last until sleep comes.

The following day begins with the usual procedure: Kenny throws coiled rope over her shoulder, climbs up, and throws one end of the rope down so we can hoist the pulley to the next shelf. But today is a little different.

"I made it to the top!" Kenny shouts down to us.

When they've hoisted me to the top again, I climb out of the boson's chair and look around. To the north, the direction we're traveling, the ground rises steeply, but the hike up is mild enough for a one-handed ET to climb without being winched.

We climb for two days and then, unfortunately, find a new set of cliffs. So it's back to the boson's chair. Two more days of winching leave us atop the last of the cliffs. From here on, the terrain is flat and level. To the south, there's a beautiful panoramic view of the cliffs and forest we've passed through. We can't see the edge of the forest, even from here. We've done a lot of traveling.

The temperature is much cooler at this altitude. The trees up here are a combination of lodge pole and ponderosa pines, with a few aspens on the slopes above us to the east. The roaring of the river seems to be behind us, so we work our way to the west until we find the river again.

We find it and pause, awestruck. Up here, the river is a mile wide. It narrows to the south, and we can see a series of beautiful waterfalls where the water drops precipitously to the raging river thousands of feet below.

"Now we know why the river down there churns the way it does," I say.

On the far side of the river, there's another broad river, a tributary to the one we've been following. It flows into our river from the west. The tributary seems to flow west to east. Chase climbs a ponderosa pine and confirms our hypothesis.

"The map drawn by Johnny shows a river that runs from west to east. We have to cross it on our way north," I say.

"And I'm willing to bet that's the river over there," says Chase, pointing at the tributary.

"How on earth are we going to get across *this* river?" asks Kenny. "If we get my water purification powder wet, it'll ruin it. The jars I've stored it in have a tight seal, but they're not waterproof, so they're gonna leak if we dunk 'em in the river."

"For that matter," observes Grizz, "how can we swim across that thing wearing swords and backpacks? That river's a mile across. We'll be lucky to swim it at all, let alone carrying our weapons."

Grizz is right. A mile is a long way to swim. "Let's explore to the north," I suggest. "Maybe the river will be narrower there. Let's camp for the night and explore tomorrow."

* * * * *

The river narrows to about a half mile ten miles to the north. We walk north the rest of the day, and the day after that, but the river shows no sign of narrowing any further.

"Well," I say, "it looks like we'll have to build a raft."

"To build a raft big enough to carry the four of us and all our gear, we'll need to hack up what's left of our rope to bind the poles together," Grizz observes.

"But we still have a mountain range to cross," I say. "I'd rather keep what's left of our rope intact. Can we use vines to build the raft?"

We explore the pine forest around our camp, and find absolutely no vines.

"I hate to say it," says Kenny. "But if we want vines, we're gonna have to go back down the cliff to the forest below. We know there are plenty of vines down there."

Chase, Kremke, and Grizz groan at the prospect of working their way back down to the forest below.

"We'll need at least two days to climb down and another two days to climb back up," Chase complains.

"Can't be helped," says Kenny.

"I'll stay up here," I volunteer. "That way you won't have to hoist me up again."

We make camp for the night, and next morning, Grizz and Chase begin the long walk back down to the forest below.

"I'll stay with you," says Kenny. "So you won't get lonesome. Our strapping, big males can carry enough vines to build our raft."

Grizz leaves his machete with us. He can cut through the vines we need with a knife. Using the machete, Kenny and I hack down several slender trees we'll need to build the raft. When we have a couple dozen, Kenny begins to cut them to the same length. This is two-handed work, so I leave Kenny and decide to do a little exploring.

The cooler air and the beauty of the broad river make our camp a wonderful place. For a few minutes, I take a break and sit on the riverbank watching the river roll by. I throw leaves in the water to test the strength of the current. Watching my little leaf ships float southward, I conclude the current is not particularly fast, but our raft will definitely wind up a mile or two farther south on the west bank.

I turn my back on the river and climb up the hills to the east. This being the height of fall, the aspens are a beautiful yellow. I pick my way slowly through the trees until aspens give way to ponderosa pines. The forest here is darker, with very little sunlight filtering through the dense growth overhead. Still, the air is sweet with the smell of pine trees, and full of birdsong.

Ahead I see a huge black rock. Black is an unusual color for a rock, so I move in closer to take a better look. I'm within ten feet when the "rock" rises. I look into the multi-faceted eyes of a spider. The spider towers above me, easily twenty feet from the ground to the top of its cephalothorax. Its mandibles are razor-sharp, each one easily four feet long, and are opening and closing, as if in anticipation of a tasty snack.

# 20

My immediate impulse is to run. But with its long legs, the spider would catch me in a matter of seconds. I feel fatalistic. So this is the end, I think. I'm considering the wisdom of pulling my sword. At least I'll do some damage before I die.

"Hello," says the spider in a thin, reedy voice. "Welcome to my home."

My jaw drops. I'm at a loss for words. I'd have been equally surprised if the spider had begun to tap-dance.

"Hello," I stammer at last. "My name is ET."

"I'm pleased to meet you, ET. My name is Yuri. From the look of surprise on your face, I believe you've never met a talking spider before." The spider's high-pitched voice makes it hard to understand, so I must listen very carefully.

"That's true," I say cautiously. "Nor have I met a spider that's twenty feet tall. Do you intend to eat me?"

The spider makes a noise that I can only interpret as laughter. "No, ET, I do not intend to eat you. I only harm humans who attempt to harm me."

I'm glad I didn't pull my sword.

"Where did you come from?" asks Yuri.

"My friends and I are traveling near the river, just west of here."

"Spiders don't like rivers," says Yuri. "We don't swim. I never go in the direction of the river. It frightens me."

I imagine there are not many things that frighten twenty-foot-tall spiders. "Yuri," I say, "how did you get so big? Back in my time, spiders were seldom bigger than my palm." I open my hand to illustrate the size.

"Ah," says Yuri, "that's a long story. If you have time, I can tell it to you. It's quite a story, really."

"Yes. I'm very curious." It's only early afternoon, so I have plenty of time.

"Why don't you have a seat on that stump over there," Yuri says, turning his head toward a comfortable-looking stump.

I take my seat and watch as Yuri folds his legs beneath himself. I've never seen a spider do that, either, but it makes him seem less threatening. His head and mandibles are now only six feet above me.

"How to begin?" Yuri says, mostly to himself. "Well during the wars that ended civilization, many nuclear bombs were dropped, several of them quite near here. The radiation from the bombs created many mutant creatures. In the case of spiders, a few of us had mutations in our glands that govern our growth. Sort of like the pituitary gland in humans.

"Within fifty years, a few of us had grown to the size of house cats. By this time, most vestiges of civilization had vanished, but scholars at the University of New Mexico heard stories of us. The faculty and students had found a means of survival. They moved to a huge mesa with incredibly steep sides, and they managed to create a small commune on top of the mesa, safe from the wandering groups of brigands that prowled the land. Indeed, the commune still exists today.

"But I digress. The scientist who came to see the amazingly large spiders was an arachnologist, a scientist who studies spiders and other arachnids. He discovered that our brains had grown at a pace with our bodies. Those few spiders with the genetic mutations had become highly intelligent.

"The scientist, whose name was Dr. Kornikova, set up a field laboratory just behind those trees." Yuri moves his head in the direction of a cluster of trees to my left. "In fact, I'll show you what's left of his lab after I finish the story, if you'd like."

"Thank you, Yuri. I'd like that very much."

"Slowly and painstakingly, Dr. Kornikova taught us to speak. This was more complicated than you might think, because spiders have no ears. We pick up vibrations from our legs. So, where humans hear vibrations with their ears, spiders 'hear' with their legs. When Dr. Kornikova began to repeat the same patterns over and over, my ancestors caught on to the fact that the vibrations *meant* something. Spiders do not have vocal cords, but we do have other organs that can vibrate and make sound. Dr. Kornikova also taught us to avoid eating humans. At the time, we were too small to threaten a full-grown human, but over the next thousand years, our mutant glands caused us to grow steadily larger.

"Fifty years ago, the egg sacs of our females became barren, probably because of our mutations. My wife, Svetlana, and I are the last of the mutant spiders. Svetlana's egg sacs are infertile, so the giant spider race will end when we die. I hope you will stay and meet Svetlana. She'll be back momentarily."

"Yes," I reply. "I'd love to meet Svetlana."

Yuri begins to tremble. "Har!" he says. "Har! Har!"

The change that overcomes Yuri is sudden and dramatic. Spiders have multifaceted eyes, and they're quite unlike human eyes. His eyes change. They look wild, insane even.

I rise from my stump, alarmed. I turn to flee, but find myself unable to run. Yuri's spinnerets are pumping out copious amounts of silk, and within moments, I'm unable to move. I'm wrapped in silk as tight as a mummy.

"Yuri!" I say. "Why are you doing this?"

Yuri's voice has changed. "Pathetic little human. Svetlana and I will feast on you when she returns. Do you know how spiders kill? We sink our mandibles through your skin and suck out your insides. Just the way you humans drink a soda through a straw. Our victims scream while we eat. I understand it's incredibly painful."

"But what about Dr. Kornikova?" I plead. "Didn't he teach you to avoid eating humans?"

"Kornikova was a martinet. A blabbering, devious, simpleminded human. He wanted to exploit mutant spiders for his own gain! He pretended to love us, but what he really wanted was to make us into circus freaks!"

With this, Yuri turns and stalks off into the woods to the east.

I struggle against my bonds, but spider silk is sticky and strong. I can't weaken the bonds no matter how hard I try. I struggle mightily, but I can't move my hands or feet a fraction of an inch. I can't imagine a worse way to die than to be eaten by two spiders. I turn pale and go clammy with sweat at the thought. I wonder if Kenny will come looking for me. The sun tells me it's still early in the afternoon. Kenny won't miss me for hours.

It seems I've run into a schizophrenic, multiple-personality spider. The pleasant Yuri morphed into psychopathic Yuri very quickly. I struggle to remain calm. Perhaps the "nice" Yuri will return.

\* \* \* \* \*

An hour later, Yuri returns.

"How did you manage to get all wrapped up?" he asks in surprise. "Here, let me cut you free."

With his razor-sharp mandibles, he easily slices through the silk that binds me. I pull the spider silk from my body, but it's sticky and leaves a tacky residue on my skin and clothes.

"Do you know how to make spider silk?" he asks skeptically.

"No," I reply. "You wrapped me up."

"Oh, my dear girl, that *is* funny! I've never in my life wrapped up a human!"

"Well, *I* didn't do it," I reply. "How could I possibly wrap myself in spider silk?"

"It must have been Svetlana who wrapped you up! That little comedian. She must have done it as a joke."

Yuri begins to tremble again. "Har!" he says. "Har! Har!"

His eyes turn wild once more, and before I know it, I'm wrapped in spider silk once more.

"Svetlana and I will feast on your innards as soon as she comes home! Enjoy the last minutes of your pathetic little life, you insignificant worm."

Yuri lowers himself by folding his legs beneath his cephalothorax. He appears to nap.

I try to fight down panic, but am unsuccessful. I thrash around, desperately trying to loosen the silk bonds. I'm going to be eaten from the inside out by spiders. In my panic, I'm unable to think rationally.

And then I see Jules again. Jules is looking at me with an expression of calm and compassion. She holds her hands out, palms down. *"Calm down,"* she seems to be saying. She disappears, but I feel much more composed.

What do I know about spiders? What weakness do they have that I might be able to exploit? From some long-ago class taught by my fifth-grade teacher, Mr. Lawrence, I recall spiders have very poor eyesight, and they must touch something with their feet in order to "smell" it. If I can scurry up a tree, perhaps Yuri will be unable to find me. As a plan, it's not elegant, but it's better than nothing. I vow that if "nice" Yuri frees me again, I'm going to head for the hills.

Yuri awakes.

\* \* \* \* \*

Yuri looks at me again, tilting his head to one side. "Wrapped up again, I see," he says, puzzled. "Well, let's free you again." His thin and reedy spider voice betrays his confusion. He slices through my bonds with his mandibles.

I shuck the spider silk as best I can. My skin is extremely sticky, but there's nothing I can do about that right now. I watch Yuri cautiously.

"That's twice you've been wrapped up," he says absently. "How can that be?" He begins to pace back and forth.

The minute his eyes look elsewhere, I'm up the nearest pine tree, moving as quietly as I can, given my terrorized mental state. I'm forty feet above the ground when Yuri turns to look at me.

"Now where did that girl go?" he asks himself. "Terribly rude to leave without so much as a fare-thee-well. And she seemed like such a nice girl. Oh well, Svetlana will be home soon."

I watch Yuri as, once again, he is transformed from "Yuri the Nice" to "Yuri the Bloodthirsty."

"Har! Har! Har!" he shouts once again. He stomps around the clearing, mandibles working, looking for something to eat. He stalks off to the east again.

I wait several minutes so I can be certain Yuri is gone. I climb down from the tree. I run west as quickly as the forest will permit. Behind me, I hear him return to his clearing. He must hear me, because he changes direction and comes directly after me. Spiders may have poor eyesight and a limited sense of smell, but there's clearly nothing wrong with Yuri's "hearing."

Because of Yuri's long legs, the race is a mismatch. I can hear the sound of him crashing through the trees. No matter how hard I run, he narrows the distance. I'm going to have to climb back up a tree.

No sooner have I processed this thought than I come around a large pinion pine and fall flat on my face. I scramble to my feet and see a huge black spider in the clearing in front of me. Svetlana! I'm surrounded! I fight down my fear and find the nearest tree, a sixty-foot-tall ponderosa pine. Pumped full of adrenaline, I climb to a height of forty feet in seconds flat. I know spiders can climb, but I don't think the really big ones, like Yuri, will be able to climb a tree.

Ignoring my fear of heights, I peer down into the clearing from my perch. The spider in the clearing has not moved. In fact, the spider in the clearing looks dead; it is lying on its back, and its legs are curled up. As I look closer, I can see the forest scavengers have been working on it. The spider's eyes and mandibles have been eaten, and there are chunks missing from its huge cephalothorax.

Yuri, who was split seconds behind me, charges into the clearing. Seeing Svetlana dead, he comes to a crashing halt. For a moment he stands still, taking in the evidence before him. Having realized he's looking at the corpse of his wife, he collapses. I hear him wailing, a bleak and anguished sound.

"Svetlana!" he cries.

I momentarily forget the fact that seconds ago, Yuri was chasing me with the intent of wrapping me up and eating me. I can't help but feel compassion given the depth of his misery. Spiders have no tear ducts, but Yuri's thin, reedy voice is choked with misery. He approaches Svetlana's corpse and gently touches her face with two of his legs, and then he collapses again.

I begin to think about Yuri's mood swings. They were always precipitated by a mention of Svetlana. He spoke of her as though he expected her to return at any moment. Yuri said he never went near the river, so it's quite likely this is the first time he has seen Svetlana's body. Looking at her corpse, it's clear to me that she has been dead for quite some time. Is it possible that her absence had pushed Yuri into a psychotic break? He and Svetlana had been the last of their breed. Was Yuri simply unable to contemplate life alone, the last of his kind?

There's a part of me that yearns to climb down out of my tree and comfort Yuri. But I don't know which Yuri I'm likely to find. Will he be kind and gentle Yuri or the bloodthirsty killer? I feel terribly sad for him and what he must face, but I decide to watch in silence.

Yuri grieves for hours. I begin to worry that I'll have to spend the night in the tree. But as the sun sinks in the west, Yuri begins to move Svetlana's body. He probably wants to bury her near their home. He gently nudges Svetlana to the east.

When they've been gone over an hour, I scramble down out of the tree and run back toward our camp by the river.

I tell Kenny of my experience with Yuri. Had I spun a yarn like this in Tucson, Kenny would have called the men with the white coats and straitjackets. In this world, my story is one strange tale out of many. I consider traveling back to see how Yuri is doing, but Kenny talks me out of it.

"From your story," she says, "Yuri sounds like one seriously deranged spider. Finding his wife dead may have pushed him over the edge. 'Nice Yuri' may be a thing of the past."

I forget Yuri and, using my one good hand, resume hacking down trees for the raft.

# 21

The men return on the fourth day with yards and yards of vine. Kenny and I have cut down many trees, and Kenny has cut them to the size of a raft fifteen feet long and ten feet wide. Lashing the logs together is not difficult, and Kremke works on tightening the knots. We don't want vines coming loose in the middle of the river.

We all work on fashioning oars and oarlocks, and Chase, who is clever with wood, hews a log into a rudder. We manhandle the raft into the water, and Chase lashes the rudder to the stern. We wade out into thigh-deep water and load our equipment. I take a last look around our campsite to be sure we're not leaving anything behind, wade out to the raft, and clamber aboard. We fit the oars into our improvised oarlocks and push off from the eastern shore.

The weather is ideal. Up here amid the pine trees, the temperature is much cooler than it is in the scrub forests below. The sun is shining, and the broad blue river is beautiful, fringed on both shores by tall evergreens and brilliant yellow aspens. There is a slight breeze blowing from the south, raising tiny ripples in the water. I man the rudder because it's a job that can be done with one hand. The others row vigorously.

Just moments after we cast off, we hear a whistle from the far shore. Moments later, we hear a series of answering whistles. I've never heard a birdcall anything like the sound of those whistles. There must be humans on the far shore.

"I really hope that's not the zealots," says Kenny.

"I don't think so," I reply. "Johnny's map didn't show the zealots this far north. And when they want to communicate, they use drums."

"If there are people over there," says Kremke, "they could have been watching us for days. We camped right by the river's edge, so we'd have been easy to see."

"Nothing to do but wait and see," I say.

I had checked the speed of the current near shore by throwing various floating objects in the water and had determined the current was swift, but not a problem. We soon discover that the current in the middle of the river is much stronger. We're miles upstream of the waterfalls, but we paddle industriously, just in case.

The trees on the far bank grow larger, and I scan the west shore for possible landing sites. I've just located a likely-looking spot and adjust the rudder to carry us ashore.

We're within fifty yards of shore when the arrows begin falling around us.

\* \* \* \* \*

"Whoa!" I shout. Oars go up as we anxiously scan the shoreline in front of us. I can make out tiny men clad in loincloths launching their arrows in a high arc. The arrows are falling all around us, even though we're close enough for them to target us accurately. They're just warning us off. "Don't come closer" is the message they're sending. If that's the case, then we'll oblige them.

"Let's turn this thing around!" I cry. I jam the rudder as far to the left as I can. "Stop rowing on the port side!"

With the rudder locked and all our forward propulsion on the right side, the bow of the raft slowly swings around and points downstream. I keep the rudder locked a few more moments to take us well out of range of the men onshore.

The current carries us rapidly to the south. Once we've traveled a couple miles downstream, I jam the rudder to the right, and we're once again aimed at the shore. As we approach the bank, we hear whistles, and arrows once again begin to fall around us.

"Jeez!" exclaims Kenny. "How far downstream do these people go?"

"Hopefully not all the way to the waterfalls," I reply.

We head out toward the center of the river once again. Twice more we try to land, and twice more we are greeted by volleys of arrows. After the last volley, we turn downstream again. I hear the distant roar of the waterfalls.

The current strengthens as we travel south. We begin to shoot past the trees on the west shore. We must be moving at thirty or forty miles per hour. The distance between us and the falls shrinks by the second.

"We're gonna run out of river!" Chase hollers. We're close enough to the falls that we must holler to be heard above the thunderous falling water.

"We have to get ashore!" I jam the rudder to the right and lock it. "Everybody row on the left side!"

Kenny and Kremke, who were rowing on the starboard side, remove their oars from the oarlocks and move to the left side of the raft. This sudden movement of weight to the left causes the port side of the raft to dip precipitously, and, for a moment, the raft threatens to capsize. Thinking quickly, Kenny and Kremke throw backpacks and weapons to the starboard side, and the shift of weight stabilizes the raft. Even without oarlocks, Kenny and Kremke can use their long oars as sweeps.

Just when I think we're going to make safe landfall, we reach the broad tributary that flows into our river from the west, just north of the falls. The current from the tributary pushes us back toward the center of the river. My friends redouble their efforts, and we begin to close on the shore just south of the tributary. We're still one hundred yards from shore when I see the telltale white foam of the first waterfall off to the south.

I resist the temptation to push harder on the rudder. It's already locked, and all I could hope to achieve with added pressure is a broken rudder. My friends are visibly tiring, their strokes not as deep or powerful as they were fifteen minutes ago. They see the white foam ahead, and fear provides an extra shot of adrenalin. The combined current of the two rivers has us moving south at an incredible speed. The trees on the shore pass in the blink of an eye. I begin to contemplate the wisdom of leaving the raft and swimming to shore, and dismiss it as a bad idea.

I've almost given up hope when we crash into a submerged rock. The impact of the collision splinters the wood on the front of the raft and throws Kenny, who is farthest forward, into the river. Quick as a cat, Grizz grabs her by the collar and, with Kremke's help, drags her back aboard. Kenny's oar is lost, over the waterfall and gone in seconds.

For the moment, the raft is hung up on the rock, but the river's current is pushing the stern of the raft slowly back out into the mainstream. If we don't do something quickly, we're going to go over the falls backward. We're only ten yards from shore, but we're also just fifty yards from the cataract. The thunder of hundreds of thousands of gallons of water falling makes it impossible to be heard. I grab Kremke's oar, which is about six feet long, and push it tentatively into the river off our left side.

The oar touches bottom! Following my lead, Grizz and Chase pull their sweeps out of the oarlocks and push off the bottom as well. Kremke reclaims his oar, which is a good thing because he has two good arms and is much stronger than I in any case. We can't be heard, so Kenny, who has lost her oar, counts with her fingers, one, two, and on three, we push with all our might. The stern moves slowly toward the shore. Kenny counts again, and again we push. We're going to make it!

With a half dozen more pushes, the back of the raft comes around, and the current roaring around the west side of the submerged rock pushes us up onto the shore with a bone-shaking thud, further splintering the raft's timbers.

Kremke and Grizz leap to shore and begin to tug the raft out of the water and onto dry land. A second later, the rest of us are onshore and helping, although with only one hand, my contribution is minor. Within a matter of minutes, the raft is safely ashore, and my friends lie flat on their backs, chests heaving, desperately pulling in oxygen to relieve the pain racking exhausted muscles that have been pushed to the point of collapse.

We're going to have to cross the tributary again to get to the north side. And there's no way we can row our battered raft upstream against the current.

\* \* \* \* \*

My friends need a good twenty minutes to catch their breath. The roar of the water makes it impossible to talk, so I gesture with my arms to go farther inland so we can talk. With reluctance, my companions lurch to their feet and stagger unsteadily into the forest. We find a clearing far enough from the river to make conversation possible.

"I'm as weak as a baby," says Chase. "I can't lift so much as a feather." He sinks to the ground.

Grizz lurches to a tree, where he collapses and sits with his back against it. "What's next?" he asks.

"Looking at you guys, 'what's next' is ET gathers wood, makes a fire, and cooks you dinner," I reply.

I hear murmurs of gratitude.

As I gather kindling, I mull over the alarming thought that we're on the zealots' side of the river again. *Perhaps*, I think positively, *they haven't settled this far north.* I make a point of collecting only aged, dry wood. Dry wood burns without producing much smoke.

When I return with an armload of wood, the menfolk are staring intently at nothing while Kenny, behind them, changes out of her wet clothes. Looking at the sky, I see it's still an hour or two from sunset.

I drop my armload of wood, pick up my bow and a quiver of arrows, and go hunting. Managing a bow with a wounded wrist is tricky, but I'll have to find a way. I find a good blind in a thicket and wait patiently. A few minutes later, a plump young squirrel makes an appearance, and I bring him down with a well-placed arrow. In less than half an hour, I bag three more. After paddling all day, my friends will need some real protein for dinner.

Returning to the clearing, I say, "Let's set the fire now. I don't know if there are zealots around, but a fire after dark would be more visible."

I see tired nods, so I clean the squirrels, gather a little more wood, and light the fire. I purify some river water and watch as it fizzes and foams. I pour the water into our old, fire-charred skillet and then add squirrel and greens. Fifteen minutes later, we're eating squirrel stew.

"Finest meal I ever ate," says Kremke.

After dinner and cleanup, I offer to keep watch all night.

"Wake me in a few hours," says Grizz. "A few hours' sleep, and I'll be right as rain."

My friends are asleep before the sun sets.

In the morning, we discuss our next steps.

"There's no way we can paddle our raft upstream," says Grizz.

"Let's just salvage the vines, walk upstream, and find a good spot to build another raft," suggests Chase.

We agree. An hour later, we're packed and ready to travel. We hug the bank of the river, but progress is slow. Many creeks and streams feed into the river, forcing us to travel inland to find a place to ford.

The issue of where to cross the river is a difficult one. We know we have zealots to the south. And we know the hostile men who kept us from landing the raft live to the north. Johnny made no mention of the hostiles on the north side of the river, so we hope they all live close to the riverbanks they defended so energetically. Perhaps a few days' travel will put us to the west of their lands.

We travel quietly and extinguish our cooking fires well before dark. We see no signs of zealots, but we'll take no chances. After three days of traveling to the west, we decide to build another raft and cross the river. The sound of axes cutting trees will carry well inland, so we fell the saplings we need as quickly as we can. Two of us stand guard while the others work. By sunset, we have a new raft.

Nervous because the noise we made might have attracted the attention of the zealots, we consider crossing the river in the dark. We discard this notion as being too dangerous. How can we find a good place to land on the north shore if we can't see? I sleep fitfully, worried about zealots.

We're up at dawn, ready to travel. The river at this point is only about one hundred feet wide. We can see the current is swift, but we're miles from the waterfalls, so we decide to attempt a crossing here. We busily load the raft and push off. Our crossing is quick and uneventful. No loincloth-clad hostiles threaten our landing this time.

We take six days to cross the forest north of the river. On the final day, we reach a point where the trees begin to thin out. Shortly thereafter, we reach the blasted lands. The only plant life we see are tumbleweed and some scraggly-looking shrubs that grow no taller than a foot. The soil is barren, nothing but dry sand and broken rock.

In the distance, we see the range of mountains Johnny described, running west to east. In the far distance, off to our left, is the black mountain Johnny told us to look for.

"That's where we're going," I say.

The blasted lands have an eerie feeling about them. Life is not welcome here. Grasshoppers are the exception to this rule. We can scarcely take a step without crushing one or two. I can't believe they find much to eat here, unless they can thrive on tumbleweed. When the breeze picks up, we must dodge tumbleweed. Being hit by rolling weed is not particularly painful, but they stick to our clothes. A series of dry arroyos must be crossed as we travel to the northwest, toward the black mountain. Many of them are deep, and hard to descend and climb, but we're spared the problem of dodging tumbleweed, as none of it grows in the ravines.

On our third day crossing the blasted lands, we see huge thunderheads forming in the sky off to the north. The winds pick up, and wind-driven sand stings our faces and arms. Tumbleweed traveling at speed are more painful as well. We come to a steep arroyo. The climb down is difficult, particularly for one-handed people, but once we've descended twenty feet or so, we're out of the wind, so blowing sand no longer bothers us.

A filthy-looking stream runs through the bottom of the arroyo. The water looks absolutely foul. I wouldn't drink this water even if we'd doused it with Kenny's purifier and boiled it. We're anxious to cross the stream and begin climbing the other side. Desert kids are all taught that small streams like this can become raging torrents without warning in a rainstorm. And the sky above is thick with storm clouds.

We climb the far side of the arroyo and find the wind has picked up. We consider waiting out the storm there, but decide to push on. We regret this decision when lightning begins to strike all around us. Our bodies are the tallest objects around for miles. This makes us especially vulnerable to lightning. We drop flat on the ground and hug it.

Peals of thunder boom almost nonstop, and we watch as lightning bolts strike the ground all around us. Off to the south, a lightning strike has set the tumbleweed afire. We watch in awe as the burning weed travels, setting more tumbleweed afire. The wind is out of the north, so the tumbleweeds travel away from us.

I am congratulating myself on our good fortune of being upwind of the fire, when the ground to the south begins to seethe.

\* \* \* \* \*

Grasshoppers fleeing from the flames form a thick carpet traveling right toward us. The earth is alive with millions of panicked, leaping locusts. I can hear their chittering even above the howl of the wind and the booming thunder. The horde reaches us in minutes. Frantic grasshoppers cover my entire body. I can't see or hear because grasshoppers cover my eyes and ears. I can feel them as they try to crawl into my nose and mouth. I realize I can't breathe. I hold my breath as long as I can, and then I open my mouth to breathe. In an instant, my mouth is full of grasshoppers. I spit and claw, trying to clear grasshoppers away long enough to catch a breath. I can't. No sooner have I scraped a layer of grasshoppers off than another takes its place. The darkness of suffocation begins to overtake me. I begin to give up hope, when, without warning, the grasshoppers suddenly disappear.

I watch as the horde of insects travel north. I gasp, sucking in cool, blessed air. My relief lasts only an instant as I realize that a lightning strike has ignited the tumbleweed to the west of us as well. The distant wall of flame moves closer as I watch. Fiery blowing tumbleweed ignite more tumbleweed as they travel.

We're on our feet and running for the cover of the ravine when the horde of grasshoppers reaches us again. Once again, I'm coated in them. Clawing at grasshoppers does no good. I can't see where I'm going. I can only pray I'm headed toward the ravine, because the other directions all lead to fiery death. I find I've reached the arroyo when there is no longer earth beneath my feet. I fall and land hard. My broken wrist takes part of the weight of the fall, and the pain is severe. I struggle to arrest my fall down the side of the arroyo and succeed. The grasshoppers are gone, and I say a prayer of thanks until I realize why they've left. From the west, a torrent of muddy water forms a tsunami bearing down on us. I scramble up the side of the arroyo, but when I near the top, I feel the intense heat of fire above. I retreat a few feet back down into the arroyo and watch as the wall of brown water churns past a few yards beneath my feet.

The wind is blowing at gale strength from the north. This is good because, since there is no tumbleweed in the arroyo, the firestorm will travel above us. Occasionally, flaming tumbleweed roar over the edge of the ravine and down at me, but I'm able to scramble away before they strike.

So I sit, unable to move, a traveling inferno above me, a churning maelstrom below. A few isolated grasshoppers leap around, too slow to keep up with their mates. The plague of locusts has disappeared, going God knows where.

The raging torrent below shrinks to a trickle, and the fire above ceases, having consumed all available fuel. I'm relieved to find my friends scattered along the side of the arroyo. Nobody is injured, except for Grizz, who has a minor burn on his arm, courtesy of flaming tumbleweed. We wash, disinfect, and bandage his burn.

We peer over the top of the arroyo and find a wasteland above. Nothing has survived the storm and the fire. As we walk, we kick up clouds of ash, and we are soon covered from head to toe in gritty cinders. I must blow my nose repeatedly to keep my nostrils clear.

Several hours later, we find a patch of ground that has somehow been spared from the fire. We decide this is a good place to camp, even though there are a couple hours of daylight left. The thought of sleeping on ashes and cinders convinces us to take this good campsite because there may not be any others.

Two days later, we leave the blasted zone and stand near the foot of the black mountain. As Johnny directed, we climb its western shoulder. The climb proves to be an easy one. I'm relieved, because I have no desire to be hoisted in the boson's chair again. We camp on the mountain, and because of the cold, we risk building a fire. We build it behind a wall of sheltering rocks, hoping that it won't attract unwelcome company. By noon the next day, we've crossed the mountain and stand looking at Los Alamos.

# 22

Los Alamos is separated from the rest of the world by deep chasms. The one on our side is over one hundred yards wide and so deep that I can't see the bottom. A quarter mile to the northwest stands a man who gestures for us to come closer. We walk along the edge of the crevasse until we are standing opposite the man, separated by one hundred yards of seemingly bottomless chasm.

"State your business," the man shouts. His tone is businesslike, but friendly.

"We're here at the invitation of Johnny Grainseed," I reply.

"If that's true, where's Johnny?"

"Johnny was badly wounded by people called 'the zealots.' By the time he reached us, there was nothing we could do to save him. But he gave us directions to reach you."

"Yes. We know the zealots well. Unfortunately. How do I know you didn't torture Johnny into giving you directions to Los Alamos?"

"Johnny gave us a code word," I reply. "The code word is Oppenheimer."

The gatekeeper picks up what appears to be a radio and speaks into it. His voice is too soft for us to hear from our side of the chasm, but the gist of the message becomes clear when five armed men appear and stand near him.

"OK," says the gatekeeper. "Your leader may come across."

As he says this, he throws a switch, and a bridge slowly emerges from the far side of the chasm. It rumbles toward us with the hum of well-tuned machinery. It locks into place on our side.

"If anyone but the girl tries to cross, I push a button, the bridge flips over, and you die on the rocks miles below."

I pause, but I understand their need for caution. There are a lot of wicked people in this world.

I look at my friends. "What do you think?"

"We don't have much choice," says Grizz. The others nod.

I would have crossed the bridge regardless of what anybody said, but it's nice to have everybody singing the same song. If these people are malicious, I realize, I'm done for.

Careful not to look down, I begin to cross the bridge. It's wide and sturdy.

When I reach the far side, the gatekeeper shakes my hand. "Follow me," he says.

So far, so good. I look back at my friends and wave. They all look worried, Grizz most of all. I follow the gatekeeper until we reach a broad set of stairs heading down.

We reach the bottom and find a small city with hundreds of people scurrying about industriously. A few pause and look at me as I descend. The city is belowground and invisible to anyone on the other side of the great crevasse.

"We built our city underground during the time of the collapse," says the gatekeeper. "We were protected from the outside world by the chasms, but the chasms could be breached by a determined foe. So we made ourselves as invisible as possible. We grew our crops behind natural-looking rock walls back then."

Although the city is underground, it is as bright as day. I look at the ceiling and realize it is made of some clever material that looks like earth from above, but turns out to be bright sky from down below. We walk down a series of corridors, passing dozens of busy-looking people.

"Please," says the gatekeeper, gesturing toward an open door.

I enter and find a dozen men and women seated around a conference table. There is water in a pitcher, empty glasses, and a plate of doughnuts near my seat.

"Please help yourself if you are hungry," says a man opposite my seat.

The doughnuts are almost irresistible. My mouth is producing so much saliva that I must swallow twice. I conquer my urge to stuff six or seven in my mouth at once, and instead say, "Thank you, perhaps later." I don't know these people, and I don't want to make a negative first impression. I'll eat a doughnut if they eat a doughnut. I smile my most charming ET smile at the man across from me.

"I'm the director," he says. "Perhaps you'd be willing to answer a few questions so we may get to know you better?"

"Of course," I say.

Over the next half hour, I'm submitted to the most intense grilling of my life. Where do I come from? Where are my people? What form of government do we have? Do we have electricity? What forms of technology have we mastered? What do we eat? Do we have any enemies? By the time they're done, they know everything there is to know about the villagers, the blacksuits, the Court, Helen, the workshop, the chem lab, the arsenal, the mines, the forts, the Sons of 1776, my meeting with Johnny, and every other detail imaginable. The only story I withhold is the one about the brane. I'm not sure whether that part of my story would be credible.

"So you've come here for the grain?" the director asks.

"For the grain and also for the chance to become a node in the civilization network you're building," I say. "Once we defeat the Court, we'll restore democracy and a respect for individual rights. We'll become a good ally and will do whatever we can to help you restore civilization as it was."

I must have done well because everyone around the table is smiling.

"Then you shall have both," says the director. "But first, let me tell you about our history so you will know us better."

"I'd like that," I say.

"The chasm you saw that divides Los Alamos from the rest of the world was created quite by accident," the director begins. "When the world was collapsing, the United States government was desperate to tap new sources of fuel. Our community here at Los Alamos was the center for nuclear weapons development. There was great pressure on us to set off nuclear explosions at ever-increasing depths to provide access to oil and coal deposits buried far beneath the earth's surface.

"Against our better judgment, we built tens of thousands of extremely powerful bombs. They were exploded at unprecedented depths. The bombs provided access to fuel, but they also had the unintended consequence of disturbing the earth's tectonic plates. We set the plates in motion, and millions of years of normal tectonic activity occurred over the span of just over one hundred years. Mountains formed. Vast new seas were created. Rivers disappeared while new ones emerged. The face of North America was forever altered.

"Here at Los Alamos, we found ourselves surrounded by deep chasms on three sides. What a blessing it was that the chasms were formed around us and not directly below us. By the time the chasms were created, the world was in turmoil, and we knew our only hope of survival lay in isolating ourselves from the chaos around us. It was a simple matter to blast a crevasse on the fourth side, and Los Alamos was effectively cut off from the outside world.

"Life in this new world was brutal. We had to grow our own food, and the desert hereabouts was not the most fertile environment imaginable in the old days. The days of every man, woman, and child at Los Alamos were consumed with the need to produce food. We are physical scientists here, but a few of us had some experience in agronomy. Our lives were hard for a long, long time, but gradually we learned to amend the soil, apply fertilizer, and breed newer hybrids more suitable to a desert biome.

"The climate changed over time as well. The weather became hotter, the monsoons wetter. We were gradually able to feed ourselves with less work, which allowed us to pursue science again. We've rediscovered electricity and many other lost technologies. But it was not until nearly one hundred years ago that we developed the grain cultivar that truly freed us from the need to spend the majority of our time on subsistence.

"Ten years ago, we began sending out seekers. If our little civilization could survive, perhaps others were out there as well. We've found a few: the Canadian government exists, and they've preserved many books; the city of Denver survived, although it has only one hundred thousand inhabitants, and their level of technology is quite primitive; and we've discovered another group of survivors near Austin, Texas. We've had no luck whatsoever with seekers sent to the south or west. All of our explorers have disappeared except for one. The woman who came back was near death, but she lived long enough to tell us about the zealots."

The director stops and takes a long drink of water.

"Your story inspires me," I say. "I can't wait to share some of the technologies we've recovered with you."

"We will share the new grain cultivar with you," says the director. "We'll also send eight people back with you. The grain they carry will be enough to seed one hundred acres of farmland. Three months after you plant, you'll have enough grain to seed thousands of acres."

"You're extremely generous. What can we give you in return?"

"The military technology you described at your armory sounds useful. In a dangerous world, sending out seekers who can defend themselves will help us locate even more advanced communities. Perhaps the people we send with you could visit the armory on their way back."

"Of course. We'll share everything we've learned with them. Perhaps they'll want to bring back some weapons that would be immediately useful. We lost our AKs when we were captured by the zealots, or we'd demonstrate them for you. But believe me, AKs will help your seekers defend themselves. We have other useful weapons as well."

"It sounds like we have a deal," says the director as he stands.

He offers his hand to me, and I shake it.

"Now," he continues, "bring your friends in, and eat from our tables and sleep in real beds."

We spend three days with our new friends in Los Alamos. We eat bread and meat for the first time in ages. We sleep in beds that are much more comfortable than the ones in the dormitories of the chem lab and the workshop. The director and his associates give us a tour of Los Alamos, and I'm impressed by the level of technology they've achieved. They're using wind turbines to generate electricity. They lack the raw materials to build solar collectors and are thrilled when I describe our solar farm.

My favorite tour was of the wheat fields, hidden from the outside world behind natural-looking rock barriers. They have wheat in every stage of development, from seeds just planted to stalks so heavy with grain they bend over and touch the ground.

But we're well aware that we have only a limited amount of time before the Court gains the upper hand in our struggle. So we leave much sooner than we would have liked. We need to get the new grain planted soon.

* * * * *

We pass over the bridge leaving Los Alamos and receive a pleasant surprise. Waiting for us are our old friends, Steve and Edie, the entertainers.

"Does your offer to join your community still stand?" asks Steve.

"Of course," I say. "What made you change your mind?"

"Edie and I talked after you had left. You and your friends seemed so genuine, we felt almost certain you would treat us well if we joined you. The story of the battles you are fighting inspired us. We've lived on the road for a long time now, and while we enjoy traveling and entertaining, we decided it's time to do something new, something valuable and worthwhile. The prospect of joining good people in a fight against evil seemed very appealing. You had told us you were heading to Los Alamos, so we decided to wait for you here. So, here we are."

We embrace and shake hands with Steve and Edie.

"Welcome," I say simply.

We are a large group now with the addition of Steve and Edie and the eight men and women from Los Alamos hauling grain seed. We grow acquainted with one another on the long walk south. Even Kremke gets along well with our new companions.

We reach the escarpment that I was hauled up in the boson's chair. I decide to test my injured wrist. Kenny carefully removes the splint. Once it comes off, I gingerly try to flex the wrist. I find it stiff, but can move it without too much pain. I enjoy descending the cliffs under my own power. As I use my wrist, most of the stiffness disappears, but it's definitely not as good as new. Its range of motion is severely limited. I hope it'll improve with time.

One immediate benefit of adding Steve and Edie to our party is their skill in traveling quietly. They've had a long and successful career wandering the wilds, and they've learned to find other people before other people find them. We walk single file and well spread out, with

Edie and Steve taking turns leading our column. Kremke, with his marine background, refers to leading the column as "walking point." With our new friends walking point, our journey homeward passes with few incidents. We run across the occasional zealot village, but Steve and Edie steer us safely around them.

I mark our position on my map every evening. I work with the compass and my pedometer religiously. My task is complicated by the fact that we're taking a slightly different path on our homebound leg. This is OK because it gives me a chance to use my trigonometry, although calculating sin and such is difficult without a calculator. Still, I feel reasonably comfortable that I know where we are with some small margin for error.

We're only three days from the place we left the balloon when disaster strikes again.

# 23

We believe we are well to the southwest of the zealots, but we build our fire from aged wood well before sunset, just in case. We've been fortunate in our hunting today, so we feast on both rabbit and partridge. We carefully extinguish our fire well before dark. Our larger group makes it possible to post more sentries. We have four people awake at all times.

I'm on watch an hour after midnight when the shrieking begins. The howl is loud, high-pitched, and predatory. My blood runs cold. Only a creature born in agony could issue such an awful cry.

The screaming wakes everybody in camp. We look fearfully at one another as the creature's shrieks grow ever louder.

"What is it?" I ask urgently.

"It's the banshee," says Chase.

"No, it's not," says Edie. "It's the wendigo."

The look of sheer terror on her face confirms my fear that we're dealing with something terrible and deadly.

"The wendigo is an ancient evil beast," Edie continues, her voice quivering, "and it won't rest until it's consumed a human in its fire."

The screaming continues to grow louder. The beast is getting closer. I've faced some fearsome things in this world, but the earsplitting howls of the wendigo frighten me more than anything I've experienced before. The shrieks are a horrible combination of unbearable agony and the excited cry of a vicious predator closing in on its prey.

"Should we run?" I ask.

"No. The wendigo will find us no matter what we do."

We're all standing. Those of us with swords are clutching them. We form a circle, facing outward.

"You won't kill the wendigo with those swords," says Steve. "You can't kill fire with a blade, even a sharp one."

The wailing grows louder. The creature is getting nearer.

"I see something," says Grizz.

We look where Grizz is pointing, and we see it: a pulsing blue-white flame heading right toward us. The wendigo moves rapidly. It reaches us before we can even blink.

The wendigo is made of fire, a fire burning white-hot that constantly flares and changes. The most horrible thing about the creature is its face. Malicious glowing red eyes glower just above terrible, sharp fangs. Like its body, the wendigo's face is made of blue-white fire. But the facial fire blazes and rages more rapidly than the body. I can make out horns of fire atop the horrifying head.

The wendigo circles us, screeching as it goes. It moves so quickly that I can't follow it no matter how fast I move my head. It makes dozens of circuits around us. Finally it stops and focuses its malign glare on one of the men from Los Alamos. Seeing the terrible gleaming red eyes intent upon him, the man screams. In a move so fast I can't be sure I actually saw it, the wendigo seizes the man with its razor-sharp claws, long as carving knives, and uses its long, fiery arms to enfold him in a flaming embrace. The man screams, obviously in terrible pain, and disappears.

The wendigo shrieks with joy and shrinks away, disappearing into the forest.

Our fear is palpable. None of us is able to speak for long minutes.

"What the devil was that?" asks Kremke in a trembling voice.

"The wendigo has stalked the forest for ages," says Edie. "Before the collapse, it haunted the forests of Northern Canada, far to the north of most civilization. But now, it ranges south at will. We've only seen the beast once before, and it took a victim just as it did tonight. According to legend, the wendigo takes only one victim per night, so it won't visit us again until tomorrow night."

"You say it stalks the forest," I say. "Does that mean the wendigo won't bother us once we're out of the forest and into the desert?"

"Yes. The wendigo seems to draw its strength from the energy of the forest. The last time we ran into it, we left the forest the following day, and we never saw it again."

"By my calculation, we have at least one more night in the forest before we're out of the trees and into the desert," I say.

"That means another of us will die tonight," says Steve, his voice stiff and haunted.

"Perhaps we should travel all night," I suggest.

"The wendigo will find us whether we are moving or not," says Edie.

"And the footing in this forest is so treacherous, we'll have sprained ankles and broken legs for sure," says Grizz. "Then, at least some of us would be in the forest for a lot more than one night."

\* \* \* \* \*

Despite Steve's assurance that the wendigo strikes only once a night, nobody sleeps a wink. At the first hint of dawn, we pack our things and travel southwest, as fast as we can move. We're almost certainly south of the zealots' territory, so we make no effort to walk quietly. We each take a turn carrying the dead man's grain sack.

We don't stop for lunch. We eat as we walk.

There's no conversation today. Each of us is wondering whether we'll be the one the wendigo claims tonight. I walk next to Grizz and reach out to grasp his hand. Somehow, the touch of another person seems to make the fear more bearable. I see Chase grab Kenny's hand as well. Our fear has turned us from heroes back into what we really are: frightened kids.

\* \* \* \* \*

We walk until it's too dark to see the ground before us. We gather wood and start a blazing fire.

"Fire won't frighten the wendigo," says Edie.

"Maybe not," I say, "but it makes *me* feel better.

There will be no sleep for us tonight. I sit with my back against Grizz's. The warmth of human contact is somehow reassuring. We wait, each minute an eternity. I glance at my watch for the thousandth time and am surprised to see it's five o'clock. Perhaps the wendigo will not come tonight. Dawn is only an hour away.

Moments later, my hopes are dashed. We hear the fearsome cry of the wendigo faintly in the distance. I listen, hoping the sound will go in another direction. Perhaps there's another unfortunate party in the woods tonight. My hopes turn to ashes as the seconds tick away. The sound grows louder, and we all know the wendigo is headed in our direction.

Some of the men and women from Los Alamos begin to cry quietly. Grizz squeezes my shoulder, trying to reassure me, but he can't hide the terror on his own face. Kenny and Chase have closed their eyes tight. They're kids again, thinking that if they can't see the evil beast, it might go away.

The wendigo roars into our camp again and circles us dozens of times. I throw my arms around Grizz, and he clings tightly to me. If the wendigo wants one of us, the other will go as well. Nothing can break our embrace.

The wendigo chooses a woman from Los Alamos tonight. It grasps her in its terrible claws and embraces her. She screams in agony.

After selecting its victim, the wendigo shrieks again with joy and fades slowly away, disappearing into the forest.

\* \* \* \* \*

Grief-stricken at the loss of another, we leave before dawn. With a good dayswalk, we'll leave the forest and the wendigo behind. By noon, the trees begin to thin out, and by mid-afternoon, we're back in the desert. The trees behind us grow smaller, and soon we can't see them anymore. I feel ecstatic. A terrible weight has been lifted from my shoulders. Our group begins to talk, and we find we can even begin to laugh. We feel awful for the loss of our friends from Los Alamos, but can't hide our sense of exhilaration at being beyond the awful reach of the wendigo.

An hour before sunset, we reach the arroyo where we stashed the balloon. Kenny inspects it and declares it flight-worthy. We light a huge campfire and eat the scrawny desert rabbits we were able to bring down once the forest was safely behind us.

"The balloon won't be able to take all of us along with eight heavy bags of grain," Kenny says.

"The grain is our first priority," I say. "We need to get those seeds in the ground. It'll take three months to produce our first crop, and we'll need the seeds from that crop to plant the thousands of acres we'll need to feed all our people. So at best, we'll have our first bumper crop in six months."

"ET is right," says Grizz. "We need to get those seeds planted."

We continue our discussion and decide that Kenny, the grain, and two of the people from Los Alamos will go first. The two from Los Alamos who go on the first flight will supervise our people as they the plant the seeds. The rest of us will work our way west on a straight line, aiming at the saddle. After the grain has been unloaded, Kenny will bring the balloon back for the rest of us.

We stay awake late, talking. The euphoria that accompanies release from intense fear buoys us even after two sleepless nights. Chase wants to check the work on the fort at the armory. Kenny wants to work on bringing the solar farm across the mountains. Kremke volunteers to give the survivors from Los Alamos, along with Steve and Edie, a tour of our installations. Grizz and I need to meet with Falstaff and Helen to find out what's transpired during our long absence.

\* \* \* \* \*

I'm on watch in the middle of the night when I hear a sound that causes my heart to hammer with dread. The wendigo shrieks with the obscene laughter that marks the end of another human life. A male human screams in agony. I spin around in time to see the wendigo disappear in the distance. Kremke, who was on watch with me, is no longer at his post.

"I thought the wendigo never left the forest! Why didn't it howl as it was coming?" My thoughts are a jumble.

"I don't know," says Steve, tears rolling down his face, voice quivering with fear. "Maybe it couldn't scream because it was far away from its energy source, the forest. Maybe it had just enough energy to approach us quietly and steal one of us away."

We're all awake, milling around in confusion. How could this happen?

My next discovery brings me physically to my knees and emotionally to the brink of hysteria.

Grizz is gone as well.

www.ingramcontent.com/pod-product-compliance
Lightning Source LLC
Chambersburg PA
CBHW020725210626
46807CB00016B/71